CHILD'S PLAY

When 16-year-old Caitlin Reynolds fails to return home from school, Detective Inspector Sarah Quinn soon realizes this is no ordinary missing persons case. How could a schoolgirl vanish in broad daylight with no witnesses? Why is Caitlin's mother so unhelpful and hostile to the police? Then the note arrives, referring to a crime committed more than fifty years earlier – and it becomes clear that someone is playing a childish – but all too deadly – game with the police. To make matters worse, journalist Caroline King has got hold of the story – and Sarah Quinn's troubles are only just beginning.

CHILD'S PLAY

A DI Sarah Quinn Mystery

Maureen Carter

Severn House Large Print
London & New York

This first large print edition published 2014
in Great Britain and the USA by
SEVERN HOUSE PUBLISHERS LTD of
19 Cedar Road, Sutton, Surrey, England, SM2 5DA.
First world regular print edition published 2013 by
Crème de la Crime, an imprint of
Severn House Publishers Ltd., London and New York.

British Library Cataloguing in Publication Data

Carter, Maureen author.
   Child's play. -- (The Sarah Quinn mysteries)
   1. Quinn, Sarah (Fictitious character)--Fiction. 2. Women
   detectives--England--Birmingham--Fiction. 3. Missing
   children--Fiction. 4. Women journalists--Fiction.
   5. Detective and mystery stories. 6. Large type books.
   I. Title II. Series
   823.9'2-dc23

   ISBN-13: 9780727897251

Severn House Publishers support the Forest Stewardship Council™
[FSC™], the leading international forest certification organisation. All
our titles that are printed on FSC certified paper carry the FSC logo.

Printed and bound in Great Britain by
T J International, Padstow, Cornwall.

The lyrics from 'Femme Fatale' are reproduced with kind permission of The Toy Hearts. Thank you Hannah, Sophia andStewart Johnson.

My thanks for editorial expertise and insight go to Kate Lyall Grant, Anna Telfer and the exceptional team at Crème de la Crime and Severn House. I thank my wide range of contacts for their expert knowledge and priceless input and – as always – I thank readers everywhere.

ONE

August 1960, Moss Pit, Leicestershire

Picnics and pooh sticks. Hide-and-seek and pirate ships. It was that kind of blue-skies summer, long days with no school or stupid rules. Susan didn't want it to end, would happily spend the rest of her life in shorts and t-shirts messing about outside. Scabby knees and nettle stings were a non-occupational hazard for a ten-year-old who loved climbing trees, squeezing through hedges, rolling down grassy banks. Not that it was all rough and tumble: sometimes she and Pauline just lazed in the long grass, threading daisy chains, blowing dandelion seeds, listening to the birds and bees. If she'd spared a thought about it, Susan might have described the last few weeks as idyllic, but the little girl's focus was on more down-to-earth subjects and her vocabulary didn't stretch that far.

Indeed, idyllic wouldn't have been entirely true and it would not have painted the full picture.

On the edge of the village, new building was underway. Thirty, maybe forty redbrick slate-

7

roofed council houses. Little boxes, most of the oldies reckoned. But Susan rather liked the sparkling windows and shiny yellow doors. Compared to the row of old stone cottages where she lived, Susan thought they looked smashing. She might even make new friends. A handful of families had already moved in, clothes flapped on washing lines and she'd spotted a couple of children's bikes lying in scrubby front gardens, but most of the houses weren't finished yet, and a lot of the site was still fenced off.

She and Pauline sometimes pressed their faces against the wire to have a nose. It was all bare-chested men with brawny arms and beer guts busy over wheelbarrows and concrete mixers. The site was what Susan's mum called an eyesore: littered with piles of bricks and mounds of sand, half-empty sacks and spades shoved anyhow in the ground. Keep-out notices in huge red lettering were dotted round the fence, as if they'd deter some of the lads from sneaking in for a dare. Not Susan. Her dad had told her to keep away: setting foot inside would have been more than her life was worth.

No. Most of her days were spent larking about in the open fields backing on to the farm labourers' cottages. Right now, she stood on top of a rotting tree stump, shielding amber eyes from the sun's glare, sweeping the landscape with a narrow gaze. Constable could have paint-ed its straggly hedges, quilted fields, muted

8

greens and browns. To the left stood a copse of ancient gnarled oaks and, just beyond, sunlight glinted off a sluggish stream; in the heat haze the church steeple glimmered and the big farm where Susan's dad worked was bathed in gold. But apart from cows and crows there was no sign of life.

'What you doing, Sukie?' Pauline, wildly swinging a sturdy little leg, squinted up at her playmate. Susan ignored the question but suspected if Pauline didn't calm down she'd do herself an injury. Oblivious, the little girl swapped legs, swung even harder, then stuck her thumb in her mouth for good measure.

Standing on tiptoe, Susan was still trying to spot where the other kids had gone. She always seemed to get landed with Pauline and, truth be told, sometimes the girl could be more of a pain than a pal. It mightn't be so bad but she was only five and supposed to stay within earshot of her mum's house, anything further than the copse being out of bounds. It was like baby-sitting without the pay. What with the baby twins and that, Pauline's mum had her hands full and Susan's mum was big on helping neighbours. Well, big on Susan helping neighbours. Her mum had drummed it into her enough times how it wouldn't hurt to take the kid under her wing. What was she? A flippin' bird or something? She wouldn't care but Pauline had a big sister. Grace was a good bit older but she never wanted to play or help out or anything. Wasn't blood supposed to be thicker than water?

Still, Susan had to admit that Mrs Bolton was pretty generous with treats and stuff: this afternoon she'd given them pop and sandwiches for a picnic. Pauline was supposed to be laying the goodies out on the blanket. Like she ever did as she was told. She might be just a nipper but, according to Susan's mum, with her Shirley Temple curls and huge blue eyes Pauline could be a right little madam. What's more, to Susan's way of thinking, the kid had a touch of the Violet Elizabeths. Scream wasn't in it. Yet to look at her, butter wouldn't melt. She sneaked a quick glance remembering how, ages and ages ago, she'd heard her parents talk about how Pauline got away with murder at home. She could smile about it now, but for days Susan had pictured blood-stained bodies propped all over the place. She'd eventually mentioned it to her mum and got a clip round the head for ear-wigging and being thick.

'Sukie!' Pauline swung the leg even harder; she was going to ruin those sandals. 'I said what—'

'Nothing.' She used the hem of her t-shirt to wipe her glasses. 'I'm not doing nothing.' She'd bet Sally and Brenda were off playing vampires again. They were always hanging round that creepy graveyard; obsessed they were. Mind, the Dawson girls were only nice when they wanted sweets or a ride on her bike, things like that. She'd heard the names and sniggers behind her back: fatso, four eyes, smelly-poo-Sue. Fair-weather friends her mum called them. At least Pauline wasn't into name-calling. Well, not the nasty sort.

'Sukie!'

'Don't call me that.' The little girl's lisp made Sukie sound like thoo-key and it drove her mad. 'How many times do I have to tell you?'

'Can if I want. You're not my mum.'

Thank God. Susan hiked up a once-white ankle sock then puffed out her already pigeon chest. 'I'm the king of the castle and you...' She waggled a finger at Pauline.

'I am NOT so.' She took a swing too far and toppled over. What with all the grass, it couldn't have hurt that much. Susan reckoned the welling eyes and quivering lip were purely for show. Again.

Sighing, she jumped down and helped the little girl to her feet. 'Come on, don't be a cry baby.' The fall had damaged the dress more than her bum: grass stains were a devil to get rid of.

Pauline made heavy weather of wiping her eyes then flashed a hopeful smile. 'Shall we play tick?'

'OK.' She prodded the little girl's shoulder. 'You're it.'

'Not playing then. You're mean, you are.' Head down, she toed the ground. The white sandals were scuffed now as well as dirty; she was going the right way to get a smacking from her mum. 'I *always* have to be it.'

'Always moaning, that's what you are.' Susan sniffed and turned on her heel. 'Come on. I'm starving. Let's do the picnic.'

'Can I be mum?' Didn't take much to distract her; she skipped alongside, happy enough.

'Don't be daft.'

'Why not?'

'Why d'you think?' Susan halted and turned, hands on hips. 'I'm older than you and twice as big.'

''Snot fair.' Pauline kneaded her eye with a knuckle. Cor, it looked dead painful.

'All right then.' Relenting, Susan smiled, reached down and ruffled the little girl's curls. 'Just this once.'

'Ow!' Pauline recoiled, rubbing her head. 'That hurt.'

'No it didn't. Stop whinging. You're...' She bit her lip. What was the point? The kid was never happy unless she was moaning. Spoilt rotten was Princess Pauline.

Laying the spread on the old tartan rug kept them both quiet for a while. The make-shift tea set comprised chipped mismatched crockery donated by their mums. Susan filled a cast-off teapot with dandelion and burdock pop while Pauline sorted the food: jam sandwiches cut into quarters, a packet of Midget Gems and two slabs of fruit cake. Apart from a dog's bark and the occasional cracking twig and creaking branch they munched in companionable silence, the sun warm on their flesh, the smell of cut grass wafting even in the still air.

Susan sat as cross-legged as chubby thighs allowed and watched a now kneeling Pauline pretend to feed her doll. The thing was propped against a tree, glassy eyes staring straight back at Susan. She grimaced. It hadn't struck her before but the doll looked a bit like Pauline. How spooky was that? Mind you, Susan could not be doing with dolls at the best of times; they made her skin creep. Give her a teddy bear any day.

'Now be a good girl, Carol,' Pauline coaxed. 'Eat it all up.'

Susan rolled her eyes. Stupid name for a doll. And look at the waste. Stuffing food in its mouth like that. Crumbs were flying everywhere and the shiny pink face was smeared with jam. God, it looked a right mess.

Still, gift horse and all that – with Pauline otherwise occupied, Susan inched forward and sneaked the last sandwich.

'Hey, you.' She'd caught the movement out of the corner of her eye and spun round fast. 'That's Carol's.'

'Not now it isn't.' Susan gave a fulsome smile before cramming the bread into her mouth.

Pauline sat up straight, folded her arms and screwed her eyes tight. Talk about killer looks. Mind, the little Miss Sulky pose was so over the top it was comical. If her mouth wasn't still full, Susan would have laughed out loud.

'You're a greedy pig, Susan Bailey.'

The older girl stared back, took her time chewing and swallowing before making a sudden grab for the doll and lifting its skirt. 'Carol's had enough already. Look at her. What a porker.'

Pauline's lunge took Susan by surprise, winded her as she fell back. The little girl scrambled up, hiking Susan's t-shirt with both hands. 'Let's look at yours then, shall we? See how you like—'

Frozen at the sight, Pauline gasped then stared open-mouthed. 'What's that, Sukie?' Gingerly the little girl made to stroke the jagged damson mark that spread over much of her friend's stomach.

Susan shoved her to one side and straightened, tugging at her top. 'Mind your own. It's nothing.' She sensed Pauline's confused gaze but refused to meet it. The silence was no longer companionable; it was painful.

'Does it ... hurt?' Pauline asked.

'Course not, dumbo.' Not so much, now.

'It looked like a ... a...' Still hesitant, Pauline whispered, 'A big ... nasty ... bruise.'

She shrugged. 'Yeah, well. Shows what you know. Let's clear this lot up.' She started gathering the plates and cups, greaseproof paper. 'Come on, don't just sit there.'

'Sukie?' Gentle, still unsure of herself, she placed tiny fingers on her friend's arm. 'Did you ... did you ... fall over again?'

'Yeah.' She dropped her head, eyes smarting. 'Dead clumsy me. Don't tell anyone, eh?'

'Course not.' Susan wrapped her arm as far as it would go round Pauline's sloping shoulder. Both were kneeling now, heads together; neither spoke. Neither noticed the man's dark figure lurking in the shadows of the copse.

'It'll be OK, Sukie. Don't cry.' Gently, she patted her friend's shoulder, trying to gee her up. 'Look, we don't have to go home yet. We've got bags of time to play.'

Susan lifted her head, gave a tentative smile. Pauline was right. There was no point sitting round moping, and in an hour or so, hopefully the kid would have forgotten all about the bruise. 'Course we have. Bags and bags of time. What'll we play?' She cut a sly glance at the copse before raising a knowing eyebrow. 'Anything you fancy?'

'Hide and seek? Yeah!' A broad grin broke across her features as she leapt to her feet.

'Off you go then.' It was Pauline's favourite game.

'No peeping,' the little girl yelled over her shoulder.

Susan's back was turned already. She closed her eyes and pressed sticky hands over her pink National Health specs. 'One ... two ... three...'

TWO

'And you've no idea where she is? Who she might be with?' The woman fought to keep her voice calm, her knuckles clamped round the handset looked as if they were about to split. It was nearly eight o'clock and this was the sixth call she'd made since arriving home. Nicola hadn't even sat down yet, still wore a thick car coat. She'd been late herself – she picked up the weekly shopping after work on Thursdays – but her daughter should've been back hours ago.

'Sorry, Mrs Reynolds, Caitlin never said anything about meeting anyone. Far as I know she was heading straight home after school.'

It was a half-mile walk from Queen's Ridge comprehensive. She pictured Caitlin weighed down by her schoolbag, strolling along in her own little world, probably listening to some pop pap on her iPod. The fond smile on Nicola's face froze. Surely she'd not been in an accident? She told herself to cool it. The roads were quiet, mostly residential. Besides, she'd have heard by now.

'Are you still there, Mrs Reynolds?'

'Sorry, Lauren, I'm...' She glanced round the

16

sitting room on the off-chance a note had gone astray somewhere; there'd certainly been no texts sent to her phone. Something had seemed amiss as soon as she stepped inside the house – it had been too quiet, a pile of junk mail lay on the mat and Caitlin's blazer wasn't hanging skewiff from the banister. After dumping five Tesco bags on the floor in the kitchen, Nicola's quick scout round suggested Caitlin hadn't been back at all.

'Mrs Reynolds, are you there?'

Distracted, Nicola dragged her fingers down a cheek leaving pale trails in the sallow skin. Caitlin was no angel – what teenager is? – but usually she'd let Nicola know if there was a problem or she was running late. Surely this wasn't payback time for the minor spat this morning?

'Mrs Reynolds, are—'

'Sorry. I'm still here, Lauren.' And miles away. She glanced towards the bay window, caught her reflection in the glass. The frazzled features were nothing new but were the lines on her face deeper? *Don't be so bloody melodramatic, woman.* That was the trouble with an overactive imagination. Not the only one, given some of the scenarios running through her mind.

'Millie might know something,' Lauren suggested. 'Have you had a word with her? I've got a number if—'

'No, she doesn't. I've tried.' And Charlie and Liz. Caitlin's best friend Millie had been top of the list. She'd not even been in school today, flu or something. The other two had stayed behind for chess club and said they'd seen Caitlin around four o'clock packing books into her school bag.

'What about Chloe?'

Nicola suppressed an impatient sigh. *And Uncle Tom Cobbly.* The grandfather clock in the hall started chiming the hour. As if she needed a reminder.

'No one knows anything, Lauren.' She'd even phoned Caitlin's granny over in Small Heath, hoped the call hadn't worried her too much. 'Tell me, love, is Luke back on the scene? I'll not give her a hard time again.' Caitlin had kept the fledgling romance a secret until she'd been casually dumped and needed a mum's shoulder to cry on.

'Not as far as I know, Mrs Reynolds. Could you hold on a minute, please?' The girl had used a similar expression before. Significant? Nicola had no idea, nor had anyone else she'd spoken to: the clueless state must be catching. She heard muffled voices, a snatch of telly then Lauren was back. 'I'm really sorry but Mum says dinner's on the table.'

'No worries, love. But, hey, if you hear anything?'

No worries? Was she out of her mind? Nicola raked both hands through light brown shoulder-length hair before resting them briefly on top of her head. What now, for crying out loud? A

18

message alert beeped on her mobile. Thank God. She scrabbled in her coat pocket but cursed under her breath when she saw a workmate's name. She double checked her messages: still nothing. No response either from the two voicemails she'd left on Caitlin's iPhone: the fact it was switched off was alarming enough in itself. She bit her lip. What about the police? Was it too early to call?

Yes. Better to hang fire an hour or so. She strode to the front door, scanned both sides of the tree-lined street: Edwardian villas, satellite dishes, shiny cars. She liked Moseley, reckoned if you had to live in Birmingham ... Stepping further out, Nicola stood in the middle of the pavement, willing Caitlin to appear, longed to see her familiar figure heading home, sheepish smile on her lovely face. Tall and shapely with long dark hair, Caitlin was a knockout, could easily pass for eighteen, nineteen.

The young mother who lived across the road flashed a smile as she drew the curtains. Nicola managed a token wave, her focus elsewhere. She and Caitlin were close – occasionally it crossed Nicola's mind they were too close. Hardly surprising given the girl had never known her dad. Brian had passed away before Caitlin even drew breath. Until relatively recently, it had been just the two of them. And though Nicola had been seeing Neil for a while now, neither was in an all-fired rush to live together. It would be time enough when Caitlin left for college.

Nicola screamed when something cold touched the back of her leg.

'Sorry 'bout that, missus. He's a bit too friendly for his own good sometimes. Come here, Frodo. There's a good lad.'

She glared at the portly middle-aged man struggling to control a chocolate Labrador that was still trying to get pally with her thigh. The man's name was Ronald. Ronald Gibson if she remembered right; he lived a few doors down the street and was nosy with a capital N. She gave a thin smile before stepping aside. His corresponding manoeuvre – and the dog's – mirrored hers three or four times and they ended up in some sort of weird Excuse Me street dance.

'By 'eck, love.' Gibson's beam showcased a dental graveyard of sepia tombstones. 'They'll have us on *Strictly* next.' Tapping the brow of his trilby, he made to move off. 'By the way, how's that lovely girl of yours?'

Innocent enough remark, so why were her hackles rising? 'Fine. Why?'

'Just wondered why she wasn't at school today.'

'Sorry?' She felt a trickle of ice down her spine.

'Oops. I don't want to get her into Mum's bad books or anything, but I saw her with some chap down the—'

'Hang on there one minute, will you?' A phone was ringing inside the house. She was already halfway to the door, a desperate mantra on a mental loop: don't hang up, don't hang up, don't hang up. 'Caitlin?' Her gasping breath must be God's way of telling her to stop smoking. 'Is that—?'

'This call is urgent. Within the last six months, have you been sold...' Tinny voice, taped message.

'Get lost, damn you!' she screamed, slammed down the receiver, took a deep, calming breath, lost in thought for several seconds, until: 'Gibson. Bugger.'

The old boy had gone, but Frodo's faecal legacy lay steaming on the pavement. Gibson's sly innuendo rang in her ears. Had Caitlin wagged off school? And was she still messing around with that loser? If so, the minute she got home she'd find herself in the doo-doo, up to the neck in it.

Anger now mixed with concern, Nicola slung her coat on a hook in the hall and headed for the drinks' trolley. She'd earned a stiff one, poured a generous measure of Gordon's into a glass and ferried it through to the kitchen. It was when she stooped to tackle the first couple of shopping bags that she noticed it. A white envelope slipped under the back door. She frowned, would have sworn it hadn't been there earlier. She stood to open it, found a photograph and a message. Nicola almost fainted, felt her legs give way. No, it wasn't too early to call the police. In fact, with every fibre of her being, she prayed it wasn't too late.

THREE

Caitlin had stopped crying hours ago. At least she guessed it was hours: keeping track of time was difficult, counting away the seconds only possible when conscious. Her water must have been spiked because she'd never have fallen asleep willingly. She blinked then winced when the blindfold scratched her eyes again. She had only the vaguest idea how she'd got here; no idea where 'here' was. Nor, more pressing, how she'd get out. Not with her ankles lashed to wooden chair legs, the tight white cable cutting into her flesh. More cable bound her wrists at the small of her back. She'd stopped struggling too; movement only exacerbated the pain.

'Why are you doing this?' she croaked, her throat sore.

'Button it, girlie, or the gag goes back.' The soft mocking voice sounded sibilant, slightly muffled. She had a sudden vision of Hannibal Lecter in that god-awful mask in *Silence of the Lambs*. If her abductor's aim was to increase tension, hike the fear factor, it so wasn't needed.

Caitlin licked already dry, cracked lips. God knows what the cloth had been used for before, but the inside of her mouth tasted vile; bits of fluff stuck to her tongue, lodged between her teeth. She felt a slight movement of air. He must be closer. Yes, his breathing sounded louder, more laboured. Something touched her face. A finger. Now slowly tracing her jaw line, then her neck. She stiffened but the stink made her flinch: stale smoke, vinegar, something rank she couldn't pin down.

Warm breath near her ear and the soft humming started again, the harmless tune creepier than his direct threats. She pictured him crouched over her, ogling, mentally stripping her, all the while hum, hum, humming.

'De-dum-de-dumdum-de-dum-de-dum. Dum-dum-dum-de-dum-de-dum.'

The damn thing rang a distant bell, a kids' song she thought, couldn't remember what it was called. Christ on a bike. As if it mattered. She sighed, impatient, tried blanking it out, concentrated instead on why he'd brought her here. What he intended doing. She'd caught no more than a glimpse of his face; he'd gone out of his way not to show it. Surely that was a good sign? If she couldn't describe him, he was more likely to release her. Wasn't he?

'Please ... tell me...'

He pressed his finger hard against her lips. 'When I'm good and ready, girlie. De-dum-de-dumdum...'

The tune ran in her head now; she doubted she'd ever get it out. 'Please, look, my mum...'

Will be going out of her mind.

'Don't you worry about a thing, babe. Momma knows you've been – how shall I put it – detained?' *He'd contacted her? Had she called the police?* 'I let her know you're ... tied up, as it were.' His snigger in her face released a wave of toxic breath that made her gag. 'What's up, missie? Feeling a bit queasy, are we?'

She nodded, retched violently, this time for effect. Hopes rising, she made to straighten in the chair. The restraints cut deeper but the pain would be a small price if he untied her, removed the blindfold. At the very least she'd be able to scope out the place, work on a way of getting out.

'Please. I need the bathroom fast.'

'I think not.'

'But—'

'But nothing. If you barf, you can sit in it and stink. I don't give a monkey's. Momma won't be too happy though. She'll think we're not looking after her pretty little girl, won't she?'

Caitlin frowned, myriad thoughts racing. Why was he doing this? Did she know him? Did he know her? Or had she just been in the wrong place at the wrong time? For once, she was glad of the blindfold; it concealed her confusion and concern. More than that, her increasing terror.

'Lost your tongue, missie?' She recoiled when his fingers chucked her chin. 'Hope not. You're gonna need it in a minute.'

Her tongue? Why? His voice was still muffled,

but sounded further away. She heard a zip? Opening? Then clicks, metallic clicks. What the hell was he doing? 'Please, please, I need the loo.' This was no act.

'De-dum-de-dum-de...'

'For God's sake, tell me what you're doing.'

'...de-de-de-dum-de-dum-de...'

'Please!' she screamed. No way could she hide the panic now. 'Let me go, I won't tell—'

'Ready? Steady?' Trembling, she braced herself, eyes squeezed tight. 'Go!' Her head snapped back when he snatched the blindfold. She stayed completely still, whimpering. 'Open your eyes.'

If she saw his face...

'Open your fucking eyes.' Saliva hit her cheek. She gasped when he grabbed a handful of her hair, yanked it back.

'Please, no.' The intended scream lodged in her throat, she stared wide-eyed, open-mouthed. The mask hid all but dark pupils glinting through holes in thick black fur. Had she not been scared beyond belief, the gorilla mask might almost have been funny.

'What do you want from me?'

'Watch the birdie, little girlie and say ... cheese. A snap for the family album, eh? Another little surprise for momma.'

FOUR

'And you're absolutely certain it wasn't here when you got home, Mrs Reynolds?' 'It' was a black and white print now inside a clear plastic envelope that lay on the tacky Formica kitchen table. Detective Inspector Sarah Quinn's cool grey eyes focused on the woman slouched in the chair opposite, hoping the body language might give away more than she'd so far said. Since the detectives' arrival, Nicola Reynolds had barely torn her gaze from her daughter's image.

'What part of the word "no" don't you understand? I've told you and the other lot three times now.' She tossed a head in the direction of the door. Two uniformed officers were currently ensconced in a patrol car waiting on the DI's orders. As a matter of course, the attending officers had checked the premises before asking for plain clothes' back-up.

'Is it remotely possible you just didn't notice it?' Sarah tapped her lip. Risking the woman's wrath was worth it: establishing a time-line could be important.

'Christ Almighty.' Nicola's voice dripped contempt. 'Do I look stupid?'

26

Sarah glanced up at DC Dave Harries who leaned against the sink thankfully out of the woman's eye-line. She doubted his nod would have gone down well. As to 'stupid', the DI's jury was out. On the other hand she had no doubt that Reynolds looked like a woman on the edge, teetering on a greased cheese-wire over hot coals. Grey-faced and gaunt-featured, she compulsively raked trembling fingers through a bad dye job. The other hand clutched a mobile phone as if it had life-saving properties. She seemed to be ageing before Sarah's eyes.

'I didn't say that, Mrs Reynolds.' Still watching closely, she waited for the woman – as far as she could – to collect herself. 'Tell me about the photograph. What disturbs you so much?' Sarah regarded the shot as fairly innocuous. It showed Caitlin Reynolds in school uniform mid-stride walking along a street. It looked like a snatched shot, the girl probably unaware of the camera. The typed message attached was less clear: *Hey momma, you're in for a big surprise.* More surprising to Sarah? DCS Baker asking her to turn out on what could be some sort of routine domestic. She might be wrong but the chief's calls seemed increasingly erratic these days.

Mrs Reynolds raised her head, finally met Sarah's gaze. 'You've not said much at all, have you? Coming here, making judgements, disapproving. I can see it in your eyes.'

Unlikely. Sarah's face rarely showed emotion. It was one reason the station clowns called her the Ice Queen – among other things – always behind her back. She suspected the woman's hostility stemmed from several sources: fear, for sure; concern, of course. Guilt certainly couldn't be ruled out. And not just at the disaster area surrounding them. The small tatty kitchen was a tip, ashtrays overflowed on several surfaces and the empties stacked by the bin could've been props for a rendition of 'Ten Green Bottles'. Though going on Reynolds' breath, she'd been hitting the mother's ruin tonight. The woman's alcohol consumption wasn't high on Sarah's priorities.

'It's not my job to judge you.' Unless the woman knew more about her daughter's apparent disappearance than she'd let on. Sarah waited as Nicola checked the damn phone yet again. Either she was distracted or it was a distraction technique. 'OK. You were telling me about the photograph.'

'What is your job then?' Nicola grabbed the crumpled pack of Marlboro, twisted her mouth when she realised the contents had already gone up in smoke. 'Shouldn't you be organizing a search, calling the papers and the telly? Caitlin's out there somewhere and you're just sitting on your backside asking me stupid questions.'

Media friendly already? Sarah gave a thin smile. 'It's my job to ask questions, Mrs Reynolds. We need to know what we're dealing with, how best to go about sorting it.' So far, they'd learned that Caitlin went to Queen's

Ridge comprehensive, that she was an A* pupil who worked hard and had lots of friends. At this stage it might be nothing more sinister than a headstrong girl and a family row. And the mother still hadn't answered the last question. Sarah's cocked head acted as a cue to Harries to record the omission.

'What we're *dealing* with? You make it sound like a game of cards. My daughter's life could be at stake here.'

'Could' being the operative word. Surely giving parents grief was part of a teenager's job description? The girl was sixteen going on seventeen and had only been absent a few hours. 'Why are you so convinced she's at risk, Mrs Reynolds?'

'For God's sake, I don't know where she is. She never stays out, not without calling me.' Her fingers tightened round the phone.

'So she has stayed out before?' The woman's flapped hand was no answer, but sent a signal to Sarah. The silence, bar dripping water and ticking clock, lasted ten seconds. Nicola jumped a mile when Harries shifted to tighten the tap. 'Well, has she?' Sarah persisted.

'Trust me. She wouldn't do this to me.' *Would-n't she?* Besides, it was only half-nine, at Caitlin's age it was hardly 'staying out'. Sarah shuffled slightly in her seat. Nicola was swift to interpret the movement. 'You don't believe me, do you?'

Realistically, she'd no way of knowing. At the

moment Nicola Reynolds, like her daughter, was little more than a blank sheet to the DI. And like most cops, Sarah's experience taught her to suspect her own granny. 'Is Caitlin's father around, Mrs Reynolds?'

'Only if you've got a Ouija board.' Unnecessary and over-the-top antagonism. And Harries was getting more cocked-head prompts from Sarah than an amnesiac actor. This time she threw in a barely perceptible tightening of the lips as well. 'OK, do you have a current partner?'

'What's it to you? I'm her mother. Are you saying I'm not good enough?'

'Stop putting words in my mouth, Mrs Reynolds. We'll get nowhere if you don't co-operate. You called us in, right?' She paused, let the point hit home. 'Have you a recent picture of Caitlin?' Something they could use, just in case.

She nodded, hauled herself up, ambled out of the kitchen. Sarah rolled her eyes at Harries. As it happened, she thought it too early for alarm bells. What teenager hanging out with mates religiously remembered to call home? Caitlin's phone could have been nicked; it could be out of credit. The girl may have just lost track of time. Or for once might not want her mother to know where she was or who she was with.

'This is a good one.' With the ghost of a smile on her lips, Mrs Reynolds handed the pic to Sarah. Dark, glossy hair framed an oval-shaped face, flawless complexion. It was the sort of image that sold toothpaste, or skincare products.

Harries strolled across to take a look over Sarah's shoulder. 'Has Caitlin got a boyfriend, Mrs Reynolds?' His smile and chatty delivery were deceptively casual.

'What sort of question's that?' she snapped.

Sarah glanced up, now knew what was meant by a steely glare. As for the question, it was perfectly reasonable, patently obvious. And if Reynolds couldn't see that she was either dense, in denial, or both.

'It's fair enough, Mrs Reynolds.' DC Chatty Man again, ostensibly oblivious to the impact of his remarks. 'She's a pretty girl. She'll break a few hearts in her time, I bet.'

Going by the glower and clenched teeth, it looked as if breaking kneecaps was more Nicola's baby: Harries' kneecaps.

'What the hell are you implying? That she's out with some lad? Clubbing it?'

'Could she be?' Harries raised an eyebrow.

'I'm not lowering myself to answer that.' She checked the phone again before hauling herself up to reach a new pack of baccy from a shelf. Deliberate or not, she'd skirted virtually every question. Harries had quite a list going. Sarah waited until the cigarette had been lit and the woman re-installed in her seat.

'Is there a reason she may have decided not to come home?' Sarah asked. Reynolds' concrete-curdling glance spoke volumes. But she said nothing. 'Mrs Reynolds. Was everything OK

31

between you and Caitlin this morning?'

Staring at Sarah, she picked a fleck of tobacco from her tongue. 'Fine. Absolutely ... dandy.'

'Sure about that?' Because sure as hell, Sarah wasn't.

'Look, I don't know if you have kids, but my instinct tells me my girl's in no position to make decisions.' She jabbed the cigarette at the plastic envelope. 'This isn't her doing. And if anything happens to her, I swear I'll swing for you.'

So help me out here. 'I can't do it alone, Mrs Reynolds.' At a signal from Sarah, Harries tore a page from his notebook and placed it on the table next to the woman's ashtray. Sarah rose, pointed at the list. 'If Caitlin's not been in touch, I'll need answers to those first thing plus names, numbers, addresses of her friends, male and female.' Placing a card on top of the list, Sarah told her to ring the minute she heard anything.

'What? That's it?'

'For the time being. Think on what I've said.' She glanced at Harries. The woman didn't look up from her phone. 'Stay where you are, Mrs Reynolds. We'll see ourselves out.'

The only response was wavering smoke from the cigarette dangling in her fingers.

Nicola waited until she heard the detectives leave the house, waited until she heard car doors closing then with a trembling finger reopened the email on her phone. Through scalding tears she could barely make it out. Seeing wasn't necessary: every word was burned into her brain.

Naughty, naughty girl. You called the cops, didn't you? If you want to see your precious daughter alive again, I wouldn't advise you to share all my little surprises. The pictures are our secret. Savvy? Play ball with me, and I might play ball ... or something ... with Caitlin. Mum's the word, eh, Nicola?

'It's not some fucking game, asshole.' Face screwed in contempt, Nicola ground out the butt in the ashtray. But what was it? Five minutes after dialling nine-nine-nine, an even starker warning than the one she'd found in the kitchen had arrived on her phone. And a gut-wrenching photograph. Knowing Caitlin's life was at risk upped the ante, she'd been at a loss how to deal with the police. Scared to show them the abductor's latest offerings, desperate to galvanize them into action. Lying and dissembling, Nicola had been treading the finest of lines to buy time. Sobbing now, she stared at the image again; her daughter's terrified face virtually filled the screen. As if she could wipe away the glistening tears, she traced a finger under Caitlin's eyes, and prayed to God time hadn't run out.

Harries hunched over to fasten his seat belt as Sarah fired the engine. She'd told the attending officers to keep an eye on the place, and the girl's description had been circulated to patrol cars. There wasn't a bunch more they could do until morning. Shivering, Sarah pulled up her coat collar. The March wind had dropped by now but so had the mercury; it was brass-monkey grade.

'Reckon it's too late, boss?' Harries must be feeling the chill too, given the way he rubbed his hands.

'For what?' she asked, slowing down to let a mangy black cat slink across the road. Meant to be lucky, wasn't it? Good or bad? She couldn't remember.

'That Indian you promised me on the way over.' The permanently starving and stick-thin DC grinned and patted his six-pack.

She arched an eyebrow; her recollection of the exchange differed. 'What I actually said was let's see how it goes.'

'And?'

'On a scale of one to ten?' She tapped the wheel with an index finger. 'Minus twelve.'

'That's a no-no, then?'

Not buying. Not peckish. Not in the mood. The interview – if that's what you could call it – with Nicola Reynolds had left a bitter taste in Sarah's mouth. The woman's apparent obduracy still rankled. 'Who's a clever boy?'

'Thanks, mu–a'm.'

She twitched a lip at the swift switch from maternal to formal address. Mind, her patronizing tone had asked for the former. 'Nice recovery, Batman.'

'Hey, does that make you—'

'Don't even go there, Dave.' She caught his broad smile in the wing mirror. It didn't take much to keep the guy happy. All she had to do was laugh at his jokes, tell him occasionally he still resembled a young Keith Richards and re-assure him that one day he'd make senior detective. After working with him for three years, she had no doubt of the latter.

'Funny though, 'cause there was me...' There was a glint in her eye when she met his glance. 'There was me, thinking your mind was on the job and you were asking whether it was too late for Caitlin Reynolds.'

'Boss! My mind's always on the job.' Dave's innuendo was as subtle as a flying brick with flashing lights and landing gear. Two or three times now he'd made his personal feelings clear. She knew she only had to say the word and their relationship would go beyond the professional. The potential pitfalls and myriad complications that could ensue – *would* ensue – were all that stopped her from crossing the thin blue line. As for the bottom line? He was well fancy-able. Not that she'd told him. She'd only recently admitted it to herself. She also knew that a relationship, fling, liaison, whatever was increasingly tempting. Like a lot of cops, Sarah was sick of going back to an empty house, lonely bed, solo breakfast. Maybe if fit guys were falling over themselves beating a daily path to her door?

'OK, you win, DI Quinn.' He had in mind the verbal stand-off. 'What about the girl? Is it too late?'

'You're the budding Rebus. You tell me.' The faux goading was more of a prompt; she'd formed her own take, didn't want to colour Dave's.

'Mole. Mountain. Storm. Teacup. Crown. Jewel.' He stretched impossibly long legs into the footwell, laced fingers in his lap. 'A looker like Caitlin? My money's on her being with a bloke. Christ, if my ma had been anything like Nicola Reynolds, I'd have legged it way back.'

'You're all heart, Dave.'

'You did ask.'

'Fair point. Well made.' His assessment of the woman was even harsher than Sarah's. Had he hit the nail on the proverbial? Nicola Reynolds to say the least had come across as flaky. But apart from gratuitous hostility, 'least said' had been the woman's fall-back stance. Sarah hadn't been able to read her at all. Surely if Nicola really thought her daughter was in danger, she'd have moved heaven and earth with a toothpick to help, not stonewall every question? Sarah waited while Dave, who was on a call, brought whoever was on duty in the squad room up to speed, then said: 'So, you reckon the girl might've done a runner?' He waggled an either-way hand, said it wouldn't surprise him.

They drove in silence for a while, Sarah mentally digesting Harries' input. With all the moles

36

in mountainous teacups, he clearly thought the mother was making too big a thing of Caitlin's absence. She narrowed her eyes. 'I don't follow, Dave. Why jewel, crown?'

'Jewel *in* the Crown, boss. The Indian on the Moseley Road? Mind dropping by? I could murder a biriyani.'

Smiling, she shook her head. 'OK. You win.'

'Fancy playing something else, boss?'

FIVE

Susan used her sing-song voice again. 'Where ... *are* ... you? I'm ... *coming* ... ready or not.' She giggled softly. Pauline's high-pitched squeal had just rung out from the copse. The silly little kid got so lathered up with excitement she could barely contain herself. Susan raced across the long grass and hid behind the gnarly old oak tree. Its massive pitted trunk was smothered in dark green moss. Susan hated touching it when it was damp, but it was hardly slimy at all now. Her glance darted to all the usual hidey places, but she couldn't spot any tell-tale sign. Usually she'd catch sight of Pauline's tiny white sandal or glimpse her curls. Not to worry. Susan only had to bide her time; she knew it wouldn't be long before she heard rustling or another squeal.

Head cocked, she pricked her ears, held her breath. A fat bumble bee flew near and Susan swatted it away. Was there jam on her face? Do bees even like jam? The bee was still too close for comfort. She flapped both hands until it buzzed off.

Still not a sound from ... Susan stiffened. What was that? A splash in the stream. And another. She angled her head towards the noise. It wouldn't be Pauline; the kid knew better than to go near water on her own. Years ago a toddler had drowned in that stream and every parent in the village warned their kids not to play there. Anyway it had stopped now. Susan relaxed. It would've been a frog or a bird or something.

She dashed to the next tree then slowly peered round the trunk. Her nose wrinkled when she caught a whiff of smoke. She knew it was from a ciggie 'cause her dad smoked and she hated the smell on him. Odds on it was Alfie Marsden. He'd built a den in the copse and was always skulking there having a crafty fag. His mum had caught him last week puffing away on one of her Woodbines. Betty Marsden was only four foot ten but she'd marched the big lummock straight to the village bobby who'd given him a right telling-off. He probably wouldn't have understood though. Susan's mum said Alfie had the mind of a child. Other folk called him a gentle giant. Susan had overheard lots more comments but those were the kindest. She reckoned a lot of

38

the village kids were cruel to Alfie but he couldn't help being a bit slow. Besides, he was always kind to her and Paul—

Pauline. Where the devil was she? The little madam must have found a new hiding place. Darting keen glances left, right and centre, Susan sneaked to the next tree then the next then the next. Not so much as a peep. She did clock a dead useful bit of wood near a clump of dusty nettles though. Crouching down, she disentangled the fallen branch from the weeds and stripped off a few twigs. She held it this way and that. Abracadabra! It could be anything she wanted: walking stick, cane, sword, rifle, spear. Susan was pleased as punch with the find – just wait until she showed Pauline.

Clutching the stick, Susan tiptoed into the clearing and stood very still, just like the statues in the churchyard. A smile played at her lips. She'd have to sprout wings to be like those statues. She strained her ears so hard she thought her head would burst.

Right. Only one thing for it, she'd have to play the usual trick. Never mind squeal, Pauline sometimes wet her pants when she heard Susan's scary voice. Taking a deep breath, she cupped her hands round her mouth. 'I'm coming to get you. Come out, come out, wherever you are.'

The birdlife emerged all of a flap. The sudden loud cacophony of squawks and snapping twigs startled Susan so much she ducked instinctively and very nearly lost her footing. She felt a right idiot and just knew she'd have beetroot cheeks. Thank God no one was watching. Pauline certainly couldn't have seen or she'd have split her sides laughing. Susan frowned. She couldn't have heard the monster voice either. She must've ventured further than normal.

Susan cupped her hands again and yelled louder. 'Come out, come out, wherever you are.' Waiting. Listening. She'd have to shout even louder: 'I'm coming to get you.' Not a bean. But the scary voice *always* worked. Cross now, Susan stamped her foot. What was Pauline playing at? The little madam had better look out or she'd be in for a damn good slapping.

SIX

Sarah studied her face in the bathroom mirror. Nordic colouring was all well and good but a whiter shade of pale? Either she'd looked better or new lighting might be a sound investment. Hands round the sink, she leaned forward and peered closer. The mauve shadows might well colour co-ordinate with the dove-grey eyes but the combined effect put her in mind of an anaemic vampire. She fumbled round in a minuscule make-up bag until her fingers found the Touche

Éclat. The DI usually eschewed war paint, left it to the likes of her old – for want of a better word – friend, the journalist Caroline King, but this morning a little slap was definitely called for.

Her lip curved as she blended in the cream: Dave had been lucky not to get a little slap last night with his tongue-in-cheek suggestion about playing mummies and daddies. They'd not just dropped by the Jewel in the Crown – over the space of a couple of hours they'd shared a table and a lot of laughs. She couldn't recall in what context he'd come out with the quip but she knew she'd brushed it off. Knew too that the spicy food and two Cobras would mean a disturbed night. Had it been worth it? Yes. No. Probably. She rolled her eyes. Make your mind up, woman.

Either way, twice she'd had to get up to use the loo, taken the opportunity to check her phone at the same time. That there'd not been a peep out of Nicola Reynolds, she read as a good sign.

She examined her face again. *Result.* Forget the lighting; the concealer had worked its magic. Reaching for the mascara wand, she decided she might as well go down the King route for once. After a quick coat of lip gloss, she took less than a minute to expertly twist her long blonde hair into a well-behaved bun. Talk about fine art. Smiling, she saluted her reflection: DI Quinn reporting for duty. She looked down. Actually, clothes wouldn't be a bad idea. Still smiling, she retrieved her phone, padded back to the bedroom. The ivory satin duvet was barely crumpled; only one pillow bore a dent. Sarah pursed her lips. Mummies and daddies? There were far worse games to play.

'What on earth were you playing at, Nic?' Neil Lomas dangled the mobile at arm's length as if it held the lurgy. Nicola thought he might be going down with something already: a pink flush darkened the dusting of freckles across his nose and a line of sweat glistened over his top lip. He'd inadvertently raked his sandy hair into unflattering tufts. 'You so should have given it to the police.'

The remark stung, as did Nicola's eyes. Blowing out smoke, she appraised Neil through the haze, hoped she wasn't seeing him properly for the first time. Over the last ten hours, she'd beaten herself up so much, the last thing she needed was the man who supposedly loved her weighing in too. She'd thought he'd understand her actions, or lack of them. Brushing a layer of ash from her skirt she murmured, 'Thanks for your support, Neil.'

His mouth tightened almost imperceptibly. Contempt? Anger? Disgust? Nicola couldn't read the signs, currently didn't care. She took a final drag on her umpteenth cigarette and ground the butt in a saucer. It had taken courage to confide in Neil, confide in anyone. He'd probably have come to the house earlier if she'd phoned, but she'd convinced herself the psycho holding Caitlin was spying, monitoring her calls. When she eventually rang, she'd been cagey, asked him casually to drop by before college. And when she'd showed him the images, she'd studied his face as he scanned the emails and notes. She'd hoped for a few words of comfort, not a bloody lecture. Slumped in her chair now, she watched him rest an elbow on the table, close his eyes, pinch the bridge of his nose. The Thinker pose was marred by shaving nicks on his neck oozing tiny pearls of blood.

The silence unnerved her. She reached for the radio, tuned to a local news station, just in case. Stupid, really. The police would have told her if...

'I'm sorry, Nic.' She flinched when he laid his hand on hers. 'Seeing her like that ... I can't bear to think of it.'

'You can't? What do you think it's doing to me?' Fractured sleep. Mental torture. The very thought of food made her gag. She'd gone over it again and again in her head, wracked her brain for reasons why this was happening. Who could be so cruel?

'Then why...?' He swallowed. 'Why the hell didn't you tell the police what's going on?'

'I was scared, goddamn it.' She whacked the table with the edge of her fist. *'Am* scared.' She dropped her head in her hands, couldn't let her mind go there. She heard him get up, move across the kitchen, fill the kettle. Great. Tea but no sympathy...

'I'll make coffee. You look as if you need it.'

The little sleep Nicola had snatched had been head down at the kitchen table. Stale smells clung to yesterday's crumpled clothes and vestiges of make-up lingered in the lines round her eyes. Not that his dig was aimed at her appearance. She knew the mouthwash had done little to mask her gin breath. She drummed the table with her fingers. 'Don't hold back, Neil.'

He stiffened momentarily. 'You're the one who held back, Nic.' Turning, he held her gaze for the first time that morning. 'If you want my opinion, you need to call the police now. Work out what to say, why you failed to put them in the picture.' He raised a palm in apology for the unintentional pun.

'Christ, Neil, you've read the email.' She snatched another cigarette. '"If you want to see your precious daughter alive again ..." I can't take that risk.' Trembling, she couldn't hold the flame steady.

'Nic, sweetheart.' He knelt, gentler now, held the lighter for her. 'Whoever's doing this is toying with you, playing mind games. I bet he's just taking a punt that you called the police. He couldn't know for sure, could he? Unless...'

'What?' She grabbed his wrist. 'Unless what?'

He paused, stroked a strand of hair from her eyes. 'Is there something you're not telling me, Nic?'

Christ, he didn't believe her. Three times she'd said it and now, four: 'I have no idea who's

44

doing this, Neil. Or why.' She fought to keep calm, couldn't afford to give in to the incipient hysteria, or she'd collapse completely. She needed to stay strong for Caitlin's sake.

'Then bring the police in on it, Nic. It's their job.' He wiped away a tear with a thumb. 'And time's passing.'

'Like I don't know that?'

'So the sooner the better. They have procedures in place to deal with this sort of thing.' He glanced at the phone. 'Think how bad it'll look if they find out you lied to them.'

She widened her eyes, realized it had been a telling pause. 'Lied? I didn't—'

'OK. Misled. Failed to mention. Kept them in the dark. Call it what you will. It boils down to the same thing. They'll not like it.'

'And what about me? What if I don't like it?' Far from helping, Neil had made her feel worse. He'd done sod all to make sense of it and not even tried to see it from her point of view. 'Just whose side are you on, Neil?'

He frowned as if the question was beyond him. 'Caitlin's of course. Who else?'

The man cupped Caitlin's face between his hands, twisted it roughly this way and that. 'Wakey, wakey, rise and shine.'

Disorientated, she snapped her eyes open. 'What?' she gasped as pain tore through her tethered limbs. 'What is it?'

'Not "what", you silly bitch.' Looming over

45

her, he jerked her head right then left then right again. She caught glimpses of a tripod, a laptop, a bulging rucksack; otherwise the room looked the same: grimy white walls, stone floor, steel desk, filing cabinet, no window. 'I'm asking, "which?" Which is your best side, eh?' The thick fur mask concealed all but the darkly glittering eyes, but she heard the sly smirk in his muffled voice. 'Hey, it rhymes: which bitch, which bitch, which bitch.' He looped his thumbs through his belt, thrust his crutch forward. 'Know what, girlie? I don't reckon you've got a good side. Have to do a full-on mug shot, eh?'

The twat could do what he liked. He'd dicked her around for the last time. 'Go fuck yourself, monkey man.'

Dead silence. Stock still. The gorilla head looked unintentionally hilarious. She could piss herself laughing, except she'd wet herself in the night. She was past caring about that too. Before the drugs he'd forced down her throat kicked in, she'd worked out the guy's pathetic game. Obviously, he got off on scaring the shit out of her and if he was hell bent on killing her, there was little she could do about it however she played it. At least she'd go down fighting.

'What did you say, bitch?'

'Are you deaf as well as brain dead, monkey man?'

'Oh, Caitlin.' He crossed his arms, tapped a foot. The black cargo pants and Converse train- ers were rough clues to his age, but gave nothing

46

else away. 'You naughty, naughty, girl.'

'Yeah? Tell someone who gives a shit.' Her mouth was dry or she'd have spat in his stupid face.

'I'll tell your ma then, shall I?' He leaned towards her, couldn't get any closer if he tried. 'That her precious daughter needs a damn good slapping.'

'Your breath stinks, monkey man.' She gave a wide-mouthed yawn. 'Go clean your teeth.'

Tutting, he slowly shook his head and walked away. Heart racing, she watched until he was out the door. She heard a drawer, maybe a cupboard being opened. Then a sound like something cutting through air. Whip? Ruler? Neither. He came back brandishing a thin tapering cane. 'I'd so hoped it wouldn't be necessary.' He stood in front of her, gently tapping it against his palm.

'Do one, douche bag.'

The air whistled as he whipped back the cane, held it aloft. She closed her eyes, braced herself but, really, what was a bit more pain anyway? *Get on with it, psycho.* What the hell was he doing? It took a few seconds for Caitlin to identify the noise. Wary, she opened an eye. The mad bastard was laughing, clutching his sides, bent double with it.

'Nothing's that funny, mate.'

'Oh, it is, Caitlin,' he spluttered. 'Believe me that was dead funny.'

Then he straightened and snatched off the mask.

SEVEN

'Late night was it, Quinn?' Baker sniffed. 'Watch the wind don't change. Or you'll stick like that.' No preamble. No, God forbid, 'Good morning'. The chief had spotted Sarah in the corridor, beckoned her in to his office with a stubby finger and now lounged back in a leather executive chair, hands on head, size twelve brogues up on the desk. Sarah stood in the threshold open-mouthed, machine coffee in one hand, phone and keys in the other. Cheeky git. Baker could bloody talk; he could do with more than a touch of *éclat* himself. She puckered her nostrils when a waft of his Paco Rabanne entered her airspace but her motionless stance wasn't down to olfactory overload; she was mentally censoring come-back lines that wouldn't get her fired. 'Sod off.'

'Sod off, *sir.*' He whipped his feet down, patted his tie, pointed to the seat opposite. 'What have you got on today, Quinn?'

She briefly toyed with the idea of describing her rather fetching ensemble of taupe linen trouser suit, ivory cashmere crew neck and calf-length camel coat. But he'd probably have her sectioned; besides, he wasn't making polite inquiries about her gear. Knowing Baker, he'd already have read her initial report on Caitlin Reynolds' supposed vanishing act and have something more pressing up his sleeve.

'I need to put in a call to the missing girl's—'

'Yeah, I caught the drift.' He waved a disparaging arm. 'You reckon she's playing away?'

'Or gone AWOL. Well, absent without her mother's leave, that is.' Sarah blew on the coffee, took a quick sip. 'I'll pick up the O'Malley investigation, there's a stack of outstanding interviews and I need to prepare papers for the Lawson trial next week. After that there's—'

'Yeah, yeah. Nothing to write home about in other words.' He plucked a bulging file off his desk, handed it over. 'There you go.'

Her heart hit her court shoes at the initials on the cover. 'Police and Crime Commission?'

'It's a routine meeting. No sweat.' Liar. Either that or his face was leaking. She also registered that Baker's thick black mane wasn't so much subtly streaked as shot through with white. Mind it was about time the old goat gave up the Grecian 2000. 'It's this afternoon, Quinn. You can pretend to be me.' She'd seen sincerer smiles on a clinically depressed grass snake. 'It'll be good experience for you.'

'You're too kind, chief,' she murmured. She'd walked right into it. The prospect of x number of hours in a stuffy room packed with y number of sweaty bodies equalled one seriously pissed off

DI. And given the size of the file: 'I'd better get on, skim through it.'

He waved her down. 'Hold your horses, Quinn.' Stifling a sigh, she sank back into the chair. Baker's American ranching holidays had a lot to answer for, including the equestrian lingo that nowadays peppered his vocab. *Yeehaw.* 'How's Davy doing under your mat— wing?'

Maternal? She spat out a mental mouthful of feathers. 'Were you about to say maternal?'

'Calm down, dear. It's not always about you. I'm after a professional run down on the boy wonder.' He'd assigned the nickname on Dave's first day in CID. Like a lot of Bakerisms it had stuck. 'How tight a rein's the lad on these days?'

Biting her tongue, she rose above the David Cameron meets Michael Winner jibe. The chief's query had set more serious antennae quivering. 'He's a good cop. Shows a lot of initiative. Why?'

'Thought so.' Baker steepled his fingers. 'Far be it from me to party poop, but isn't it about time the lad put in for his stripes?'

Cheeky sod with double knobs on. Every detective constable who passed the sergeant's exams had to go back into uniform for a spell. So in one fell – make that foul – swoop Baker had not only categorized her working relationship with Dave as cosy, but also questioned her professional judgement as to his progress up the career ladder. She clenched her fists: if she bit her tongue any more, she'd lose the power of speech. 'Are you saying I'm not pushing Harries enough?' Did Baker have a point? Was she subconsciously holding Harries back because she didn't want to lose him as her bag man?

'I've no idea which bit you're holding, Quinn. You tell me.'

'I'm sorry.' She jumped to her feet, just stopped the chair toppling over. 'I don't have to listen to this.'

'You're not sorry. And you're not going anywhere.'

Pursing her lips, she sat down again, felt like a frigging Jackie in the box.

'I've got both your interests at heart, Quinn. Dave clearly needs stretching. And you're not getting any younger.' Her mouth formed a perfect 'O'. Could he be more offensive? 'You've been DI how long? Five years. Six? Time for you to think big career wise, too. It's not like you're dying to be a yummy mummy any time soon, is it?'

Offensive? He'd barely started. She shook her head. 'I don't believe I'm hearing this.'

'Take the wasp out your mouth. All I'm saying is: time waits for no man, Quinn.' He caught the look on her face and raised a hand. 'OK, or woman. You know where I'm coming from, but ... You're not stupid.'

'Can I go now? I need a word with the squad.' Not to mention time to think on what he'd said.

'I'll tag along.' She heard a wince as he struggled to his feet and grabbed his jacket.

51

'You OK, chief?'

'Never better, lass.'

He was breathing heavily by the time they reached the squad room. He stood to one side, played doorman. 'You know, Quinn, I'd never have said maternal about you.'

'Good.' Sarah smiled as she squeezed past. 'I'm glad to hear it.'

'Nah. Word I had in mind was "mature".'

If only he'd come out with it a couple of seconds sooner – she'd have stamped on his bloody foot. Harries, who was on the phone, lifted a finger when he saw her. She waited at his desk while he jotted a line or two before replacing the receiver. 'Good timing, boss.'

Good timing, bad news. The words were written all over his face, it was the fine print she couldn't make out. 'The missing girl,' he said. 'That was control. They've just taken a call.'

Sarah frowned. 'From Nicola Reynolds?'

'No. From Caitlin.'

EIGHT

A dozen squad members sat in shocked silence round a hastily set-up incident room. Operation Vixen was up, if not quite running. The recording had been played twice now. It hadn't taken long to get a copy of the triple-nine exchange but given the new impetus, every minute counted; God knew how many had been squandered. Features impassive, Sarah perched on a desk at the front, arms folded, ankles crossed: a subconscious attempt to stop a self-inflicted kick up the backside?

Though efforts were underway to trace the call, door-to-door inquiries on-going along Caitlin's route home from Queen's Ridge and two teams of detectives currently interviewing up at the school, to the DI's mind they were playing catch-up: the nigh on twelve-hour delay caused her professional grief. Mind, that was nothing compared with the grief she'd be giving Nicola Reynolds.

'Poor bloody kid.' Propped against his favoured patch of off-white wall, DS John Hunt voiced what was probably communal thinking. The sergeant's balled fists were telling too, but Caitlin's words had the bigger impact.

Though a few ideas had been bounced round and tasks mostly assigned, Sarah reckoned another airing wouldn't do any harm. It could only serve to underline the urgency, reinforce the nature of the beast they were up against. She nodded at the squad's other long serving DS. 'Once more please, Woodie.'

'With feeling, ma'am.' Office Manager Paul Wood spoke through gritted teeth; there was no irony in the remark. Burly, broad-shouldered and butch with it, he was known affectionately round the station as Twig. Sarah had watched the colour drain from his face when he listened before. Beth Lally, a newish DC not long back from maternity leave, was still making heavy weather of blowing her nose. Even the chief, who'd taken up squatter's rights on a corner of the next desk, looked uneasy. What Caitlin said tore the heart; the pleading, almost resigned tone froze the blood.

'Help me, please help me.'

'Caller, can you—?'

'My name's Caitlin. Caitlin Reynolds. The man. He's holding me prisoner.'

'Caitlin, can you—?' A female operator. Calm. Authoritative. Reassuring. Probably trying to coax the girl to speak louder.

'I've sneaked his phone. I've not got long. He says he's going to kill me.

'Caitlin. Where—?'

'He says he's contacted my mum. He says she

54

knows everything. I'm really scared. Please, come and get me...'

A stinging slap, a scream. Silence. Even third time round, a couple of officers flinched. The soundtrack was difficult to marry with the girl's smiling image blue-tacked to the whiteboard. The 'just in case' picture Sarah had taken from Nicola Reynolds last night would soon be out on general release on the Net, in the news, dominating bulletins, drawing out witnesses, prompting memories, pricking consciences. Without intelligence, locating Caitlin in a city the size of Birmingham made needle tracing in a barn full of burning hay look like a piece of piss. And that assumed the girl hadn't been whisked away – for all they knew she could be in Brighton, Belgium, Belize.

'Does it sound echoey to anyone?' Brow furrowed, Harries sat at the front, hunched forward, elbows on knees. 'Maybe she's in an empty house, some sort of derelict building?'

'That narrows it down then.' The drawled aside came from a balding skinny guy at the back. Sarah could never remember his name.

'You.' Baker snapped his fingers at the clown, pointed at the door. 'Now.' The chief swept his gaze over every member of the squad as the detective slunk out. 'We pull together on this. No taking pops. No dicking around. Got it?'

Sarah glanced through the window waiting for the shuffling and throat-clearing to subside. A blank slate of a sky, not even a glint of sun. Said it all really. 'Dave, can you get a copy to the audio boys?' Maybe they could shed a ray or two.

'Already in hand, boss.'

Fingers crossed then. If specialist equipment picked up anything extraneous, it could provide a pointer. Sound of a train maybe, church bells, seagulls, call to Mecca. Straw being clutched? She sighed, supposed a talking parrot big in neighbourhood watch was out of the question.

'You'd think she'd sound terrified, wouldn't you?' Beth Lally's smooth cheeks hollowed as she sucked a pen, slowly circled a slim ankle. Talk about cartoon pensive. To Sarah, the DC was playing to an audience again. The pose screamed 'look at me', and the blonde's customary wardrobe of power suits and pearls was doubtless part of the act. Maybe if Lally ditched the dramatics, Sarah would have more time for her occasional pearl of wisdom. 'Go on, DC Lally.' The prompt was long overdue.

'I don't know ... It's worse somehow, isn't it?' She tilted her head at the player. 'Her ... acceptance, almost? Like she knows time's running out.'

Sarah's patience was on the same page. 'Your point being?'

Two blobs of blusher deepened a shade: pique-pink. 'It was just an observation ... ma'am.'

The pause was deliberate. Sarah let it go this time; she'd played the same game often enough with senior officers. 'Thanks for sharing.' And if she believed that ... 'Right, if there's nothing else?' Sarah slipped an arm into the sleeve of her jacket, watched as they all took their cue. Most would join the teams out in Moseley establishing Caitlin's last known movements, sightings.

The chief hadn't budged. Sweat beaded his pale face; he really didn't look too hot. Out of the corner of an eye, she caught him lift his cuff, glance at his watch. It was usually a get-on-with-it-woman warning. Not this time. Like her, like everyone on the case, he was chomping at the proverbial for the woman of the hour's late arrival. Nicola Reynolds hadn't been in when uniform turned up at the house first thing. Out walking, clearing her head, apparently. God knew why when her daughter was missing. Not that it was Sarah's most pressing question. It barely made the cut on to an ever-lengthening and increasingly urgent list.

'Should be any time now, chief.' Sipping from a bottle of water, she saw a tiny muscle flex in his clenched jaw. It was Baker's only perceptible response. Maybe, like Sarah, he was thinking on Caitlin's words: *He's contacted my mum. She knows everything.*

If Caitlin had it right, Nicola Reynolds had it in her grasp to help them solve the case almost before it got off the ground, not to mention save her daughter's life. So why the hell hadn't the bloody woman opened her mouth last night? *And why the hell*, Sarah thought, *hadn't I pushed her more?* Baker probably sensed she was giving herself a hard time; even she had to admit the old dinosaur displayed the occasional sensitive streak.

'Yeah, well.' He sniffed, slid off the desk, paused in front of Caitlin's photo on the whiteboard. 'For her sake, Quinn, you'd best hope I get a damn sight more out of the mother than you did.'

NINE

With Baker in the lead interview chair, pussyfooting around was rarely an option; with a girl's life at risk a pulled punch wasn't even on the table. Sarah checked the audio and video gear then sat back, glanced at the chief, who was running through his notes, last-minute homework. They were in Interview Room One's metaphorical starting blocks, ready to roll soon as Nicola Reynolds showed. 'We're good to go, chief.'

'Bring it on.' Straightening, he pushed back a shirt sleeve. Hirsute or what? She reckoned you could plait the hair on his arms. 'I'll give her five minutes to come clean, Quinn.'

Before you play dirty? The carp was unjustified. 'Fair enough.' Her kid glove treatment last night hadn't worked. And Caitlin sure needed someone on side. The mother hadn't exactly pulled her weight. If Reynolds had even an inkling of what...

'Look, just what's going on here?' Nicola was in fine voice in the corridor. Finer than Caitlin's for sure. 'Get your hands off me. You said...' As little as possible had been uniform's brief. Forewarned and all that.

Sarah had shot out of her seat to open the door. 'Mrs Reynolds. Come in, sit down.'

'You again?'

The DI caught a whiff of sour flesh and eau de smoke as Reynolds brushed past, headed straight for the chief. God help her if she thought he'd be a softer touch. 'What's this all about? I was on the verge of putting in a call when your lot turn up and drag me down here.'

The chief held out a chair, gave her his name and rank, and a tight smile. 'Call us about what, Mrs Reynolds?'

'Caitlin, of course.' Still standing, she tugged a fleshy ear lobe. 'She's absolutely fine.'

'OK.' Baker stretched the two syllables. 'Take a seat please.' Sarah would give a lot to see his expression but her brief was to watch Reynolds and she hadn't shifted her gaze from the woman's face. The lines appeared deeper and the red-rimmed amber eyes looked sore.

'So where is she?' Baker laced podgy fingers in his lap.

'I ... I'm ... not sure.' Head down, she picked a bit of loose skin near her thumb.

'But you know she's fine?' The smile was not warm. 'How does that work then?'

'She rang.'

'Course she did.' Like it went without saying. 'And when was this?'

She glanced up, mouth turned down. 'Couple of hours ago?'

'You're asking me?'

'I never wear a watch, like, but it'd be around seven.'

'Right.' The grating noise was the scratching of stubble, the chief clearly not in a hurry. 'Remind me, DI Quinn, what time did Caitlin call us?'

Sarah held the woman's wide-eyed gaze. 'A little after seven.' She saw shock for sure and something that could have been fear. 'Thirteen minutes past, to be precise. And quite frankly, "fine" isn't a word that springs to mind.'

Reynolds dropped her head in her hands, kneaded the scalp with her nails. Through her jagged sobs and heaving breaths, Sarah caught muffled words: God. Help. Forgive.

The big man in the sky might, she thought, but the big man at the desk would need a hell of a lot more persuading.

'You're not just wasting my valuable time; your daughter's is at a premium too.' A puce-faced Baker paced the floor, hands jammed in trouser pockets. Sarah reckoned the distancing was deliberate: it kept Nicola Reynolds out of arm's

– and harm's – way. Even the DI itched to shake some sense into the woman. Baker had suspended the earlier session, had to wait until Reynolds calmed down: PACE had a lot to answer for in the chief's book. The Police and Criminal Evidence Act, not the speed of his questioning. After being brought back to the interview room, Reynolds had slumped in the chair and, almost without prompting, opened her mouth and belatedly handed over her mobile. Comms were now examining the phone; copies of the photographs and emails lay on the scuffed desktop.

Reynolds wiped snot from her nose with a crumpled tissue. 'Please believe me. I've told you everything now.' The self-pitying wail grated on Sarah. It was Caitlin who needed the pity and a parent who wasn't a congenital liar.

'Like you told DI Quinn everything last night?' Baker reinforced the remark by pointing at his watch. 'More than twelve hours ago.

'I was scared.'

'*You* were scared?' Lifting the pic of a cowed, shackled Caitlin, he studied it for a few seconds then slid it across the table. Enough said. But not by Reynolds. If Caitlin was correct, her mother knew more, knew everything. She'd already been caught out withholding crucial evidence and could face charges down the line. Baker had guessed correctly that if the woman wasn't under arrest she'd not feel the need for a lawyer or, as Baker invariably put it, a bollocking time-waster wig-wearing brief. He'd trotted out the

61

old 'helping police inquiries line' – not to keep Reynolds sweet but because he wanted full disclosure soonest. And Sarah knew that if the woman continued holding back, he'd play the tape of her daughter's voice.

'I was protecting her. Can't you see that?' Reynolds, perhaps unwittingly, was shredding the tissue, and white flecks of paper joined ground-in ash on her skirt. 'He said I'd never see her again if I showed you the stuff he sent.'

'Said?' Sarah snapped. 'You've spoken to him?'

She waved what was left of the tissue. 'Figure of speech.'

'Slip of the tongue?'

'You're twisting my words.' She jabbed a finger at the printout. 'I meant what he says in that.'

Baker picked up the paper, read the last part of the message aloud: *The pictures are our secret. Savvy? Play ball with me, and I might play ball ... or something ... with Caitlin. Mum's the word, eh, Nicola?*

Going by Reynolds' reaction, it could have been a shopping list, or a phone book. Sarah played a pen between her fingers. Incongruous laughter from the corridor broke the near silence.

'He calls you Nicola,' Baker mused. 'Sounds pretty pally to me.' Her shrug provoked his jaw's tell-tale twitch. 'Are you sure you've no idea who sent it? Why he's doing this?'

'I wish.' The tone sounded glib.

'So do I, love.' Mr Nice Guy, but the twitch in his jaw was like a burrowing maggot. He leaned in as close as he could get, lowered his voice even further. 'I wish your daughter wasn't being held by a psycho. And I wish you had the sense you were born with.'

'That's not fair. I want to help, but—'

'Good. Here's your starter for ten: where's your daughter being held?'

'Here we go again.' She sighed, shook her head. 'Do you not think I'd tell you?'

'Got it in one, Mrs Reynolds. It's a bad habit. Lying.' Bane of a cop's life, Sarah reckoned. Like a lot of people, Reynolds had looked them in the eye and lied through her bridgework. Hardly surprising their trust in the woman was in short supply. 'And for the life of me, love, I don't know why you're doing it.'

Nor Sarah. If it were her child, there was nothing she wouldn't do to help.

'I'm not lying.'

'Easy for you to say.' Baker sighed, sat down again, smoothed his tie.

'Look, I know I should've been straight before, but—'

'You weren't.' He pulled a file closer. 'What if I tell you I have evidence from someone who says you know where Caitlin is?'

'Bollocks to that.' She clamped her arms across her chest. 'Whoever it is, they're lying.'

'You reckon?' Baker tilted his head. 'Let's

63

hear it, inspector.' Both detectives had hoped it wouldn't come to this, but Reynolds' intransigence plus a ticking clock limited their options. The edited version contained only Caitlin's voice. Even without the scream, Sarah had found it distressing. God knew what it would do to the mother.

'My name's Caitlin Reynolds. The man. He's holding me prisoner. I've sneaked his phone. I've not got long. He says he's going to kill me. He says he's contacted my mum. He says she knows everything. I'm really scared. Please, come and get me.'

Nothing. Then Reynolds' breathing became more laboured as her eyes narrowed to dark slits. Shit. She was about to pass out. Sarah half rose, ready to grab her before she hit the tiles. 'Keep away from me.' She spat out the order, dragged the back of her hand across her mouth. 'What are you trying to do?' Saliva glistened on the desk.

Baker shifted in his seat. 'Meaning?'

'That's not Caitlin. I've never heard that voice before in my life.'

'She's still a lying bastard, Quinn.' En route to their cars, Sarah had to lengthen her not-in-considerable stride to keep up with the chief's single-minded strut across the tarmac. The rattling pace would do him no harm if the size of his paunch showcased by the flapping jacket was anything to go by. 'If she'd not withheld the emails and the photos...' He jabbed a finger in the DI's direction.

Sarah nodded. No need to spell it out. With Reynolds' cooperation from the get-go, conceivably the inquiry would be further forward. As it stood, Operation Vixen wasn't even back to square one: the shock revelation pointed to a whole new board game. Less Clue-do, more Clue-less. It seemed now as if the perpetrator wasn't just pulling Reynolds' strings, he clearly believed he could jerk the police round as well. Quite the comedian. And part of a double act? No wonder the girl on the tape didn't sound scared: if she'd been reading his script cracking a laugh would be a bigger fear. Mind, if the cops decided to release the tape to the media, joker man and his straight girl might laugh on the other side of their faces.

What concerned Sarah most was the use of a stand-in to make the call. Did it mean the original was no longer available? Was Caitlin not up to it? Had she – God forbid – already been silenced? She'd certainly not phoned home. After further questioning Nicola had broken down again, admitted the call from Caitlin had been a fabrication, another cack-handed attempt to buy time to protect her daughter.

'What kind of mother is she, for fuck's sake, Quinn?' Finding out everything they could about Nicola Reynolds, plus background on other players – main or not – were lines being actively pursued by the squad. Given that motive was key to most cases, they needed to put flesh on these people's bones to establish why Caitlin had been abducted. It was almost inconceivable the perp had just picked the Reynolds' name out of a hat.

For her part, Nicola had at last supplied a few of the names they'd asked for: Neil Lomas, her current partner; Luke Holden, Caitlin's one-time boyfriend; a whole bunch of school besties plus the girl's grannie, Linda Walker. Of her own volition, Nicola had offered up the name of a neighbour who claimed he'd spotted Caitlin on the day she disappeared. Ronald Gibson reckoned the girl had been on the wag but according to witnesses at the school she'd been there all day. It was a loose end that needed tying.

'Stupid sodding woman,' Baker muttered, opening the Merc door, chucking in his brief-case. *Give it a rest, man.* Nicola Reynolds had certainly rattled the chief's cage but Sarah reckoned his anger was down to more than that. She sensed he blamed himself for letting the woman wrong-foot – *back*-foot – the inquiry. What did they say about the best form of defence? Sarah knew the feeling: been there, done that, shrunk the t-shirts. Course, it might have something to do with the imminent PCC meeting. New developments meant Sarah couldn't sit in for him this afternoon.

She held the driver's door as he struggled into his seat belt. 'Yeah, well, Shona won't take any shit, chief.' At Sarah's suggestion, DC Shona

66

Bruce would pick up the Nicola Reynolds' interview where they'd left off. Apart from Baker and the DI having fresh fish to grill, squad legend had it that Brucie could get a corpse talking. Beth Lally's interview technique wasn't in the same class; hers was a watching brief. Sarah smiled to herself. Bruce and Lally. Sounded like the next TV cop show. Eat your hearts out, Scott and Bailey, Cagney and Lacey. Scrub the last one, it showed her age.

Baker pulled the door to, wound down the window. 'Something amusing us, Quinn?'

'You know me, chief.' She wiped the smile off her face. 'Always looking on the bright side.'

'Regular ray of sunshine you, missus.' The wink meant he knew he was pushing his luck.

'Yeah, well, I can't see Reynolds pulling another fast one.'

'Fast one?' He started the motor. 'Over my dead body. And get that bloody news conference sorted, will you?'

TEN

Caroline King knew how to give good sound bite. Live TV interviews beat recorded every way, every time: the adrenaline buzz, the immediacy, the margin for on-air error and all that. But beggars can't be choosers and for once, network journo Caroline wasn't calling the shots. The not-so-big gun today was Colin Ford, a BBC regional reporter who, Caroline suspected, harboured delusions of adequacy. Still, needs must. She'd smile, be a good girl and say all the right things for the wannabe. But then Caroline, an award-winning journalist as the back flap trumpeted, would do almost anything to promote her first book. Pressing an artless slender finger against her expertly painted lips, she thought she just might baulk at selling her soul. But renting parts out? What's not to like?

Her wandering notions prompted a wry smile, though soon as Ford got his act together, she'd sharpen hers. Shiny-suited, shifty and a touch shambolic, Ford was tailor-made for a part on *Drop the Dead Donkey*: he even looked a bit like hapless hack Dave.

'Sorry, 'bout that, Caz.' Rolling conspiratorial

tawny eyes, Ford stowed a smart phone in his single-breasted jacket pocket. 'News desk. Still, you know all about that, don't you?'

A damn sight better than you, sunshine. 'Not a problem, Col,' she gushed, flashing a beam that could put Blackpool illuminations in the shade. Glancing round she wished it could work its magic on a grey gloomy Friday in Birmingham New Street. Waterstones' Georgian façade provided a decent enough back-drop for the interview, but in Caroline's metaphorical book, Ford's choice of location was lazy and predictable. As for her actual book, well, *Bad Men* hadn't yet set the world alight. The signing she'd just done inside had gone OK, probably down to the posters plastered across town. Even if she did say so herself, she looked pretty damn hot in the Armani suit and author pose. That plus a simpatico piece on the telly could only grab more readers and kick-start sales. She'd inveigled Ford's boss for the airtime: Eddie owed her a favour or five.

'Lucky you're a Birmingham girl, eh? Born and bred? Home grown?' Ford winked. Cocky sod. Caroline could probably give him ten years and from what she'd seen he'd be lucky to set foot out of the place. She'd fled the family nest at eighteen, only to inherit it from her mum two years back. Fed up with trying and failing to flog a Selly Oak redbrick, she'd taken it off the market and now acted as mostly absentee land-lady to lodger Nat, another old mate in the news trade.

'Why's that then, Col?' She cast a surreptitious glance at her reflection in the lens. Yep, the red jacket teamed brilliantly with the jet top, the glossy black-ink bob was still silk-smooth. The reporter cocked an eyebrow, like he was about to let her in on a state secret.

'Local interest, isn't it? We don't do plugs as a rule.' He made the money sign, rubbing together grubby thumb and fingers. 'Free advert for you, isn't it?'

Bloody nerve. Her fulsome fake smile very nearly faltered. In his shoes, scuffed desert boots as it happened, she'd probably feel similar cynicism: 'author writes book' wasn't going global any time soon. On the other hand, she needed all the coverage she could get and she had the sort of industry clout Ford could only dream of. 'No worries, Col. If you have a problem interviewing writers about their work, let's call it a day, cut our losses, eh?' She made scissor motions with two fingers then turned away, left a two-second gap before calling over her shoulder. 'Oh, and tell Ed I'll pick him up at seven.' Eddie the editor. Sounded like something out of Thomas the Tank. Caroline smiled. She'd teased Ed about it a few times; they went back a very long way. If she'd read Ford right, she'd not be going anywhere any time soon.

'Hey, Caz, stop, I didn't mean...'

Slowly, she retraced her steps, licked her lips. He had the look of a one-legged rabbit caught in a laser beam. She sashayed closer, very close, in-your-face close. 'Word of advice.' It wasn't a question. 'Say what you mean. Mean what you say. Don't try and be clever. And don't ever call me Caz.'

The interview lasted ten minutes; it wasn't Ford's finest hour. Caroline knew she'd have elicited twice as much in half the time. She was editing it mentally as she strode towards the station car park, simultaneously hoping her BMW would still be there, preferably with a full complement of wheels.

She'd already told Ford which bits of chat were worth using and which dumb-ass questions to drop. *Where'd you get your ideas?* Pur-lease. *Are your characters based on real people?* Really? *Bad Men* was a hard-edged exposé of street groomers featuring rare interviews with schoolgirl victims and input from senior cops, social workers et al. She glanced at the copy peeping from her shoulder bag, stupid really but she carried the book everywhere. It was the first she'd seen in print, and held in her hands, it gave her huge professional pride. Ford hadn't even read it, the little shit. Reckoned he could write one though. She shook her head. As a parting shot, he'd bragged about turning out a block-buster soon as he 'had the time'.

Yeah right. Chuckling, she unlocked the motor. Her mirth wasn't entirely down to the fact the car was still in one piece. She was re-calling the look on Ford's face when she'd

71

delivered her final not-so *bons mots*: For you, hun, there's not enough time in the world.

She slid behind the wheel, checked her face in the mirror. Yeah, the lippie was still good. She aimed the bag at the passenger seat but misjudged and as it toppled over, *Bad Men* slipped to the floor. She might have left it there – you could eat dinner off the carpet – but she spotted a loose page sticking out. Shit. The damn thing wasn't falling to pieces already, was it? She leaned across, lifted the book and frowned. It wasn't a page from *Bad Men*. It was an envelope with her name on. And it hadn't been there when she left the house. So how and when did it get there and who'd played postman? Her frown had deepened. Christ, she'd need Botox if she didn't open the bloody thing soon.

Hey Ms Ace Reporter
A Birmingham schoolgirl's been snatched off the street. Why no police hunt? Why isn't it all over the news? Why aren't you giving the cops a hard time? The tip-off's free – this time.
From a secret admirer.

'Flattery will get you nowhere, pal,' she muttered. After reading the note a second time, she tapped it against her teeth, brow still in ploughed-field mode. No matter how much she loathed being manipulated, the content begged a bunch of questions and piqued her reporter's curiosity.

72

Not least, how and who had gained access to her tote? Still pensive, she slipped the note back in the envelope, fired the engine, reversed the motor. She'd been meaning to give the Snow Queen a buzz anyway, ask if she liked the book; might as well drop by the Ice Palace. As for giving a cop a hard time, she'd been there, done that with dishy Dave Harries. Shagging almost on your own doorstep wasn't good news. Like a lot of other actions in her past, it had pissed Quinn off royally.

With relations less frosty nowadays, would Caroline really want to risk the fragile rapprochement for the sake of an exclusive? Lip curved, she glanced in the wing mirror, addressed an imaginary Mr Whippy. 'Make that two scoops, pal.'

ELEVEN

'Where'd you get it, Pauline?' Susan was so cross she could barely speak. No wonder she'd not been able to find the little madam. The sneaky little so-and-so must have run home, grabbed an ice lolly and scoffed it when she was supposed to be hiding. Susan would bet any money Pauline had nicked it from behind her mum's back. Mrs Bolton was dead fair about treats and sharing and that; she'd never see Susan go without. Unless the greedy little beggar had polished off a lolly meant for Susan as well as her own.

'Get what, Sukie?' Eyes wide, she had a thumb in her mouth, sucking away like there was no tomorrow. She must think Susan was born yesterday.

'Don't play the innocent with me, Pauline Bolton.' The evidence stared Susan in the face. From the kid's garish clown mouth to the red juice snaking down one of her skinny arms; even a few curls were tinged pink.

'What's "innocent", Sukie?' The little girl toed the grass with her sandal.

God, the lisp was getting on Susan's nerves.

74

She'd a good mind to shove the kid over and leave her to it. Instead she raised the cane and started decapitating dandelions. 'Innocent is being good.' Whoosh. 'Innocent is telling the truth.' Whoosh. 'Innocent is not going round thieving.' Whoosh.

'I didn't thieve nothing.' She pointed to the cane. 'Can I have a go?'

'No, get lost.' Whoosh. Whoosh. More weeds lost their heads. 'Not until you tell me where you got it.'

'Got what?' It was a bare-faced lie, unlike the kid's own mug. The clown mouth gave her a mocking lop-sided grin. Maybe that was what made Susan see red.

'Are you laughing at me?' she hissed. God, she could have done with that lolly. She was boiling.

'Course not. Come on, let's play.' A wheedling tone had crept into her voice. 'Please, Sukie.' She stretched out a grubby hand, snatched it back sharpish when Susan made to whack it.

'Not till you tell me where you got the lolly, Pauline Bolton.'

She stared at her feet. 'Not had one.'

Whoosh. Whoosh. She was beginning to like the sound of it. Whoosh. What really bugged Susan was Pauline's dirty trick, the trying to make a fool of her; the thought of a little kid trying to get one over. She cut the air with the cane again. 'You pinched it, didn't you? I'm gonna tell your mum on you.'

'An' I'll tell Grace on you. An' she'll beat you up again.'

'Oh yeah?' She drew the cane back. 'Your snotty sister doesn't scare me.'

'Anyway you're wrong, so there. I didn't nick it.'

The cane stilled. 'You did have one then.' Susan's eyes glinted behind her specs. 'You little liar. Did you eat mine too?' Pauline teared up and her bottom lip went through the same old quivering motions. The histrionics cut no ice with Susan. 'You know what happens to naughty little girls who tell whoppers, don't you?' Advancing on Pauline, she tapped the cane gently across her own palm.

'I didn't nick it, Sukie. He give it me. He said—' Eyes wide, she slapped a hand to her mouth.

'He?' Susan froze. 'Who's he?'

'Dunno.'

She'd taken stuff from a stranger? If she had, she was in big trouble. 'This man. What did he say to you?'

'Can't remember.' She couldn't even look Susan in the eye.

'What did he look like?'

Swinging a leg. 'Can't remember.'

Yeah right. Must've been the invisible man. Like heck. It was more big fat porkie pies. 'Okay. I believe you. Let's forget it.' She'd get the truth out of her eventually.

Pauline looked up, an uncertain grin on her

mucky face. 'Do you mean it, Sukie? You won't tell anyone?'

''Course not.' Smiling, she took the little girl's hand. 'We haven't played schools for ages. Let's play that.'

The little girl skipped along as they made their way back to the copse. It was like taking candy from a baby, Susan reckoned. Only in this instance it was the baby who'd done the stealing, and the baby who needed to learn a lesson. 'Sit there, Pauline.' Susan wielded the cane, whipped the head off a foxglove. 'I'll be Miss.'

TWELVE

'By Christ, lad, they didn't make 'em like that when I was at school.' DC Jed Holmes dabbed a grubby hankie round his rubbery lips. Harries shifted slightly in his seat, distancing himself from what passed as a wisecrack while keeping his gaze firmly fixed on Jude Fox's pert buttocks as she left the office, one of two at Queen's Ridge comprehensive currently commandeered into service as an interview room.

'Keep it down, man.' Harries flapped a tetchy hand. It was bad enough being teamed up with the human equivalent of Mogadon for a few

hours but for Holmes to deliver a line like that
when the woman was almost certainly in earshot? Would the stupid sod never learn? At
getting on for fifty, probably not. Little wonder
Baker had long since christened him No-Shit.

'I'm trying, lad.' Smirking, he wiped the limp
hankie round a lens of his horn-rims. 'It's hard
mind.'

Harries rolled his eyes at the ceiling, knew
where the old lech was coming from. He groaned inwardly at Holmes' word play and the mental picture it prompted. The more-than-portly
Holmes with a hard-on wasn't a thought to hold.
Unlike an image of the lovely Miss Fox. The
young blonde looked more like a movie star
than Caitlin Reynolds' drama teacher. Bright,
bubbly, big b ... blue eyes.

'Well, knock it on the head, eh, Jed? She'll be
back in a tick.' The interview had barely started
when she'd had to rush out to take a call, some
parent on the school secretary's phone demand-
ing words about little Johnnie or Jenny. Harries
hoped Miss Fox would have some decent
input/insight on Caitlin when she got back but
given she'd only been on staff since September,
he'd not hold his breath. Nor inhale too deeply.
Not with undertones of sweaty socks and over-
ripe cheese wafting in the air. Cracking open a
window crossed Harries' mind but a hockey
match was in full swing outside and the accom-
panying sound track was like something from a
slasher movie. While No-Shit strolled over to

take a closer butcher's at the action, Harries ran through the notes from earlier sessions, statements from the head, Caitlin's personal tutor, three more teachers and two of her closest friends. The picture emerging appeared to be that of a well-liked intelligent young woman, confident, fun-loving, witty, great sense of humour. Yada yada. She probably loved animals and wanted to save the world. Goody-too-good-to-be-true-shoes?

In Harries' experience no one was perfect but so far not one person had a bad word to say about the girl. No one could offer up even a guess why anyone would want to harm her. Caitlin, everyone agreed, hadn't an enemy in the world. Well, how could she? A girl with six-hundred-plus Facebook friends? Sighing, Harries shook his head. He could count his mates on the fingers of one hand, and he knew each one like the back of it. And in reality, it didn't matter what anyone said – Caitlin patently had one enemy.

'Hey, Dave.' No-Shit strolled back, tucking a sludge-coloured knitted tie into a too-high waistband. 'You want in on the sweepstake?'

Sighing, Harries tossed his pen on top of the notes. 'What sweepstake?'

'Slow off the mark, aren't you, son?' Coming from No-Shit that was rich. 'The date the chief's gonna ride off into the sunset.' It was an apt analogy given Baker's predilection for all things Wild West. If you asked Harries it was all a bit big boys' cowboys and Indians. John Wayne eat your Stetson.

'He's definitely going then?' Harries turned his mouth down, far as he knew there'd been nothing official, just a load of rumour and gossip doing the rounds.

'Trust me.' Holmes tapped the side of his distinctly crooked nose. 'I'm pally with that big bird in HR.'

'Big bird, officer?' Jude Fox arched a perfectly plucked eyebrow as she re-entered the room. 'I take it we're talking the winged variety? And tell me –' She smiled sweetly as she took a perch – 'what did they make when you were at school?' Harries felt his lip twitch. 'Quill pens?' she asked. 'Penny farthings? Faux pas?' Harries had to drop his glance but not before he caught a twinkle in her turquoise eye.

'Sorry, Miss...?' Holmes hung his head. He sounded like a thick kid apologizing. Still, it might teach him to remember names in future.

'Miss Fox.' Harries smiled, made eye contact, her twinkle still in situ. If she was flirting, it was fine by him. 'Caitlin Reynolds? You were about to tell us more.'

She took her time, crossing shapely legs, smoothing a creaseless skirt. The little black dress was straight out of *Breakfast at Tiffany's*; the silver hoop earrings could've doubled as bracelets. Harries wondered if she enjoyed an audience, hoped it was more a case of giving the subject serious thought.

'I haven't known Caitlin long.' Proper news-reader's voice. 'But she works hard in class, puts in the hours after school too.' Smiling, Miss Fox brushed a strand of hair from her cheek. 'Actually she's one of the leads in my end-of-term production. She's playing Abigail in *The Crucible*.'

Harries nodded: for all his vast theatrical knowledge, she could've been playing snooker in Sheffield. 'How would you describe her personality?'

Pensive, she reached for a bottle of Evian and held it to her lips for a few seconds before drinking. If it was a distraction technique it had partial success. Harries kicked No-Shit's foot under the desk: he was supposed to be taking notes.

'Sorry.' She balanced the bottle on her knee. 'Just marshalling my thoughts. I'd hate a careless word to point you in the wrong direction.'

'Understood.' Harries reckoned a lot of punters didn't give a toss about misdirection, though right now any direction would do. 'Take your time, Miss Fox.'

She did, and another dainty swig. 'She's a bright, popular girl, eager to please, willing to help, seems happy and bursting with confidence. Loving drama, she's a pleasure to teach.'

'"Seems"?' Harries queried. 'You said "seems" happy and confident.'

'Sometimes, I wonder if the happy-go-lucky Caitlin we all know and love is the real deal. Or if it was partly an act, you know?'

81

He didn't. And no one else had come any-where close to making the same suggestion. 'Go on.'

'It's tricky to pin down.' She re-crossed her legs.

'Try.' His smile of encouragement faded as she related vague concerns, formless fears. Apparently, Caitlin stared into space a lot, sad expression on her face, tears in her eyes. She spent quite a bit of time alone in the library, deliberately distanced herself from friends but paradoxically was the sort of girl who had to be liked by everyone and the most casual remark could cut her to the quick.

Sounded like every teenager Harries knew, unless ... He leaned forward a touch. 'Are you saying someone's bullying her?'

'No.' She paused. Was that telling? 'I really don't think so. I just find her extremely ... sensi-tive. Complex. A little moody? A bit of a drama queen.'

'As in?'

She threw her hands in the air. Harries thought the gesture pretty theatrical. Maybe Miss Fox did too. She gave a sheepish smile. 'Sorry, it's just so difficult to describe. But I guess it's a case of her always needing to be the centre of attention, always having to top everyone else's story. Not belittling people, just to get a laugh, you know?'

Not really. Maybe the boss would have an idea. They were hooking up at Caitlin's granny's house in an hour or so; he'd run it past her then. 'Tell me, Miss—'

'Please.' She raised a palm. 'The name's Jude.'

He nodded acknowledgement. 'Has Caitlin seemed more subdued recently? Did you sense anything bothering her?' Nothing, she said. 'Is there someone, a best mate maybe, she might have confided in?'

The girls she named had already been interviewed: nada on that front. He pressed further on Caitlin's background, asked whether she'd had problems at school, whether she seemed happy at home, if she'd had boyfriend bother. The teacher supplied no-yes-no answers but no real intelligence, no lines worth pursuing. Harries sensed she'd help if she could but she just didn't have anything concrete to offer. One more question then they'd hit the road.

'It's a big ask, I know, Miss Fox, but can you think of anyone who'd want to harm Caitlin?'

'Look, I probably shouldn't say this, but...' Twice, she opened her mouth to speak before finally putting Harries out of his misery. 'I think she may have been harming herself.'

THIRTEEN

'She saw Caitlin pissed?' Sarah cast an incredulous glance at her passenger. 'Is that it?' The Audi was parked a few doors up from the girl's granny's house. After wrapping up at the school, Harries had cadged a lift from No-Shit, caught Sarah grabbing a bite of late lunch in the car. Amazing what doe eyes and a rumbling stomach will do. She'd taken pity, offered him shares in her sausage roll and salt and vinegar crisps. His contribution had been filling her in on events at Queen's Ridge.

'Stoned. Pissed. Hammered. Plastered. Take your pick.' He swallowed, wolfed another bite. 'That's what Jude reckons. Not in school obviously or she'd have reported it.'

Sarah nodded, chewing slowly. That would certainly have blotted Caitlin's apparently pristine copybook. 'When you said "self-harming", I thought—'

'Yeah.' A magnanimous wave of the hand with the pastry sent flakes flying. 'Me too.'

She ducked. 'Flipping heck, Dave. Watch what you're doing with that.'

'Sorry, boss. I know what you mean though. I

thought she'd spotted cuts, scars, knife marks, something like that. But Jude's really into the health thing, reckons booze, fags, drugs are noxious substances. She's got a real downer on anything of that sort.'

Jude again? How very jolly. 'Don't tell me ... she thinks the body's a temple.'

Eyebrows knotted, mouth open, hand stilled: the double-take was almost comical. 'Do you know her, boss?'

Way Dave had been waxing on, Sarah felt she'd known the bloody woman for years. 'Let's just say I've come across people like her.' Up their own arse arty-farts. As a cop she'd witnessed real self harm: kids who'd slashed their wrists, walked in front of trains, dived off motorway bridges and had to be mopped off the tarmac. Caitlin, off her face, staggering down a back road in Moseley one night really wasn't up there. 'So what did Caitlin have to say for herself?' Jude had been driving past when she saw her, Harries said. By the time she'd parked, the girl was nowhere in sight. She broached it with her the next day at school, but Caitlin laughed it off, said she must have a double; she'd been home all night.

Sarah sighed. Fox hadn't exactly clocked the girl shooting up. Even if Caitlin was on drugs it didn't necessarily figure in her disappearance. But if Caitlin *was* using, it gave them good cause to fine-tooth comb the Reynolds' place. She reached for her phone on the dash. 'I'll get on to Woodie.'

'If it's about a search team, it's in hand, boss.' He'd already asked Twig to set the FSI wheels in motion.

Nice one. 'Ten out of ten.' Much as it irked, Baker was right: Dave had no need to wait a year or two, he was sergeant material already. 'Give the man a gold star.'

'Initiative or lateral thinking?' His hand was on the door.

'Lip more like.' Her smile faded as she reached for her attaché case, spotted a load of crumbs on her left sleeve. 'Certainly not table manners.'

'What was that, boss?'

'Nothing.' She buttoned her coat as they walked in step. 'Y'know, Dave, the teacher could've got it all wrong about Caitlin. Mistaken identity and all that.'

'Jude was pretty adamant. Her eye-sight's perfect apparently and the street lighting was good. She says she was so concerned she's been keeping close watch on Caitlin recently.'

Sarah sniffed. 'Not close enough then, Dave.'

It wasn't just the old woman's barrel shape. Linda Walker reminded Sarah of a set of Russian dolls she'd been given as a child. There had been six of the things in descending sizes and all but the last concealed a smaller version inside. Linda had the obligatory red cheeks and centre parting though the hair was in a loose steel-grey bun. Tie a scarf under her chin, wrap a shawl round her sloping shoulders and Sarah reckoned the woman would be a dead ringer for top doll. Well, apart from the Dame Edna glasses and a Zimmer frame tucked away in a corner for what she'd told the DI were her 'bad days'.

'I'd say we're very close, dear,' Mrs Walker said. 'Caitlin and Nicola lived here until a few years ago. And with Nicola out at work, it was often just the two of us. She's a dear girl. Very kind. Never gave us any trouble.' Her smile faltered as she raised a bone-china cup to pale crinkled lips. The roses on the cup had probably once been red but the colour had faded, as had the gold leaf round the rim. From Sarah's perch on a lumpy brown sofa, everything about the cluttered bungalow had a faded frowsty air. The mismatched furniture was old and cheap. The presence of a fat marmalade cat curled at the old woman's slippered feet didn't help; its fish breath vied with the acrid smell of pee. Maybe Linda Walker no longer noticed, or couldn't be arsed to do anything about it. Sarah found it vaguely depressing, wondered what Caitlin made of it.

'What about more recently?' she asked. 'How often would you normally expect to see your granddaughter?' Sipping the tea, Sarah struggled not to pull a face. She'd drunk tastier builders' brew. Mind the old dear already had the pot and plate of biscuits set out on a low table when they arrived. Harries had just seen off his fourth pink wafer. Not that Sarah was counting.

'There's no regular pattern, dear. She turns up as and when, usually with a little gift. A bunch of flowers or a puzzle book, nothing flashy. We have a natter, maybe a game of cards, or just watch a bit of telly. Caitlin and me love all the soaps and the detective series.' Her smile showcased sepia dentures that had a life of their own. 'We always try and guess who the killer is.' She pressed a liver-spotted hand to her mouth. 'Caitlin won't come to any harm will she, dear?'

'We're doing everything we can, Mrs Walker.' Sarah placed the cup and saucer back on the tray. 'Tell me, when did you last see her?'

'Let me think. My memory's not what it was.' Seemingly ill at ease, she patted her bun, glanced away. Sarah hoped she wasn't looking for her marbles. Nicola Reynolds had warned about her mother's failing health, physical and mental. She was mid-sixties, looked late seventies. 'I'm pretty sure it was Monday. No, Tuesday.'

'This week?'

She shook her head. 'Last month. She had a lot of schoolwork on, said she might not be able to visit for a while. She wants to go to university, you know. Very bright is Caitlin.' The old woman's smiling gaze had settled on a photograph of Caitlin standing in pride of place on the mantelpiece. Sarah guessed it had been taken three or four years ago. Mind it looked as if every photo Linda had ever owned was on display somewhere in the room – the walls were covered, every dusty surface crowded.

88

'Have you spoken on the phone at all?' Sarah asked.

'No ... I ... don't think so.'

Sarah's high hopes the old woman could show Caitlin in a different light were beginning to take a dive. A penchant for *Corrie* and *Colombo* was hardly revelatory. She also doubted Linda Walker's ability to recall what she'd had for breakfast let alone any confidences Caitlin might have shared.

Harries was clearly on the same page. When he casually showed her his notebook, she saw the words 'losses' and 'cut?' She was surprised he'd not drawn a pair of scissors. Sarah asked about Caitlin's relationship with her mother, whether there'd been any problems at home. According to Linda, all was sweetness and light, Caitlin and Nicola so close they were more like sisters.

'And what about Nicola's partner?'

'More tea, dear?' Sarah shook her head. Heaven forbid. Was the diversion deliberate? Apart from snapping a biscuit in half, the old woman wasn't going anywhere.

'Neil Lomas?' Sarah prompted. 'How does he fit in?'

'I'm sure he's a very nice man.' What was the saying? Damning with faint praise. The puckered lips and disparaging tone were telling too. 'I wouldn't know.'

Sarah frowned. 'You've not met him?'

'Just the once.' She brushed crumbs off her

chest.

'And?'

'He sat where you are. Stayed five minutes. I've not laid eyes on him since.'

Nose out of joint? Hurt feelings? 'Any idea why?'

She snorted. 'Nicola says he's allergic to cats.'

Given the animal had chronic flatulence as well as halitosis, Sarah could maybe see his point. 'But?'

'I got the feeling I wasn't good enough for the likes of Mr High and Mighty Lomas.'

No love lost there then. 'What about Caitlin? How does she get on with him?'

'You'll have to ask her that.' Her withered face crumpled further as she realised what she'd said, remembered why the detectives were here. 'You will find her, won't you?'

FOURTEEN

'I take it you've found her then?' Caroline took the tongue from her cheek as she pictured Sarah Quinn's expression: gormless meets clueless? The reporter had dispensed with social niceties, laid on the insouciance with an industrial trowel. The silence on the line stretched so long that for a few seconds, she thought Sarah had hung up. Like any journo, she'd have preferred a face-to-face encounter but the Ice Queen had been out doing her thing when Caroline dropped by Police HQ. Now back in Selly Oak, the reporter had done a little homework, poured a drink then put in the call.

'Found who?' Sarah's sigh was audible, so were the drumming fingers. In her mind's eye, Caroline saw the cool blonde's finely arched eyebrow, steely grey stare, tight school ma'am bun. She curved a lip. At least DI Deep Freeze was only in hedging mode; she'd not gone down the faux disingenuous 'Who is this?' path. Given their history, it wouldn't have got the detective very far, plus the fact the reporter's voice was virtually a distinguishing feature.

'The missing girl, of course,' Caroline said.

91

'Hold on, I've got her name in my notebook somewhere.' She reached across the kitchen table for a newspaper. Would rifling its kite-flying pages do the trick?

'Course you have,' Sarah drawled. 'Stop pissing around, eh?'

She sniffed. Win some, lose some. Mind, if Quinn had already resorted to swearing maybe Caroline had touched a nerve. She ditched the paper, reached for her gin and tonic. 'Pissing around?' Her bemusement was faked. 'You can talk. The inquiry's not exactly hot off the mark, is it?' Caroline's opening gambit had been heavy on the sarcasm. That the girl was still missing was an assumption on her part, her point being why – still – hadn't the cops released details to the media? A girl snatched off the street? The story should've been all over the news. Caroline had trawled the web, the local rags, but not a sniff. The cops' dilatoriness could become a story in its own right. Either way, hard news was Caroline's professional first love, what she did best, and breaking it was even better.

'I don't do riddles, Caroline. What do you want?'

'You know what I want – who, why, where.' Depending how the story panned out Caroline could well decide it wasn't worth covering personally, but keeping her hand in with the odd tip-off to an editor or two never did any harm. 'I want everything you've got. I assume she's still out there somewhere?' The question went unanswered. Mind, Quinn rarely showed her hand. 'What I can't get my head round,' Caroline persisted, 'is why you're keeping the story under wraps.'

'As it happens, we're releasing it any time now,' Sarah said. 'So your little heads-up has gone down the pan.' Damn. Caroline couldn't have put it better herself. March, stolen. Even so, the gloating was out of order.

'You surprise me, DI Quinn. A girl's missing – and you're scoring points?'

'Don't come that bollocks with me, Caroline. Tell me, this steer, where did you get it?'

Wouldn't you like to know? Hearing a muffled knock at Sarah's end of the line, she paused a second or two. 'As you well know, a journalist never—'

'Reveals a source, yeah.' Sarah sighed heavily again. 'Anyway, Caroline, pleasant though it always is to chat, time's pressing.'

Shit. She was losing her. ''Specially when it's running out, inspector. And even more so if you've already left it too late.'

Caroline suspected she'd just given the dialling tone the benefit of her wisdom. She raised her glass. 'Well that went well.'

For the first time in living history, Baker hadn't just barged in. Standing now in front of Sarah's desk, casual hand in trouser pocket, he tilted his head at the phone. 'What's Kingie after? She was sniffing round reception earlier.'

93

Sarah stiffened. 'You spoke to her?' Surely to God he hadn't tipped King the wink?

'Keep your hair on, woman. She'd buggered off by the time I got back.' Sarah winced as he did the usual thing of dragging a chair round so he could mount it like a horse. Why couldn't he just take a perch like anyone else? Oh yes. More reason to thank the holidays.

'Got back from where?'

'The little boys' room.'

She rolled her eyes, so glad she'd asked. Mind, it had been pretty dumb to think the chief had divulged anything to a reporter, even Caroline King who, Sarah suspected, Baker had taken a recent shine to. In Baker's book hacks were all granny-selling vultures in wolf's clothing. Besides, it had been the chief's call to delay a release in the first place. Word had gone out to the media in the last hour or so about a news conference they'd regret missing but no details had been disclosed. The delay and build-up were calculated risks on Baker's part; he was banking on the bait ensuring maximum turnout, saturation coverage on the major bulletins. Sarah hadn't been so convinced; they'd had crossed words on the phone earlier. Maybe he'd dropped by to apologize prior to facing the press pack. The old boy was cutting it fine given kick-off was at five.

'Is she on her way in then?' He nodded at the phone again, a smile playing across his lips. 'Your mate?'

Mate? Don't push it. Mutual daggers may no longer be unsheathed but they wouldn't be sharing girlie nights out any time soon. 'No, she's not.' Sarah dropped her glance, fiddled in a drawer. 'I was about to tell her but she threw a strop.' The heat, she knew, was rising on her cheeks.

'Funny that.' His voice held a smirk.

Still rummaging in the drawer, she said, 'Not really. She's a law—'

'Not Kingie.' He flapped a hand. 'You. I've seen post boxes with less colour. Not keeping King out of the loop are we, Quinn?'

She looked up. 'Hardly.' Baker's glib expression turned granite as Sarah told him the gist of the conversation with King, her apparent head start.

'So where's she getting the info from, for fuck's sake? Has the squad sprung another leak?' He cracked a knuckle, then another. The last mole at HQ had been booted out of the police after selling intelligence to King. But that was before Leveson and Filkin. 'Surely to God no one here's stupid enough to go down that route?' he said.

Route? Frowning, Sarah glanced at the notes she'd jotted during the call. Three words sprang out: street, broad daylight. She drummed the desk with her fingers.

'Sorry. Am I boring you, Quinn?'

'Caroline has it that a girl was snatched off the street in broad daylight.' She met Baker's gaze.

95

'We don't even know that ourselves.'

His nod said he didn't need telling. The info made a police leak look even less likely. Baker scratched his stubble. 'I suppose she could be taking a punt?'

'Maybe.' Sarah shrugged. 'But she knows we're investigating an abduction. She didn't pluck that out of the air. Someone's told her something for sure.'

'I take it she spouted the usual line? Protecting her sources and all that?'

'Natch.'

'You're gonna have to—'

'Get back to her.' She nodded. *What joy.*

The odds were minuscule but both detectives knew if the tip hadn't come from someone close to Caitlin, or anyone the police had interviewed, then the reporter could have been targeted by someone who'd witnessed the crime, or who'd committed it.

Monkey man was beginning to ring a faint bell with Caitlin. She wasn't sure if she'd come across him before or if he just had one of those faces, like some jobbing actor who popped up every five minutes on the box. She certainly wouldn't forget monkey man's mug in a hurry. Since the dramatic unmasking, she'd seen enough of it to last a lifetime. Christ. What a thought. She bit her lip to stop it quivering. Showing fear would get her nowhere. The constant uncertainty was the worst aspect; she couldn't work him out. One minute he'd be chatting away as if they were buddies, the next he'd go ape-shit as if he'd suddenly remember-ed why she was there. Which was real? Which was an act? He'd definitely shown more interest in stroppy Caitlin than pathetic victim Caitlin. Maybe her spur-of-the-moment strategy was paying off, or he was lulling her into a false sense of security. Either way, the call was im-possible to make when she still didn't have a clue why he'd abducted her. At least the only time he tethered and gagged her now was when he went out. She spent most of the day lying on an old mattress, listening to a radio he'd brought in. It had been her 'present' for the nine-nine-nine call he'd forced her to make. With a knife held to her throat it hadn't been difficult to stick to the script and maintain the thick Birmingham accent. The scream had been genuine enough; so had the stinging slap the bastard had meted out.

She cast a covert glance to where he sat cross-legged on the floor, nose down in a magazine; a bit of light reading maybe after the stack of newspapers he'd been through. Or he was leering at the pictures. He must've sensed he had an audience, as he raised his head. 'You hungry?'

Caitlin smiled and gave a tentative nod. 'Starving.'

'I'll nip out in a min. Fish and chips do you?'

'Cool.'

'Any idea when the late editions hit the streets?' He toed the nearest redtop.

Christ. Hadn't he got enough of the sodding things? 'Not my baby, sorry.'

Shrugging, he dropped his head again. He was an odd mix: dark hair, posh boy looks, nasal estuary delivery. He was probably in his thirties but today was dressed like a middle-aged anorak. She was pretty certain he slept on the premises. There was a loo but she'd not heard a shower running which could explain why he smelled bad sometimes. Not that she wrinkled her nose every time he came near any more; she'd tell him he smelled like cut grass if it got her out of here. Tell him anything really. And she reckoned if anything would help her escape it would be sweet talk, not brute force. Caitlin knew she was little match for the guy physically; she'd weighed the odds several times in her head. She also suspected he had company now and again. She could have imagined the muffled voices and laughter late at night, or the noises may have drifted in from the street. But what if he had an accomplice? Worse. What if he was just carrying out someone else's orders? Someone who made monkey man look like a teddy bear? She breathed in deeply, realized her own odour wasn't exactly fragrant either.

'OK.' He slung the magazine to the floor, sprang to his feet. 'Back in the chair.' She eyed the cable still in situ round the wooden legs and the slats; her wrists had only just stopped stinging from the last time.

'Do I have to? I won't try anything, honest.'

'Course you won't.' Grabbing her upper arm, he hauled her to her feet. 'Chair. Now. Don't force me to hurt you.'

'I really wouldn't, you know.' She sat down meekly. 'There must be a reason why you're doing this. Maybe if you told me, I could...'

He smiled. 'What?' Genuine interest? Bemused incredulity?

'I don't know.' She shrugged. Hadn't got a fucking clue. 'Help? Understand? I don't want to get you into trouble. If you let me go now I swear I won't breathe a word—'

'Got that right.' He slapped on the gag, tied it tighter than before. 'You won't breathe, period, if you try that shit again. I wasn't born yesterday, Caitlin.'

She nodded, eyes brimming. It was the only time he'd used her name. She told herself the tears had nothing to do with the personal touch.

FIFTEEN

'I presume it's a professional job?' The thin grey-haired guy on the front row had introduced himself as Seth Fielding, crime correspondent on one of the one-size-fits-all redtops. His lugubrious eyebrow and drawled delivery was a down-market Paxman, the natty grey suit and gold-framed specs owed more to John Humphrys. Axe-man meets Rottweiler. *Great.*

'What makes you say that, Mr Fielding?' Sarah's delivery was cool but her lips tightened when she slipped off her jacket. Little wonder she was feeling the heat. From the head of a horseshoe-shaped mahogany table, she faced a dozen or so reporters, acutely aware that on the screen behind, Caitlin's smiling image loomed large. Not for the first time, Sarah silently cursed the chief for leaving her in the metaphorical firing line. As a foil to hardened newshounds, the newbie press officer to her right appeared to be less use than a glass truncheon. Naomi-nice-but-dim had barely opened her mouth let alone uttered anything sound. Head down, she was scribbling away like there was no tomorrow – probably a shopping list, Sarah thought. The chief always had hacks eating out of his hand but he'd cried off, when he saw the low turnout. He'd passed the Q&A reins to Sarah. It felt more like a toxic chalice.

'It's pretty obvious, isn't it?' Fielding crossed leg over knee, ran finger and thumb down a razor-sharp crease in his black trousers. She struggled to see how he'd made the mental leap given the few facts she'd divulged.

'You tell me.' Holding the reporter's gaze, she tapped a pen against her teeth, suspected he was fishing for an even sharper angle. The media invariably seized on hooks, always attached catchy handles to major inquiries, preferably alliterative, invariably simplistic: Moors Murderers, Doctor Death, Suffolk Strangler, House of Horrors.

'Let's see, inspector. Caitlin Reynolds has been missing for more than twenty-four hours; she's abducted apparently off the street on her way home from school.' He glanced round, presumably making sure the pack was on-side. 'One might almost say she vanishes into thin air.'

One might? 'You might, Mr Fielding. I think the answer's rather more down to earth. And to find it, I need hard evidence from reliable witnesses.' She regretted the words as soon as they were out of her mouth: there was never any mileage in rising to a bait.

'And you didn't need help yesterday?' He traced an index finger along a now sardonic

101

eyebrow. She'd not be surprised if he practised poses in the mirror. 'Correct me if I'm wrong, DI Quinn, but the inquiry into Caitlin's abduction is now entering its second day and the police have no sightings, let alone leads.' *Thanks for the reminder.* It did seem weird though, not a single pointer from the scores of people who'd been interviewed.

'It strikes me,' Fielding said, 'that whoever snatched her is either a jolly lucky man or knows exactly what he's doing, i.e. a professional.' The pompous twat didn't actually say 'unlike you lot'. But the implication the cops were doing a Keystone was clear.

'I don't comment on speculation. It's why I'm seeking help from the public, Mr Fielding.'

'Again ... why not seek it earlier?'

'And I'm certainly not discussing operational policy with you.' Despite clammy palms, she threw in an icy stare.

'No, I quite see that, inspector.' He responded with a warm smile. 'That would be a waste of time. Wouldn't it?' The dig prompted sniggers from a couple of his peers.

'Anna Thorpe, *Sunday Mercury*.' A young blonde sitting behind Fielding had a finger in the air. Even without the long glossy black hair and short pencil skirt, she'd turn a few heads, *was* turning a few heads. Sarah thanked God for the diversion, reached for a carafe, nodded acknowledgement at Thorpe to continue.

'With all due respect, inspector...' *Yeah right.*

Ms Mealy Mouth. She'd not even tried to sound as if she meant it. Sarah felt sweat trickle down her spine, took a sip of tepid water. 'Though I'm sure you're doing your best –' the smile was as genuine as hen's dentures – 'I still think you should let us talk to Caitlin's mother. Real people have so much more impact with our readers, you see.'

Real people? As opposed to what? Plastic police people? For someone who looked like she could be on work experience, Thorpe's patronizing pop rate was pretty good. Her last point was on the money too. Problem was Nicola Reynolds had been under police questioning for much of the day and if the pack got so much as a sniff of that fact, it wouldn't just put them off the trail, it might point them in completely the wrong direction. Either way, it risked putting an unfair slant on the coverage. Last thing Sarah wanted right now was Nicola Reynolds facing trial by tabloid.

'You're absolutely right, Miss Thorpe. Of course you can talk to Mrs Reynolds.' She smiled, took another sip of water. 'As soon as she feels ready. Naturally, she's distraught at the moment.'

'But—'

'You wouldn't want to cause further distress, would you ... dear?' OK. Childish. The DI's customary cool had taken a couple of slides. Christ, she was only human. Besides, assuming Nicola Reynolds held nothing else close to her chest,

Sarah saw her as a trump card. The best time to parade the mother in front of the press was when its interest showed signs of flagging. Not long then. 'She'll probably be up for it tomorrow,' Sarah said. 'All being well.' Nothing like hedging your bets.

She took three more questions from the floor, repeated the time-frame and Caitlin's route, stressed how vital it was that witnesses came forward. Apart from doing a turn for the local telly station immediately after the news conference, Sarah reckoned it was more or less a wrap. But Fielding clearly had other ideas. 'Are you ruling out the professional kidnapper scenario then, inspector?'

'Neither in nor out, Mr Fielding.' Glancing down, she started gathering files. 'As in every inquiry, the police have to keep an open mind.'

He muttered something as she walked out that elicited more sniggers. Sarah only caught the last word: vacant. Reckoned she could probably guess the rest.

Naomi-nice-but-dim hung around while Sarah did the TV interview then tailed her out of the conference room. 'That reporter who was up his own backside? He was just guessing, right?'

'Fielding.' Sarah masked a smile. Naomi seemed to have found her voice. 'I reckon. Why?'

'A professional makes no sense to me. I mean Caitlin's not famous or nothing. Besides, the family's not rolling in it. So whoever it is can't be after cash. And last time I looked, Moseley wasn't exactly the centre of the white slave trade.'

'Go on.' Intriguing.

Naomi with voluble hand signals now match-ed the DI's stride. The brown mid-calf skirt and fussy orange blouse did the press officer no favours, nor the split ends in the long auburn hair, but Sarah's gaze also took in the serious expression in clear hazel eyes. Dark horse? New light? Memo to self: don't write off people too soon.

'OK, so the streets round the school and the Reynolds' house are still swamped with police, right? You've got uniform knocking doors, stop-ping drivers, detectives interviewing anyone with a pulse. But still no one's come forward, have they?'

'Go in.' Sarah opened her office door. 'Take a seat.'

Naomi perched on the edge, bit a thumbnail as she waited for Sarah to off-load files, crack open a window then lean against the sill. 'Go on.' She folded her arms.

'As far as we know, inspector, no one saw anything, heard anything, or even suspected anything.'

'And you read into that – what?' And would it match Sarah's thinking?

'Maybe there was nothing to see?' She held out empty palms. 'No scuffle, no scream, no snatch, no burning rubber.'

'You think Caitlin went willingly?'

'*If* someone took her, I think she knew who it was.' *If* someone took her? Naomi's suspicions went further than the DI's, who'd only toyed with the idea that Caitlin may have co-operated under duress; even the threat of violence from her captor could have cowed her into silent acquiescence.

'And?'

'That's why I don't buy into the abduction, kidnap, vanishing act – whatever you want to call it – being a professional hit. I see it as personal. What if she's besotted with some bloke? Had rows with her mum over him, say? Wanted to put the wind up her?' Considering how long it had taken her to speak out, the press officer certainly wasn't holding back now. Warming to her theme or what?

'You've seen the emails, Naomi, the photographs sent to Nicola Reynolds' phone?'

She nodded. 'Sure, but if Caitlin wanted to punish her mum, teach her a lesson, sending that stuff would be a piece of piss.' She coloured. 'Sorry, but for computer literate kids it'd be child's play, inspector.'

'It's one hell of a harsh lesson, Naomi.' Unless, Sarah mused, the whole thing had gone too far, got out of hand and Caitlin was too scared to call a halt. She'd certainly looked scared witless in the pics. What was it Jude Fox had told Harries? Caitlin liked to be the centre of attention, she played the drama queen. But even if she had taken part in an elaborate hoax ... 'She sure as hell couldn't be acting alone, could she?'

Naomi made eye contact, paused a heartbeat. 'Exactly.'

SIXTEEN

Standing in front of a whiteboard, Sarah ran her gaze over what she sensed was a less than delirious squad. She doubted the subdued mood had much to do with the dark night, the hail stones hammering the incident room's windows. For one thing the stunned silence had only just settled. She'd hung fire until the end of the late brief before mooting Naomi York's theory. She'd run it past the chief earlier, who'd not so much poured cold water on it as stood it under Victoria Falls in a cloudburst during the rainy season. His cavalier dismissal before knocking off for the weekend hadn't given Sarah pause; she'd waited to hear each detective's latest input, hoping for concrete developments. Their mental image of Caitlin now had a little more light and shade, but they still had no sightings, no positive leads. Clutched straw or not, Sarah had just shared the press officer's take on the girl's absence. It had gone down so well. Not.

107

Paul Wood eventually broke the silence. 'I can't see it myself, inspector.' The DS had swapped his customary patch of wall for a radiator sill, bare ham-like arms rested on his paunch. 'I mean why would a girl do something so spiteful to her own mother?' Tell that to Lizzie Borden, Sarah thought. Not that a harrowing pic or two was on the forty whacks' scale and without solid evidence any involvement on Caitlin's part in whatever was going on was pure speculation.

'Twig, I'm not taking it as read.' Sarah pushed back a sleeve of her jacket. 'I've never met the girl. None of us has any idea what the relationship's like.' Of course, if Nicola Reynolds' word was anything to go by the pair were closer than full-term twins in the womb of a size-eight model. 'I'm just saying it's possible. Got to be worth looking at, surely?'

'If she is playing silly buggers,' Wood's pause implied continuing scepticism, 'she'd need help. Where's the boyfriend?' He nodded at a photo of Holden on the whiteboard. 'Reckon he's done a runner with her?'

Luke Holden could have been abducted by aliens for all Sarah knew, but: 'You're right, Twig. We need to talk to him as a matter of urgency now.' *If only for elimination purposes.*

They'd already tried contacting Holden. As Caitlin's erstwhile or otherwise boyfriend he was always going to be a person of interest to the inquiry. Nearest and dearest and all that.

He'd not answered the numbers supplied by Nicola Reynolds and when Huntie and No-Shit had knocked on Holden's Selly Oak bed-sit the only response had been from a guy upstairs who told them Luke hadn't been around all week. Was the absence significant? Was Holden a dab hand with a camera? Had he and Caitlin hatched a hare-brained plot to get back at Nicola Reynolds?

'Has anyone put it to the mum?' Hunt asked. Sarah shook her head. Nicola Reynolds had left the station before the question rose.

DC Bruce raised a hand. 'I'm happy to pay her a house call, inspector. Me and Beth could have another word.' Lally cut her partner a 'says you' glance: the prospect of a bit of Friday night overtime clearly didn't do much for the new mum. Shona would be keen to pry again; her legendary interview technique had elicited nothing further from Nicola that afternoon.

'Cheers. Give the search team a nudge as well, yeah?' They'd heard nothing back and officers had been on site a couple of hours. Probably nothing to find, or Nicola would have kicked up more of a stink about letting them in. Sarah glanced at her watch. She didn't like rushing the squad but if she was late, her not-so-hot date wouldn't hang around. Caroline King had only agreed to a quick drink under martyr-like sufferance. Think Joan of Arc meets Saint Cecilia. Not even close.

Twig opened his mouth to speak again, but

had second thoughts.

'Huntie?' Sarah said.

John Hunt lowered his finger. 'If it's been just the two of them since the dad died, I wonder how well Caitlin gets on with her mum's boyfriend.' Sarah followed his gaze to the whiteboard where Lomas' likeness appeared next to Holden.

'You're thinking *too* well?' As in intimately; intimately enough for Neil Lomas to play cameraman? 'Are you thinking there's something going on there?' Sarah asked.

'Could be.' He shrugged. 'Who knows?'

Lomas would, and the list of questions for him was growing. The lecturer had been driving to Derby when a DC got through on his mobile. His father had apparently been taken ill and Lomas intended staying there a few days to play nurse. If need be, Sarah would send officers up to do the interview; it was too big a deal to do down a line. As Twig et al had said, if Caitlin had lead role there had to be a co-star.

'Caitlin can certainly act, boss. Her drama teacher told us that.' Slumped behind a desk, Harries had been uncharacteristically quiet. It could be he hadn't wanted to voice dissent; Dave generally gave Sarah total support in front of the troops. He probably didn't rate the theory. Either that or he was miffed she'd turned down his offer of a quick jar after work tonight.

'Hey Dave.' Jed Holmes waved from across the room. *'Call-me Jude'* would've told you anything, wouldn't she?' Holmes followed the sly dig by puckering rubbery lips into a pantomime kiss. Through narrowed eyes, Sarah watched Dave colour and his mouth come the closest she could recall to a snarl.

'Shut it, No-Shit.' The skin stretched white across his knuckles.

'Come on, man. You know she fancies the pants—'

'Go fuck.'

'After you, son.' Holmes' lascivious wink was superfluous. Sarah didn't need it to interpret the innuendo. Nor Harries apparently, who was already on his feet.

'Back in the chair, detective.' She raised a palm. 'What do you think this is? A bloody playgroup?'

'No.' Harries sank back in the seat. 'I think you're wrong about Caitlin. The way I see it, she could be Helen Mirren's lovechild, I still can't believe she'd pull off such a shitty trick. So I reckon you need to go back to the drawing board. Ma'am.'

'And you need to show respect, Harries.'

'I do. Or I'd have pissed on this Caitlin-crap-parade a lot sooner.'

Parade? The inquiry had a parade? She should be so lucky. Right now she couldn't even see a milk float.

SEVENTEEN

'You're bloody lucky I'm still here.' Caroline tapped a showy watch, shoved an empty glass across the table. Lucky to get a seat, too. Gone seven on a Friday, The Bacchus in Broad Street was already heaving. Mind, all the fake grapes draped round faux-Doric columns took up a bunch of floor space.

'Sorry,' Sarah said. 'Traffic was the pits.' Rain always slowed the flow. Five minutes wouldn't kill King though. She forced a smile, reached for the glass. 'Same again, I take it?' The lemon peel bore nibble marks and the two-thirds empty Schweppes' bottle on the table pointed to a G&T, plus Sarah had never known the reporter drink anything else in the decade and more since they'd met.

'Yeah. Plenty of ice.' Caroline had a glint in the eye. As an afterthought, she called out: 'Grab some nuts while you're at it, eh?' She curved a lip. Sarah's muttered 'my pleasure' hadn't been as *sotto voce* as she thought. The reporter lounged back on the mock-leather bench, watched a group of middle-aged suits part like waves as the detective walked to the

112

bar. Maybe they'd heard the nuts remark and feared for their sphericals. No, that was bollocks. Caroline suspected it had more to do with the cool blonde's tight-ass strut. Whatever. Five blokes' heads swivelled in sync to admire the stately process.

Still observing, Caroline swigged the dregs of the tonic. She loathed admitting it but the bloody woman had always had enviable presence. At nearly six foot in stockinged feet, who wouldn't? Not that Caroline blended into the background like a shrinking violet. In her job public recognition was par for the course. As for Sarah? Who knew? The sudden show of male interest could have something to do with the fact that her face, like new author Caroline's, had just been plastered all over the regional telly programme on the pub's widescreen.

Caroline reached for her tote, checked inside. No more fan mail; the original still nestled there though. She shook her head. It didn't take a genius to work out why Quinn had issued the drinks invite. Tucking the bag on the floor at her kitten heels, she glanced up just as the waves parted again. Talk about DI Moses. 'By the way, pal,' she said, 'I really appreciate it. Thanks.'

Sarah hadn't sat down, let alone handed over the glass. 'For?'

'Spreading the word?' Caroline, all innocence, fished out the slice of lemon, sank perfect teeth into its flesh.

Sarah took the opposite seat. 'Sorry. I'm not

with you.'

'The news conference? The missing girl? Good of you to let me know.'

'Right. Look, I'm sorr—'

'Don't.' Caroline lifted a finger. 'There's only so many apologies a girl can take in one night.'

Sarah dug the Planters out of her coat pocket, slung the pack across the table. 'Peace offering?'

'Cheers.' She clinked her glass against Sarah's, reckoned the end of hostilities would cost more than a palm full of nuts. Given the detective was after Caroline's help, for her not to have mentioned the news conference was piss poor. Waiting until Sarah took a sip of wine, she said, 'Anyway, the thanks were real. From what I heard it was a non-event, so you saved me a wasted journey. You didn't look exactly ecstatic yourself.' Face like a slapped ass was the phrase that crossed Caroline's mind as she'd watched the DI's turn on the box. Considering it was a witness appeal, the cool cop would hardly have warmed herself to viewers. Maybe Caroline should offer her some media training, mates' rates. The thought prompted a lazy grin that stretched wider when she recalled her own expert act. And the audience in the background. She doubted the tipster would be stupid enough to get in shot but she'd cast her eye over the rushes later, courtesy of Eddie the editor.

'I didn't catch the report actually.' Sarah draped her coat across the back of the chair.

'Still, since you're so happy, I'm sure you'll have no problem returning the favour?'

She'd walked into that. 'Go on.' Elbows on table, Caroline leaned forward, listened carefully as Sarah outlined how vital it was they find out more about the tip-off. If it had come from a bona-fide contact, she said, no one was asking Caroline to break the confidence. But given how few people had known about Caitlin's disappearance, how thin on the ground genuine sources could have been? 'You know where I'm coming from,' Sarah said. 'There's a chance it stems from the guy holding her.'

The reporter nodded. Like she hadn't thought of that. Whoever it came from had at least a smidgeon of inside knowledge. Caroline played for time, weighing her options along with a sip of her drink. She'd not deliberately held back; she'd kept her cards close because apart from the note, she had nothing to share. But also, if she played them correctly, the mysterious correspondent, having singled her out once, might deal a few more. *Would* deal a few more. The note had made that clear: the tip off's free – *this time*. What journalist would risk jeopardizing another steer? Certainly not Caroline.

She placed the glass on the table. 'Scout's honour, Sarah, I'd help if I could. Fact is, I haven't a clue where or who it came from.' She'd found the note in her bag, she said, after a signing at Waterstones. Someone had obviously slipped it in while she was otherwise occupied.

'Can I see it?'

'Sure.' She reached for the nuts. 'I haven't got it on me though.' Strictly speaking that was true. She caught Sarah's eyebrow arching.

'What did it say?'

'Let's think.' She ran a pensive hand through her bob, like the words weren't branded verbatim in her brain. 'A schoolgirl's been snatched off the street ... Why no police hunt? ... Why isn't it all over the news? Oh yeah...' A smile played on her lips. 'And why aren't you giving the cops a hard time?'

'Is that word for word?'

'Far as I recall.'

Sarah turned her mouth down. 'And you didn't notice anything in Waterstones? No one acting strangely?'

'I think I might have mentioned it, don't you?' She ignored the detective's sceptical shrug. 'Anyway there's no guarantee it happened there. I got into town early so I could troll round the shops, had lunch in Café Rouge. After the signing, I did an interview in the street outside the store. It's not like the bag was surgically attached to me all that time.'

'And it's always open like that?' Sarah pointed her glass at the bulging bag. 'Christ, what's in there? The fridge freezer?'

'No need to look so sniffy, pal.' She popped a couple of peanuts in her mouth, glanced round when the doors burst open and a dozen or so women in fancy dress including four in cop

116

uniform staggered in. The drunken rendition of 'Love and Marriage' was punctuated by giggles and mutual back-slapping. 'Reckon it's a police raid?' Caroline smiled. 'Or a funeral party?'

Sarah flapped a 'who gives a toss' hand. 'What I can't work out is whether the note business was planned or spur of the moment? I mean, how would he know you were in Birmingham, let alone what you'd be up to?'

'Christ, Sarah, I'm on a book tour; there's posters all over the place, a feature in last night's *Birmingham News*. Beside all that – as you well know – I've been a TV journo for years.'

She nodded. 'So you think he targeted you specifically?'

'I...' Abrupt pause. She *knew* he had; he'd called himself her secret admirer. Clearly he thought she had clout, could whip up some coverage. Unless the whole thing was a wind-up? 'I ... don't know.'

'You're sure about that, Caroline?'

'Sod this for a game of soldiers. If you don't believe me there's no—'

'That's not what I said.'

'You didn't have to.' Glaring at Sarah over the rim, she drained her glass.

'Would you...?'

'No.' Lips tight, she grabbed the bag, got to her feet and took off.

For a second, Sarah thought Caroline was stropping out, but instead she watched her weave her way past the hen party. Two nuns in minuscule habits and fish nets were clearly in a meaningful relationship. A bottled blonde in pointy bra snatched a twenty-pound note from the cleavage of a schoolgirl with holey tights and Heidi plaits. A smiling Caroline chatted away to a Lady Gaga clone standing next to her at the bar. The reporter's easy warmth helped her connect instantly. Sarah had witnessed it before. People opened up to her, confided in her. It was partly why she was so good at her job. That and the sliver of ice in her soul.

Sarah gave a lop-sided smile. Maybe they had more in common than she'd care to admit. For the sixth or seventh time she checked her phone, had expected Shona or the search team to have been in touch by now. No news is good news? Depends on the definition of good. As for the TV news, coverage of Caitlin's disappearance couldn't have prompted any useful leads or whoever was on duty in the squad room would have contacted her. Head home? Or suggest grabbing a bite with Caroline? Sarah was starving and – who knew – after another drink or three Caroline might loosen up. Either way, she was loath to leave until securing a guarantee from the reporter that if the abductor made contact again, Sarah would be second to know. Sighing, she shook her head. Given she was pretty sure Caroline had already lied three times that evening, she'd not hold her breath. Lies, half-truths, omissions. It boiled down to the same thing really: the reporter was still as trust-worthy as a hungry cat locked in a canary cage.

'Have you read it then?' Caroline thrust a glass in front of the DI. 'Still on the Sauvignon, yeah?'

'Yes, cheers.' She took the drink. 'Read what?'

'My book. *Bad Men.*' Caroline plonked herself down. 'I thought I sent you a copy?'

'Yes, I should have mentioned it.' She'd skimmed it; anything more in-depth was on her to-do list. After painting her toe nails and cleaning the loo.

'So? What did you think?'

Playing with the stem of her glass, she said: 'It's what I'd expect from you, Caroline. Well-researched case histories, compellingly written, moving stuff.' After studiously avoiding eye contact, she looked up to find Caroline with a wry smile on her face.

'Bollocks.' She shook her head. 'You've not read it, have you?'

Street grooming and the devastating effects on young victims wasn't bedtime reading in Sarah's book. Having run a major investigation into a Birmingham grooming ring the year before last, she felt she knew more than she need-ed without Caroline's take.

'Yeah well, it's your loss.' Caroline downed her drink, hoisted her bag, got to her feet. 'Don't know about you but I've got a hot date.'

She hadn't even got a cold date. Pizza for one then. 'Caro—'

'I know, I know. If I hear anything...' Smiling, she waggled her fingers. 'Ciao.'

Hot date? Cold date? Sarah grimaced. With another empty Friday night ahead, she'd happily settle for a blind date. She pushed the glass away, shucked into her still-damp coat; any more alcohol on an empty stomach and she'd regret it. Halfway to the door her mobile buzzed. She cupped a hand over her free ear to muffle the hen party's current offering: 'Sisters Are Doin It For Themselves'.

'Shona. What've we got?'

'What do you want, ma'am? The good news or ... the really good?'

EIGHTEEN

The last time Nicola Reynolds saw Caitlin they'd had a blazing row over Luke Holden. Nicola had forbidden her daughter ever to see the guy again. Caitlin's parting shot before storming out of the house? 'Back off. You don't own me.'

'So much for never a crossed word.' Sarah huddled in the doorway. Despite Friday night traffic and footfall – think ticking taxis and clacking heels – it was a damn sight quieter than inside the bar. 'Go on.'

Eliciting the admission, Shona said, had been like pulling wisdom teeth with foam pliers. Nicola eventually cracked when confronted with the Caitlin as co-conspirator scenario, tears had flowed, followed by a stream of words, mostly four-letter. 'She swore blind Caitlin wouldn't be so cruel unless, quote, "some bastard was holding a fucking knife to her throat". Well she would, wouldn't she? What mother wants to think the worst of her daughter? But it sort of stands up Naomi's theory, do you think, ma'am?'

'Maybe.' Pulling her coat collar tightly, Sarah gazed across the road. Puddles and potholes shimmered with soft-focus greens and reds and gold, Broad Street's night lights distorted in a watery hall of mirrors.

'You don't sound convinced, ma'am?'

'It's not much to go on, Shona.' Still too many unanswered questions. Primarily, why would love's young dream court publicity if they just wanted payback on Nicola? Did Luke Holden have some sort of Svengali-like hold over a besotted Caitlin?

'How about this then? Holden had apparently tried persuading Caitlin to leave home before,' Shona said. *Before?* Sarah turned her mouth down. It was hardly a given he'd done it again – this time, successfully. 'According to Nicola, when Caitlin told him she wasn't up for it, he dumped her and she was in bits for weeks. It's

121

one reason she was so keen that Caitlin had nothing more to do with the guy.'

'And the others?'

'He's a good few years older, likes a pint and he's a user. Not the hard stuff ... cannabis, E, meow meow, ketamine.'

Sarah frowned. 'Caitlin told her mum all this stuff?'

'No. She had a snoop round, found Caitlin's diary. Confronted her with the evidence.'

'Has she still got it?' Like hell. Once bitten and all that.

'No.' Her pause was deliberate. 'It's in an evidence bag in the boot of my car. One of the forensic guys found it taped under Caitlin's bed.' Sarah gave a low whistle, saw what Shona meant about news. 'A bit further along, he found a couple of wraps of dope. And as for the really good news?'

They had a potential eye witness. The neighbour Ronald Gibson still insisted he'd seen Caitlin on the day she disappeared. Shona and Beth had dropped by Gibson's place after leaving Nicola stewing. The time and location Shona had pinned down could fit. Gibson claimed Caitlin had been hanging round a bus shelter on the junction of Queen's Drive and Park Hill. He knew it must've been about 12.15 because he had a 12.30 appointment.

'So she could have nipped out at lunchtime,' Sarah said. Which would make Gibson's wag-playing assumption exactly that, an assumption.

'Yep. And Gibson's pretty sure she wasn't waiting for a bus.'

'How come?'

'Two went past while her mouth was glued to some bloke's.'

'Did he know who?'

'No. But the description's not a million miles from Neil Lomas. Dead ringer if you ask me.'

Sarah's lips parted in the smallest of smiles. *Ding dong.*

Nicola Reynolds clung to the bathroom sink aware that a faint smell of vomit lingered in the air. Maybe Neil not being around was no bad thing. He'd sounded distracted during their brief phone call, clearly worried about his father's health. He certainly wouldn't want to see her looking like this. Nicola barely recognized her own reflection: sunken cheeks, pallid complexion, haunted eyes. Swaying slightly, she told herself to get a grip. What earthly use would she be to Caitlin in this state? Nicola had to hold it together, because no way on God's earth was her daughter colluding with the sick bastard directing this real-life horror movie. Wishful thinking had nothing to do with it; Nicola knew beyond doubt her conviction was correct. Her present – the abductor's word for it – waiting by the front door when she arrived back from the cop shop had made that abundantly clear, the typed note on the gift tag underlined the message: if Nicola shared their little secret, Caitlin would pay with her life.

Doubled over, Nicola retched again and again, her stomach empty now, a vile taste in her mouth. She drank from the tap then filled cupped hands with cold water, sluiced her face, watched dispassionately as it dripped from her chin, pooled on the tiles.

She'd nearly had a heart attack when the detectives turned up out of the blue. What if he was outside, thought she'd called them in again? She'd have said anything, literally anything, to get them out of the house. She'd even owned up to the argument with Caitlin, knowing it had nothing to do with the abduction. As for Luke Holden, she'd not thought twice about dropping the little shit in the drugs mire. He'd broken Caitlin's heart, deserved everything coming to him. She saw his hopefully imminent arrest as collateral damage to avert police attention from a far greater threat. As for signing over Caitlin's diary, the detective's sweet talk had nothing to do with Nicola's decision. The scribblings were mostly of the got-up-had-breakfast-watched-telly variety. Good luck with that. At least they'd gone away happy. And out of her hair. Mind, the cannabis had been an eye-opener. Nicola would have sworn on her mother's life that Caitlin never touched tobacco let alone smoked the wacky stuff.

Not that the dope was the biggest shock. Her wary gaze strayed yet again to the Nokia phone lying on top of the cistern. It was brand new, pay-as-you-go: the unwanted present, gift-wrapped in yesterday's *Birmingham News*. Nicola had combed every article, studied every picture before realizing none of it was relevant; it would just be the sicko playing mind games again. As for the mobile?

He'd called minutes after the police left. The cultured voice, conversational delivery, made Caitlin's abduction sound like a normal reasonable act. They could've been discussing an eBay transaction or the rubbish weather, except he'd done most of the talking. Welling up again, Nicola dropped her face in her hands, replayed his words in her head.

'Listen carefully, Nicola. Please don't interrupt. Do exactly as I say and Caitlin will be fine. Once you've— Shut up and listen, Nicola.' The pace of his delivery hadn't missed a beat. 'As I say ... once you've done everything I tell you, I'll send her home and you can continue your lovely little lives. Cross me and she'll die. I think that sounds fair, all things considered, don't you?'

All things considered? What the hell? He spoke over her before she'd barely opened her mouth. 'When—?'

'All in good time, Nicola. All in good time.'

'When?' she'd shouted, immediately lowered her voice. 'Please. I'll do anything, anything.'

'I know you will, Nicola.'

'Please, tell me you won't hurt her?'

'Let's think.' Breath bated, she'd heard a sigh.

125

'If you're both very good, I'll be in touch again tomorrow. Until then ... Mum's the word, eh, Nicola?'

She'd heard a snigger as he rang off. Bastard. Torturing her like this. Lifting her head, Nicola gazed into the mirror again, scowled. Pretty little head? She must've aged ten years in two days. Christ, it could almost be her mother staring back.

Mrs Walker's arthritic knuckles gripped the arms of her favourite wing chair. The heat from the fire had turned one of her legs a mottled shade of corned beef. Lights flickered across the lenses of her Deirdre Barlow specs as she stared, rapt, at the screen. On auto pilot she reached for a Roses chocolate from the box nestled in her lap. Yeugh. Strawberry cream, she spat it back. How come the box was nigh on empty? The Bristol Cream had taken a hammering, too. Gaze still glued to the action, she took a large sip, hoping it would wash away the sickly taste coating her mouth.

'Shush.' Carelessly she nudged Ginger with her slippered foot. The fat cat – sprawled on the carpet like a Poundland tiger rug – was surrounded by photo albums that Mrs Walker had been leafing through earlier. Looking at snaps of bygone days was another of her favourite pastimes, almost as good as watching TV cop shows. But the cat's wheezy snores could raise the dead and currently grated on Mrs Walker's nerves. 'Shush, will you?' She nudged again, needed no distraction, thank you very much, not with the drama unfolding. *Prime Suspect* had always been a favourite though Mrs Walker was sure she and Caitlin hadn't caught this episode.

She waited for the ads before treating herself to another sherry. At the same time, the cat lifted its head, twitched a battle-scarred ear and fixed its beady gaze on the door. 'It's all right, Ginger. Settle down.' She'd heard the noise too, post landing on the mat. At this time of night it would be flyers for fast food or small traders pushing their wares. Take your pick. They were all the same to her: bin fodder. 'No Junk Mail' meant exactly what it said. Couldn't these people read? Same with the phone, Nicola had signed her up with some service that meant she wasn't supposed to get unwanted calls. Yes, well, it didn't work, did it?

Five minutes before the show ended, the penny dropped. A tingle ran down her spine and she felt the tiny hairs rise on the back of her neck. *Of course.* The killer was the posh bloke with the nice teeth and the fancy car. Delighted, she clapped her hands. *Who's a clever girl?* She wondered if Caitlin had worked it out too. Seconds later she slumped back in the chair. It was no big deal; the baddie was always the person you least expected. Come to think of it, she'd probably known all along. It was a repeat for heaven's sake; the solution had likely been lurking in her grey cells all the time. Sighing, she took another nip of sherry. Caitlin would remember if they'd seen it before. Would it be all right to give her a quick call? It seemed ages since they'd had a little chat.

Her hand stilled on the way to the phone and tears pricked her eyes as she remembered. Caitlin couldn't have turned up yet or Nicola – and the police – would have been in touch. They'd promised to ring with any news. Their silence had to be a good sign. Surely, it meant Caitlin was still alive? Eyes closed, she crossed herself. Dear God, don't let her come to any harm.

The business card left by the blonde detective still lay on the coffee table. What was her name? The old woman leaned forward, pulled the card closer. DI Sarah Quinn. That's right. Mrs Walker hadn't warmed to her, found her a bit stand-offish. Still, if she was half as good as Jane Tennison ... The old woman groaned, slapped her head. Stupid, stupid, stupid, it seemed to happen more often these days. If she carried on like this, the men in white coats might as well come and take her away. Maybe Nicola was right. She'd seen the pained looks on her daughter's face recently, but everyone got things confused sometimes, didn't they?

Like when she'd drawn the curtains earlier. A man had been standing opposite staring at the house. DI Quinn had told her to call if anything out of the ordinary happened. Maybe she should have a word? But no, it sounded so lame. He'd probably been waiting for a friend or something. Better to sleep on it, see how things looked in the morning. Sighing, she aimed the remote at the TV, hauled herself to her feet, toed the cat's rump. Ginger could spend a night on the tiles; she was fed up finding pools of pee every time she got up. Maybe it was time for a trip to the vet's or something. 'Come on, old boy.'

The cat hissed, bared its teeth, slunk across the carpet. Humming softly, she pottered after it, ferrying her empty glass and half-full bottle into the kitchen. The smell hit her first. Then she saw something in a dish on the table. Dear God. It couldn't be...? Tentatively, she took a few steps in, placed trembling fingers round her neck. The tongue lay in a pool of blood, frayed ends of gristle glistened moist and pink.

She heard the shatter of glass as she fainted. And a man's low whisper.

NINETEEN

'Come on, wake up.' She felt a tap on her shoulder, heard the man's voice in her ear. 'Don't dick me around.'

Caitlin slowly opened her eyes, turned on her side, found his by now familiar face hovering inches above hers. She saw concern in his gaze, concern verging on panic. Good. Maybe he'd think twice in future about the amount of sleeping pills he forced down her throat. Feeling fog-brained most of the day made it bloody difficult to get her head round an escape plan. It certainly didn't help not having set foot outside the room since the first night. She'd given up her pathetic fantasies about the cops staging a dramatic rescue. If the coverage in last night's local rag had been anything to go by they were closer to homing in on the Scarlet Pimpernel. *West Midlands police are increasingly concerned for the safety of yada yada.* She sighed. Not half as concerned as Caitlin herself.

'You OK?' He traced a finger down her profile.

Jerking her head away, she muttered, 'What do you care?' Yawning open-mouthed she hauled herself upright then sat on the mattress hugging her knees.

'Don't be like that. I bought you a pressie.' Smiling, he whipped a Primark bag from behind his back. 'Da-dah.'

Despite misgivings, she curved a lip. She'd seen good cops, bad cops in action – monkey man staged good-guy-bad-guy routines single-handedly. The kindness was almost harder to bear than the cruelty, and he could switch in a heartbeat.

Head down, she delved into the bag and found skinny jeans, clean underwear, face wipes. 'Guilt complex kicking in, is it?' She glanced up, deadpan. He'd been so late last night, she'd soiled herself. He'd found her sobbing, stinking in shit. He'd been sorry enough to help her sort it but then pissed off again, leaving her alone. The empty building's weird creaks and rustlings had scared the life out of her. But the place wasn't in the middle of nowhere: traffic noise and muffled voices floating up from the street told her that. If she could only...

'Suit yourself.' He made to snatch the bag away. 'Shame, though. You can hardly go out wearing that. Punk's so last century.'

'Big ho.' The black bin liner was better than nothing. But not for go— Frowning, she narrowed her eyes. 'What did you say?'

'Punk's so—'

She shook an impatient head. 'You know what I mean.'

'It shouldn't be long now, Caitlin.' He placed a finger under her chin. 'Things are moving on.'

'What things, for Christ's sake?'

He held her gaze for several seconds. 'Do you really want to know?'

She nodded.

So he told her – and she wished he hadn't.

TWENTY

The small brown envelope was lying on the mat when a yawning Nicola came downstairs belting her dressing gown. The contents now lay across the kitchen table vying for space with dirty plates, her phone and the Nokia. Maybe it was sleep deprivation, but she couldn't fathom the significance. Eyes creased against the cigarette smoke, she took the occasional sip of tepid tea as she reread the cutting.

BABES IN THE WOOD
Leicestershire police have launched a murder inquiry after the discovery of a child's body near her home in the village of Moss Pit. Five-year-old Pauline Bolton (pictured) had been picnicking with a friend when the assailant struck. Ten-year-old Susan Bailey, who sustained minor injuries, is believed to have wit-

nessed the brutal attack on her young playmate. Susan is currently under police guard
in hospital where detectives are waiting to
question her.

DCI Ken Southern told the *Mercury* that
Susan had had a lucky escape. "It's conceivable that had she not raised the alarm, we
could have a double murder on our hands."

Susan's screams alerted concerned villagers
who raced to the scene of the tragedy.
Badger's Copse is within sight of both girls'
homes and had become a favourite place to
play during the school holidays.

DCI Southern warned parents to keep a
close eye on their children. "A dangerous
killer is still at large," he said. "I'm appealing
for anyone with information to come forward
before he strikes again."

Frowning, Nicola stubbed the baccy in an
ashtray, picked up the cutting. In pristine
condition, it had to be a photocopy – it was
dated 13 August 1960. Nicola hadn't been born
then. As she studied Pauline's photograph, her
lip curved unwittingly. What a little doll. All
sundress and sandals with a teddy bear tucked
under her arm. She had a mop of – presumably
– blonde curls and a smile to die for. Nicola
grimaced. For God's sake, there had to be better
phrases: the kid had been brutally murdered.

But what the hell had any of it to do with her?
Unlike the Moors Murders and the Cannock

133

Chase killings, she couldn't recall a thing about the Moss Pit case. Easy enough to find out though, a few clicks should do it. She half rose before remembering the cops had removed both the desktop and Caitlin's laptop. Neil would Google it for her. The phone rang as she reached for the handset.

'Neil Lomas here. I believe you wanted a word?' Sarah scooted the chair back from the desk a few inches. She'd been at it since before seven, trying to keep on top of the admin, bringing the action book up to date, reviewing some of the eighty plus statements the squad had taken. Her flask of coffee, now half empty, had been brewed at home; the canteen toast was now mere crumbs on a paper plate. She'd have brought the food in too but her bread had turned a fetching shade of green. Nothing new there then. As for butter? Fresh out. Domestic stuff went by the stale bread board when she was working a big case. Actually, make that any case.

'Mr Lomas. Good of you to phone.' Her voice was clipped, the corollary tacit: better late than never. The guy couldn't fail to appreciate the call's importance.

'Sorry. I'd have got back sooner but you know how it is.'

'Not really.' She knew he'd not been at his father's Derby address last night. Lomas senior had told the visiting uniforms his son was out walking. According to one officer, Frank Lomas had either made a miraculous recovery or he'd not been knocking at heaven's door in the first place. Lucky either way, because Neil had apparently forgotten to take a phone on his nocturnal ramblings. She tapped her pen on the desk. He'd had ample time to elaborate. 'So do tell.'

'I needed a bit of space.' *To find himself? Purlease.* 'You must know how it is, inspector?' She heard an exaggerated sigh, imagined him soothing a furrowed brow. She stuck a mental finger down her throat.

'No. I don't find it a great necessity, Mr Lomas.'

'Lucky you.' Tetchy all of a sudden. Default mode or defence mechanism? 'But it's Caitlin you're meant to be finding, isn't it?' he said. 'How long's she been missing now?' His follow-up came more quickly than she'd expected. 'Sorry, that was below the belt. But what with Caitlin gone and my dad's collapse, it's been a crap few days.'

Tell someone who gives a shit. 'It's Caitlin I want to talk about. Where are you?'

'Yeah, your people mentioned it to Dad. I'm on the way back to Birmingham. It's easier if he stays with me. Until we know how things stand. Why don't you drop by about midday?'

Who did he think she was? Lady sodding Penelope? It didn't take long to put him straight. Unsmiling, she hung up a minute later. Lomas would be at Lloyd House. Twelve sharp.

'I need to see you. Please. Can you come round, Nicola?' Mrs Walker heard a sigh.

'Can it wait, Mum? I'm ... tied up at the mo.'

'No, I'm begging you.' The old woman darted a wary glance over her shoulder.

'What's it about?'

'I'd rather not say over the phone.' Not when the voice had as good as told her to keep her mouth shut. Standing in the kitchen now, she trembled as she recalled the low whisper in her ear last night: speak no evil. Had she imagined that, too?

'But Mum...'

Eight hours after the incident, Linda Walker had woken fully clothed in her bed, had no recollection of getting there. She'd searched everywhere, turned the place upside down, even looked in the dustbin outside. In her mind's eye she could see the tongue clear as day. The dish had vanished, too. And Ginger was nowhere to be seen.

'Nicola, please...'

'Someone must have seen something.' Sarah held out empty palms. Wished she had a penny for every time she'd trotted out the line. It was a cop cliché in the same vein as 'you're nicked'; 'make my day' and 'anything you say will be taken down'. But apart from one neighbour, no one had said anything. Well, anything worth hearing. Including, this morning, the squad. The DI ran her gaze over a dozen officers. Twelve pairs of eyes stared back. She'd known livelier briefs. She'd known livelier wakes. Which reminded her: the chief was at a funeral this morning. He'd called twice to insist he wanted filling in later. And rumour had it he was taking early retirement. Yeah, right. As for the troops? Still nothing.

'It's the route home from Queen's Ridge that's bugging me.' She turned her head to the whiteboard, traced an index finger along a street map, the picture of a smiling Caitlin was pinned next to an aerial shot. 'Shops, houses, lock-ups. It's hardly Ghostville yet she's not on a single frame of CCTV. We've not had so much as a whisper after the media appeal. Why did no one see her there?' Sarah narrowed her eyes. *Unless she wasn't on it?*

'What if she never left the school, boss? We've only heard from one source she was snatched off the street and that could've been deliberately to put us off the trail.' Sarah nodded. Harries, not for the first time, had voiced her thoughts.

'Nice try, Dave, but...' Head down, Beth Lally was rifling her notebook. 'A girl waved to her from the bus. Yeah, Lauren Bleasdale. Said she was Caitlin's best friend.'

'True, Beth, but Caitlin was still on the grounds. What if she went back in the building?' Shona Bruce was clearly on the same page

137

headed: 'long shot'. OK, no one expected to find Caitlin on site, but had they missed a pointer to her disappearance?

'Right. We'll search the premises again,' Sarah said. 'And re-interview.' She caught a groan or two from the floor: few cops relished going over old ground. Tough. Needs must when the devil drives a stalled motor. Obviously they wouldn't need to talk again to everyone at Queen's Ridge. The inquiry had neither time nor budget for a scattergun approach. The majority of students and staff could probably be eliminated immediately anyway. They couldn't afford to wait until Monday, so the rest would have to be interviewed at home. 'Dave, can you and Shona draw up a list?'

'Sure thing, boss.' He smiled. 'The usual suspects.'

Talking of suspects. She brought them up to speed on Lomas and told them she'd be doing the interview when he arrived. 'By the way, Shona, have you had a chance to look through Caitlin's diary?'

'Sorry, ma'am.' A slightly flustered DC Bruce? Rarer than a snake chiropodist.

'No worries.' Genuinely. Shona – unlike some on the squad – was a grafter; didn't watch clocks. Sarah knew the younger woman could not have got home much before ten, and the last thing she needed then was to take work to bed. 'Leave it on my desk, yes?' There'd be time to flick through before interviewing Lomas.

'What about Luke Holden, ma'am?' DC Lally asked. 'He's still AWOL.'

She nodded. 'I'd like you and Shona to call round later. Talk to the neighbours again if he's still not shown.'

Paul Wood, who'd been keeping a low profile, glanced up all innocent from a monitor. 'Didn't one of them report a gas leak, inspector?' Wood knew as well as every cop in the station that entering premises on dodgy grounds was a no-go. Without a warrant, any evidence they found would be inadmissible even if they located the crown jewels.

She gathered her files, eyebrow arched. 'I didn't hear that, Twig.'

'Course not, ma'am.'

TWENTY-ONE

'It's the truth. Please don't look at me like that.' Had she been standing, Linda Walker might have stamped a foot. Slumped in a kitchen chair, her tightly folded arms were signal enough.

'Like what?' Nicola stifled a sigh, chucked a teabag in the sink. Please, let her have misheard the old dear.

'Like I'm a total stranger or a mad old bat.' The old woman ran fluttering fingers down a sallow raddled cheek; hanks of steel-grey hair had escaped the moorings of her bun. Nicola hadn't a clue how her mother could focus through the smears on her glasses. Mind, that could explain a lot.

'Here you go.' Liquid sloshed over the rim when she banged the mug on the table. She'd dropped everything to drive over to Small Heath and listen to what sounded like the verbal equivalent of a steaming pile of horse manure. 'So you found a tongue there,' pointing, 'and you fainted. Next thing you're in bed and this ... this ... tongue's ... disappeared.'

'I know it sounds daft ... but there was a man in here.'

Nicola had considered briefly whether it could be true, of course she had. Given Caitlin's disappearance, she'd have been mad not to. But she knew her mother well and just didn't buy it: the old dear was lonely and had played the emotional blackmail card before. 'Mum, when you fell, did you hit your head?'

'I might have.' Her dentures shifted and left faint marks when she bit her bottom lip. 'But I'm sure it's true, Nicola. There was a man. He whispered in my ear.' *Jesus Christ*, Nicola thought. *My daughter's missing, a mad bastard's playing me like an orchestra and it looks as if my mother's losing her mind.*

'The same man you thought you saw over the road?' She leant across to redo the buttons on her mum's old lilac cardigan.

'No. I don't think it could have been.'

'OK.' Nicola glanced at her phone, breathed a sigh of relief. 'So this man in the kitchen? What did he look like?'

'I'm not sure. He came up from behind. I just saw a dark shape out of the corner of my eye.'

She nodded. 'Drink your tea, Mum. I need the loo.' Despite her better judgement, Nicola carried out a quick search of the house, checked doors and windows, rummaged through the bin outside. When Nicola returned, the older woman was staring into space, wringing her hands. She looked as if she'd seen a ghost, but the shakes could have a more prosaic explanation.

Leaning against the dresser, Nicola lit a cigarette, took a deep drag. 'How much did you have to drink last night, Mum?'

'One small sherry.' Her mouth tightened as far as shrivelled lips allowed. 'That's nothing to do with it. I was stone cold—'

'Mum, it stinks in here.' Booze, boiled cabbage, cat pee.

'I know. I dropped the bottle.' She frowned. 'That's another thing. When I came down, the mess had been cleaned up.'

'I see.' Like hell. 'Must be a first, that. A house-proud burglar.'

'If you're going to be sarky...' She turned her head.

'Didn't nick your Marigolds, did he?' Masking a smile, she doused the butt under the tap and dropped it in the pedal bin before sitting

141

next to her mum. 'Look, if you're sure about all this, we'll call the police.'

'No, not that. Please, Nic. I'm scared.'

'All the more reason—'

'He as good as warned me not to.' She glanced round before whispering, 'His mouth was right by my ear and he said, "Speak no evil".'

Dear Lord. Was she hearing voices as well as hallucinating? 'Is *anything* missing, Mum? Have you checked?'

'I had a quick scout round.' She traced a finger round the rim of her mug. 'I don't think anything's gone.'

'Are you sure?' The old woman still seemed preoccupied but eventually she nodded.

'OK, what do you want to do?'

'Maybe, just for a day or two ... I could...' The words petered out and she dropped her head. Nicola briefly closed her eyes. Knew where this was going. It had probably been heading there all along. 'I'm sorry, Mum. You can't stay with me at the moment. It's difficult. Caitlin's missing. The police are in and out.'

'But what if he comes back?' Her fingers clawed her neck and behind the glasses, her eyes were wide with fear.

She took one of her mother's hands, held it between her own. 'He's not going to, Mum. Trust me.' Her smile faded. She let go of the hand. The Nokia had beeped an alert.

'I'm sure you're right, love.' Mrs Walker struggled to her feet. 'You get off home. I

142

understand.'

'Understand what?' Only half-listening, she read the message again, struggled to make sense of it.

'You have your own life now.' She halted in the doorway, hand visibly trembling on the frame. 'And when Ginger shows up he won't know where I'm gone. Next door won't look out for him, that's for sure. Not with that Alsatian of theirs. Mind, the dog's run off, she come round this morning in bits, asking if—'

'Mum.' Nicola looked up from the phone. 'What do you know about Badger's Copse?'

TWENTY-TWO

Pauline's sky-blue eyes shone as she shot a skinny arm in the air. 'Miss! Miss! I know, I know. Let me, let me. Please, Miss!' Susan reckoned if the silly little beggar wriggled any harder she'd slip off the tree stump and land in a heap on the prickly grass. Her bum must be full of splinters as it was. Not that the stump was a real chair, or the fallen trunk more than a make-believe desk. Like the rest of the classroom, a lively imagination was all the girls needed. The cane was real enough though. Susan pointed it at her liveliest pupil who sat cross-legged, still waving her arm.

'Pauline Bolton. You're showing your knickers again. How many times do I have to tell you?'

'Sorry, Miss.' Focussed on her role as teacher's pet, her distracted tugs on the hem of the sundress were pretty ineffectual. 'Let me answer, Miss, please, Miss.'

Susan glowered, pursed pantomime lips, pretended to give the request serious consideration just like Miss Morris at school. 'All right, Pauline. But be very careful.' Fragments of rotting bark flew as she whacked the log with her cane. 'You know what happened last time you made a mistake.'

They both glanced at the angry red mark on the little girl's leg. Going home with that on show was a complete no-no. Pauline's mum would kill Susan. She'd have to keep the kid happy for at least another hour before it faded. Unless they lied, told Mrs B that Pauline had fallen or something. It had been an accident of sorts after all. She couldn't have known Pauline would be dumb enough to walk in the way just as she was dishing out six of the best to the naughtiest boy in the class.

'Well? Go on, girl.' Susan had almost perfected Miss's tone of voice and turn of phrase. 'Cat got your tongue?'

Frowning, Pauline turned her mouth down, her lips still blood-red with juice from the illicit lolly. 'Sorry, Miss. You took so long, I forgot the

144

question.'

'Blaming someone else?' Whoosh went the cane. 'When you're at fault?' Thwack. 'That'll never do.'

'Not so.' The skirt rode up as she squirmed. Susan caught another flash of pink cotton. 'Ask it again. Ask it again.'

''Kay. What's six times seven?'

'That's not the question,' she wailed.

'How do you know, missie? You said you couldn't remember.' Course it wasn't. Even Susan struggled with the seven times table and she'd be at big school next year. Pauline didn't stand a chance. 'It's really not good enough, young lady.' The skin chafed on Susan's lardy thighs as she struggled to her feet. 'Come on, think about it. One times seven is seven...' She continued reciting as she padded round the tree stump, poking and prodding Pauline's tiny body with the cane then halted, hands on hips, her shadow almost obliterating the little girl. 'And six times seven is...?'

'I dunno. 'Snot fair.' Tears glistened as they ran down Pauline's face, dripped from her chin.

'All right. Who's going to help Little Miss Smarty Pants? I said who's—' Eyes wide, Susan froze, cane pressed against Pauline's chest. She'd heard something. Could swear it was a voice.

'What is it, Sukie?' Pauline whispered.

'Shush!' Ears pricked, Susan cocked her head. Sounded like it came from the copse. Somebody spying on them?

Spooked as well now, Pauline said, 'Sukie, stop it.'

'Shush, I said.' She drew back the cane. A dog barked, a branch snapped.

'Please don't, Sukie,' she whimpered, then put her thumb in her mouth, sucked it like a teat.

Still straining her ears, Susan counted to ten. Nothing but the trickling stream, wood pigeons cooing, the faint drone of a tractor. Could she have imagined it? She dropped the cane, lowered her voice. 'Did you hear anything, Paulie?'

She shook her head. 'Like what?'

'A voice. A man's voice.'

'What did it say?'

Susan dithered for a few seconds, wondering if she should tell. 'I couldn't make it out.' She tousled Pauline's curls. 'Forget it.'

The little girl stood on the tree stump, gently removed her friend's glasses, stared into her eyes. 'What did it say, Sukie?'

'I told you – nothing. Come on, let's—'

She stamped her foot. 'Were you just trying to scare me?'

'Don't be daft.'

Not initially anyway. Now she saw a way of using the little girl's fear to get at the truth and hopefully allay her own unease. Because Susan really didn't think she'd imagined the voice or the words. And if Pauline had been telling the truth about the lolly...

'On your mother's life, Paulie. Where'd you

146

get the lolly?'

'Cross my heart and hope to die, a man give it me.'

Pauline hadn't been making it up then. Susan felt the hairs rise on the back of her neck. She grabbed both of Pauline's arms, forced her to make eye contact. 'Did you get it from a stranger, Pauline?'

'That hurts. Stop it.' She struggled free, rubbed the tender flesh. In the tussle, Susan didn't even notice the glasses fall from Pauline's grasp.

'I won't ask you again, Pauline Bolton. Did you take it from a stranger?'

'No,' she shouted, red-faced.

'So you know him?'

The little girl looked down, started picking at the grass wedged in the soles of her sandals. 'A bit. I seen him before. You know him too. I seen you with him in the copse.'

'When? Who did you see?' She shook her hard.

'Let me go or I'll tell on you.'

'What did you see, you little liar?'

'Nothin'.'

'If you don't tell me—'

'Sukie.' Eyes wide, Pauline pointed a finger over Susan's shoulder. 'He's there.'

TWENTY-THREE

'I'm sorry. Say again.' Sarah's biro stalled mid-hover over an almost full page of notes: name, age, address, alibis that would have to be checked, yada yada, then: wham. Had she heard him right? A quick glance to her left suggested Harries was experiencing a credibility gap too – he seemed to be having trouble swallowing. Sarah leaned back, laid down the pen, studied Neil Lomas even more closely, certainly more than he reciprocated.

The criminology lecturer lounged in the chair opposite, skinny ankle lodged across bony knee, eau de pong wafted from a scuffed Hush Puppy. Part-bemused, she watched as he plucked a sandy hair from his brown cord jacket, held it to the light then dropped it on her carpet. *In your own time, sunshine.* Considering the guy had turned up early, he was certainly wasting it now. Shame the interview rooms downstairs were full; more formal surroundings often provided a kick up a cocky bum.

'Which part can't you grasp, DI Quinn?' Finally meeting her gaze, Lomas flashed an emaciated smile at her and what looked like a wink at Harries. 'That Caitlin hit on me? Or that I had to let her down gently.'

Both, actually. Sarah hadn't seen Caitlin in the flesh but found it almost inconceivable that the striking girl in the photograph would have the hots for the tosspot facing her. It was difficult enough believing the sparse ginger hair and skin like undercooked dough ticked even Nicola Reynolds' boxes. Like Sarah's mum used to say, looks aren't everything. But to compensate for the shortcomings, Lomas must have a bloody big ... personality. Sarah reckoned he hid it well.

Harries was up to something, too. She heard a rustle, glanced down, *so* wished she hadn't. He was miming a hand-job under the desk. The gesture's timing was unfortunate, given her next question. 'Define "came on to me", Mr Lomas.'

'Do I really have to spell it out, inspector?' Pursed prissy lips.

She wondered if an expression could be simultaneously both pitying and patronizing, decided Lomas had perfected the art. Maybe it worked on his students. 'Let's think. Yes.'

He gave a laboured sigh and ran both hands through the thinning hair before revealing that he'd started spending less time at the Reynolds' house because Caitlin seemed to have developed some sort of crush. Apparently she made a lot of eye contact, gave lingering pecks on the cheek and indulged in suggestive wordplay. Big deal. A lot of people might interpret Caitlin's actions as being warm and friendly. As for suggestive wordplay? It sounded to Sarah like weasel speak for talk dirty. Why didn't he just say what he meant? Harries leaned forward; he'd clearly had enough of the guy's crap. 'Did she or didn't she ask for a shag?'

That was certainly one way of putting it. She masked a smile.

'Screw you, constable.' Lomas scraped back the chair, flecks of spittle on his lip. 'I came here freely of my own volition. I don't have to tolerate language like that or the offensive nature of the slur.'

'Please sit down, Mr Lomas,' Sarah said evenly. 'We're not finished.' She felt like pointing out the tautology but didn't think he'd appreciate the lecture. 'And you've not answered the question. Did she explicitly proposition you?'

'Not in so many words.'

'Did her alleged flirting go any further than looks and innuendo?'

The bristling was almost laughable. 'There was nothing alleged about it, DI Quinn. And it would've – if I'd let it.'

'So why didn't you?' Harries asked. 'Most men—'

'I'm not most men. Some of us don't take advantage of pretty needy girls. And more to the point, I'm in a relationship with Nicola.'

Needy? Sarah made another note. 'Is Caitlin's mother aware of what you say was going on?' Under her nose.

150

'Good God, no. Nic thinks the sun shines out of Caitlin's ar— Pardon the French, Caitlin's posterior.' The guy's arched eyebrow was so knowing, she wouldn't be surprised to see it on *Mastermind*. Specialist subject: arrogant twats.

She unscrewed the cap on a bottle of water, took a few sips. 'Let's say for a minute Nicola had found out. How would she react?'

'I'd get the blame.' He threw his hands in the air. 'I'd be out on my ear, my feet wouldn't touch.'

'Would Nicola feel betrayed, angry even?' Sarah asked.

He snorted. 'Surely you must've picked up by now that Caitlin can do no wrong in her mother's eyes?' She shrugged. Like some ham actor, he narrowed his eyes. 'Are you trying to suggest Nicola's got something to do with Caitlin's disappearance?'

No, she wasn't. But she found it interesting that Lomas had mooted the possibility.

'If Caitlin Reynolds fancies that knob-end ... sod the hat, boss.' Harries glanced in the wing mirror, pulled out to overtake. 'I'd scoff the effing wardrobe.'

The lilac-rinse wrinkly in the car ahead – a pristine powder-blue Morris Minor – was tootling along at tortoise pace. 'Watch your speed, Dave.' They were in a thirty limit: penalty points on a cop's licence weren't a good look, and besides Sarah wanted to get there in one piece.

'There' being Queen's Ridge comprehensive. The premises had been opened up by a caretaker and the deputy head would be on site too. Apart from touching base with the search team, Sarah wanted to check out call-me-Jude-my-body's-a-temple-Fox. The teacher's name didn't figure on the list drawn up by Dave and Shona but Dave just happened to mention she'd be in school painting scenery for the end of term play. Sarah hadn't asked how he knew.

'You see it the same way, don't you, boss? A girl like Caitlin isn't gonna be that desperate.'

'Sure.' She took a green apple from a pocket, started polishing it on her coat sleeve. 'But why'd he put it out there at all?' She remembered the thought bugging her at the time. Lomas had already denied being what Dave called the snogger at the bus stop, claimed he'd been lunching in the canteen when Caitlin was indulging in a tongue sandwich. If the alibi checked, he'd be in the clear. So why mention Caitlin's so-called crush? If he'd kept his mouth shut, they'd have been none the wiser.

'Come on, boss. He was blowing smoke up his arse.'

'Charming.' She took a bite, pulled a face, turned to gaze at the Saturday shoppers out in force on Kings Heath high street. That reminded her, she'd have to hit a supermarket today; she was down to her last loo roll. Back to bums then. She raised a wry eyebrow – did Dave have a point? Lomas probably had a Masters in ego-

152

aggrandisement. He'd certainly not featured yet in Caitlin's diary. The lecturer's early arrival at the station had bitten into Sarah's reading time. She'd considered passing the book/buck back to Shona but on second thoughts decided against, hoping the girl's own words might give some insight into her character. Sarah hated admitting she was little nearer knowing what made Caitlin tick now than on day one of Operation Vixen.

'You heard about the sweepstake, boss?'

Face screwed, she looked at the apple: God it was tart. Shame she'd not grabbed a banana. Mind, she'd just clocked a bloke shuffling past shoving burger and chips down his bull neck. Why did it always seem to be lard-arses who ate on the hoof? Couldn't they wait to get home before topping up the fat levels? School kids weren't much better – every lunchtime all over the city, queues outside Greggs spilled onto the pavement. Not as bad as Glasgow though. She'd spent a month there on a case some years back and the first time she'd witnessed it she thought a riot had broken out.

'Hello? Is anybody there? Knock once for yes.' Dave hadn't done his Madame Arcati act for a while.

She smiled. 'Sorry. I was miles away.'

'Never.'

'Good one though, Dave.'

'What?'

'It was like being in the same room.'

'With?'

'Margaret Rutherford.'

'Who?'

'Forget it.' She flapped a hand.

'Anyway I was saying ... the sweepstake. Are you in?'

'What sweepstake?'

She took another nibble of apple, listened as he told her one of the custody sergeants had it on good authority Baker was taking an early bath. The sweepstake was a fiver a go and winner pockets the lot. 'All you have to do is pick a date, boss.'

'I don't think so.'

'Why's that?'

'Come on, Dave, if the chief gets wind ... he'd put in for promotion.'

Harries glanced across and smiled. 'What date you going for then?'

'Fourth of July.'

They drove in an easy silence for a while. Juggling the apple, she scrolled through a few emails on her phone, put in a call to the squad room, left another message for Baker, who'd still not got back to her. When she glanced up, the school was in sight. Dave indicated left, turned into the gates.

She took another tentative nibble. 'Course, it could have been a pre-emptive strike.'

'Are we back on Lomas?'

'Yeah.' Well spotted, that man. 'You know what they say, Dave: attack's the best kind of defence.'

The knotted eyebrows meant he wasn't convinced. Thinking it through while he parked the motor, he switched off the engine, turned to face her. 'You think *he* tried it on? Not Caitlin. And Casanova was getting his version in first?'

She shrugged a shoulder. 'Could be.'

'If that's the case, I bet she told him to take a running jump.'

'Off a motorway bridge. And he wouldn't have liked that, would he?' They held eye contact for a few seconds.

'That's food for thought, boss.'

Nodding, she offered him the apple. 'Fancy a bite?'

He flashed a smile. 'Thought you'd never ask.'

TWENTY-FOUR

'Why did you never tell me, Mum?' Forget stranger or mad old bat; Nicola thought her mother looked haunted. After hearing the name Badger's Copse, she'd had to be gently led into the next room. She sat in the wing chair now, clutching her chest, struggling to get her breath.

Nicola had left the news cutting at home but it was beginning to make sense. Her mother must have been one of the children in the wood, the ten-year-old who'd been attacked by a stranger and witnessed the murder of her best friend. No wonder she'd taken Nicola's question so badly.

'I don't talk about it. It happened a long time ago.' She never talked about her family either, Nicola realized. Or her upbringing, schooling, teen years. No old photos survived; none of her children's books or toys had been passed down. What do they say about the past? In her mum's case, foreign country barely covered it. More like faraway galaxy.

Nicola leaned forward in her seat. 'But you saw the man who killed her. You helped the police and everything.' Her mum must have been quite a heroine at the time. She'd had her fifteen minutes of fame before Nicola was born, before Warhol even coined the phrase. Maybe that was why she changed her name. She gave her mum a warm smile. After all these years she saw the old dear in a new light. 'Was it exciting? Did you have to go to court? Give evidence?'

'Tommy rot,' she snapped. 'You've no idea what you're talking about.'

'Don't be shy, Mum. I read a newspaper article. Somebody pushed it through the—' Nicola froze, felt her blood run cold. Not just somebody. The psycho holding Caitlin. Her confused thoughts raced. What did her mother's part in a fifty-year-old crime have to do with Caitlin's abduction? Unless ... Had her testament led to the killer being sent down? Was he free now and seeking to exact some kind of sick

156

revenge?

'Tell me, Mum.' Nicola willed her mother to make eye contact. The old woman continued staring into the distance, biting her lip. 'Why did you change your name?'

Was she staring at the past as well as into the distance? 'Because.' A tear slithered down the wizened cheek.

'Because what, goddamnit?'

'Because they said I did it.'

'And did you?'

TWENTY-FIVE

Caroline gave a lazy smile, licked her slightly swollen lips. Boy did she need a drink and a pee. Not necessarily in that order. Hardly surprising given a quick glance at the bedside clock showed it was mid-morning and she'd yet to rise let alone shine. It had been a busy night but ... Her erstwhile editor had by no means fallen down on the job. Though neither of them, as she recalled, had been what you'd call a sleeping partner.

The ceiling mirror had certainly seen some action. She laughed out loud as she admired her reflection. Yep. You could definitely say Eddie had come good, and not just with the rushes. In fact, compared with the high-octane sex, the surplus footage had been a bit of an anti-climax. A potential tipster hadn't exactly leapt off the screen screaming, 'Bang to rights, governor, it's a fair cop.' Mind, she'd been a tad tipsy by the time they got round to a viewing. Eddie's bedroom athleticism had at least provided bonus features, and what's more he'd picked up the tab at the Thai restaurant.

Yawning, she threw off the duvet, caught a trace of his Aramis. She smoothed the black satin sheet where he'd lain, plucked a blond hair from the pillow. He was a decent bloke, and Caro occasionally needed the exercise, but out of sight, out of...

When he'd leaned over to peck her cheek goodbye, she'd feigned sleep, watched his exit through bleary eyes. Even if he'd not had to leave, she knew she'd have found some excuse to turf him out. Home territory and all that.

Barefoot she padded to the sash window, peered through the blind at the pewter sky. Same old. Christ, she could barely remember what the sun looked like. Grabbing her dressing gown, she headed for the bathroom, still pondering the irony: she made a damn good living invading other people's space while guarding her own like the recipe for Coke. She rarely invited a man back for a nightcap, let alone into her bed. Exchanging bodily fluids was no sweat, but she drew the line at home addresses. No big secret. It was a question of who called the shots. And when it boiled down to it, Caroline recognized she was as much a control freak as the Ice Queen. No wonder they had such a warm relationship.

Lip curled, she lowered the toilet seat. *Bloody men.* Course, the fact that a decade back Caroline had been sleeping with Sarah's then fiancée wouldn't have helped. Or that he was gunned down during a covert police operation after Caroline screamed at the sight of the weapon. Her more recent one-night stand with dishy Dave Harries hadn't gone down too well with the frosty cop either. Yeah, all that could have something to do with how well they got on. Caroline sighed. Flushed the loo. Why couldn't some people just let things go?

She rinsed her hands then slaked her thirst from the cold tap. As she patted her face dry, she stared critically in the mirror. Good skin, bright eyes, barely noticeable lines. She smiled, reckoned she could forego the filler for a while. Though God knew how much longer she could get away with late nights and too much booze. She was nearer forty than thirty and had already found a smattering of grey hairs among the black. TV – news or otherwise – was still a young woman's game, but she'd not go down the Cherry Blossom route. When her face no longer fitted, she'd find something else. Who knew? She might even settle down, get married, have kids. She pulled a face in the glass. Christ, she must have had a skin full.

She nearly jumped out of it when someone

banged the door. 'You in there, Caro?'

'Give us a minute, Nat,' she snapped. She'd taken on a lodger primarily to keep an eye on her inheritance while she was in London. When she was in residence, his presence sometimes seemed a high price to pay. 'I thought you were away?' she called, hoped to God he'd not been trying to sleep last night.

'I told you I'd be back today.' She rolled her eyes. Like she'd remember. 'Look, Caro, are you—?'

'Put some coffee on, Nat. I'll be down in a tick.'

'No prob. As long as you're OK.'

Something in his voice made her stiffen. 'Why shouldn't I be?'

'I saw the blood on the wall – the writing.'

'Hey, can't you read?' Even the footsteps sounded tetchy. Sarah glanced over her shoulder. Mr Angry Young Man dashed towards them jabbing a finger at yellow lettering on the pitted concrete. 'H.E.A.D, in case you didn't know, spells "head". And this isn't a public right of way.'

Unimpressed with the lecture, Harries slowly slipped his ID from a breast pocket, displayed the card at eye-level. 'And this,' tilting his head, 'is Detective Inspector Sarah Quinn.'

The classy vowels and cocky ticking off suggested deputy head to Sarah. Either way, the man's regular features softened almost immediately. 'Shoot. I'm sorry.' He slapped his forehead, aped a Homer Simpson 'Doh!' 'Given we've got more police on site than a double episode of *The Bill* I should've realized. It's just we get a lot of trouble with people parking here and if I may say so you don't look like a cop, inspector.' The guy certainly didn't lack confidence; the flirting wasn't even subtle. She'd probably pull him up on it if he looked like Jabba the Hut but she'd always been into the dark hair, blue eyes, pearly teeth combo.

'So what do cops look like, Mr...?'

'Portman. Jake Portman. Caretaker of this parish. Well, one of them.' He clicked his heels, offered a hand. 'As to cops,' he lowered his voice as if sharing a confidence, 'butch, bald, beer-bellied, Burton suits.'

Maybe he'd come in on a day off. The natty grey two-piece was clearly a cut above chain-store gear. She curved a faintly amused mental lip. 'And you base this vast knowledge on...?'

'*Crimewatch*.' He flashed a grin. 'Mind, I've not seen it for ages.' He'd clocked Harries tapping his watch though. 'Where are you heading, inspector? I'll show you the way.'

Queen's Ridge comp was a throwback to the sixties, flat-roofed concrete blocks, lots of blues and greys, open stairways visible through picture windows, everything functional, nothing fancy. Unless you counted Portman, Sarah mused. He did the guided-tour patter as they walked in step, but she'd already done her homework, knew the school's six hundred

161

pupils spoke getting on for thirty languages. And that the diversity crowd called it a multi-cultural microcosm. She guessed like any school it had its share of bullies and baddies, but the police rarely visited for anything more vital than a crime prevention talk, until recently.

Glancing back at Dave, she reckoned he looked none too happy to be here now. Through an upstairs window – complete with well-post-Christmas cotton wool snowdrift – she caught a glimpse of a couple of PCs. If the police were treating the place as a crime scene the full FSI works would be out in force. Instead, her oppo in uniform had released half a dozen officers who were carrying out a methodical search of the premises. Given no one knew precisely what they were looking for it was a bit needle-meets-haystack. Not so much nose job as nous.

'The main staircase is just down the corridor on the left.' Portman gave a mock salute as he played doorman. 'I'll love you and leave you.'

'Hold on, mate,' Harries said. 'I don't remember seeing your name on the list.'

'List?'

'We've been interviewing everyone at the school,' Sarah said. Surely he knew that?

'I've been on leave, but I guess I should've cottoned on anyway.' He spread his arms in mock surrender. 'Feel free. I'm all yours.'

'Leave in term-time?' Harries sniffed.

Portman paused a second or two, the smile no longer in situ. 'It was sick leave. I'm actually doing the head a favour coming in today.'

'How jolly decent,' Harries mumbled.

They used the staffroom. Portman had a bunch of keys. A low coffee table was littered with files, exercise books, two odd socks and a Mars bar with teeth marks. He offered a drink but going by the tannin rings in a couple of mugs on the floor, Sarah declined. As she sat, she spotted a can of air freshener in a bookcase. It patently didn't work, unless nowadays it came in sweat-laced-sprout fragrance.

After running through the basics, Portman told them he'd worked at the school since January, one of a three-strong team, who looked after the grounds as well as kept an eye on the buildings. 'Jake of all trades', as he put it. He might have seen Caitlin round the school but hadn't known anyone was missing until the head's phone call late last night. He'd been too ill to catch the telly news let alone read a paper. Reckoned he'd never touch prawns again.

'How well did you know Caitlin?' Dave tapped a pen between his teeth.

'I said...' He glanced at Harries for the first time. 'I might have seen her around. I thought you were supposed to be recording this.'

Sarah cleared her throat. 'Before Queen's Ridge, Mr Portman? What did you do?'

He'd been a full-time carer to his father who'd died six months back. Portman said he sold the family home in Rugby and moved to Birmingham just after. Sarah was on body-watch as well as asking the questions. His laid-back posture seemed as open as the relaxed manner, the twinkle in the eye a more or less permanent fixture. If he had longer hair, a parrot and a penchant for hoop earrings, she could easily picture Portman doing a passable Jack Sparrow. More easily than school dogsbody. Smoothing her skirt she said, 'You've not worked as a caretaker before, then?'

He twitched a lip. 'Is that a polite way of saying, what's a nice boy like you doing in a crap job like this?'

'Just answer the question eh, mate?' Since when had Dave turned into Mr Grumpy?

Portman didn't bat an eye, kept his gaze on Sarah. 'I've never worked as a caretaker before, but beggars can't be choosers. And when you've been out of the job market as long as I have, I was happy to take it.'

Beggar in a Boss suit? She raised a sceptical eyebrow.

'I use the cliché loosely, inspector.' Clearly he could read body language too. 'I inherited a modest estate from my father but money isn't everything. Life can be pretty lonely without work. Everyone needs to contribute, feel useful. And what better way to meet people, build a social life? Besides, we all need a reason to get out of bed in the morning, don't we?'

Full bladder usually works. 'Tell me...'

Three heads swivelled when the door swung

open and a woman reversed in, arms piled high with cardboard boxes. 'Whoops, sorry, I didn't realize anyone was here.' Not surprising given her nose was pressed against the top box. As she lowered the burden, her glance fell on Harries and her turquoise eyes lightened. 'Hello again. What are you doing here?'

From a teacher, Sarah reckoned it was a pretty dumb question. She'd little doubt of box lady's identity. Dave's hot blush wasn't the only clue. The blob of red paint on Fox's otherwise peachy cheek clinched it. Actually, Sarah ceded, on Ms Fox it was less blob, more fetching dab. 'Silly me,' the teacher unwittingly concurred. 'Seeing someone out of context, it always takes a second or two to sink in. Like bumping into your dentist at the butcher's.' The girly giggle followed by a broad smile suggested she fancied herself as a bit of a wit. And Sarah wouldn't be surprised if she was on first-name terms with her dentist.

'Actually,' Portman said. 'We're just in the mid—'

'Of course. No worries. I don't need to do this now.' She raked her fingers apparently artlessly through the long blonde tresses.

Sarah rose. 'Let me give you my card, Ms Fox. I'm Sarah Quinn.' She was a good six inches taller than the younger woman. 'If anything comes to mind...'

The teacher glanced at Harries. 'I've already got—'

'I'm senior investigating officer on the inquiry.'

'Why not.' She gave a tight smile. 'The more the merrier. Catch you later.'

Throwaway remark or carefully targeted? Harries had his head down. Sarah resumed her seat, uncharacteristically rattled. 'We were talking about your work, Mr Portman. Tell me, do you have close contact with the children?' Christ, she could've phrased that better.

His mouth tightened and the twinkle went out. 'What exactly are you suggesting?' Pique didn't cover it; he was clearly pissed off.

She raised a placatory palm. 'Not the best way of putting it. I'm sorry. What I'm trying to say is, are you in a position to pick up what goes on in school? Rumours. Playground gossip, that sort of thing. Would you know, for instance, if a pupil was being bullied, or bothered by something, someone?'

'Apology accepted.' He smiled. 'But no, not really. I've not been here long enough for that.'

'"Not really"?' she quoted. 'You're sure?'

'I've certainly not heard any buzz about the missing girl.' He anticipated the obvious supplementary. 'Or anyone else for that matter.'

She looked at Harries who shook his head. 'OK, Mr Portman. I think that's it for now.'

'Let me have a card.' He held out a hand. 'If I think of anything, I'll be sure to ring. Is your home number on here as well?' He winked. 'That was a joke. Seriously, though, I wish I could be more help. Maybe if I'd been around when Caitlin was...' He held out empty palms.

'Why?' Harries couldn't resist a final dig. 'What would you've done?'

'Who knows? But I presume an intruder entered the grounds again?'

Again?

TWENTY-SIX

'So when did they get in? And come to that, how?' Nat passed Caroline a black coffee, dragged a stool out from under the breakfast bar. 'Sit down Caro, you look like shit.'

Her mumbled 'Cheers, mate' had nothing to do with the drink. What woman liked being told she looked less than hot? After seeing the artwork on the wall, Caroline felt like puking, still hadn't taken her gaze off the bloody thing. She barely noticed her hand shake as she lifted the espresso to her lips.

'I was scared I'd find you lying dead or something.' Nat's nervous laugh failed to take the edge off what he'd said.

'Fuck's sake, Nat.' Dabbing coffee off her chin, brushing it off her chest. 'Don't mince your words, eh?'

167

'Sorry Caro, but look at it.' Hands deep in black denim pockets, Nat stood and surveyed the unwanted mural in all its gory glory. A child could have daubed it. The matchstick body, splayed legs, the corpse and limbs streaked red, the whole wall spattered scarlet. The semblance of blood had to be for shock value. It wasn't real; paint fumes still lingered in the air.

'Get the window, will you, Nat?' Shivering, Caroline drew the dressing gown round her body more tightly. Presumably, the bastards had left it open on purpose. If she'd noticed the smell earlier she might have caught them red-handed. As it was the room could've doubled as a freezer.

Nat strode across the kitchen, his thin frame not exactly instilling confidence. As a reporter, Caroline knew he punched well above his weight. As for the real world, the jury was out. She slapped a hand to her mouth. Holy mother ... What if? 'Nat, have you—?'

'The whole house.' He brushed a boyish fringe out of his eyes. 'Bathroom was the last place I checked. Whoever did it has long gone.' He perched on a stool beside her, gave her hand a tentative pat. 'And you still haven't answered the questions.'

She'd certainly been giving them thought. The intruder/intruders had to have broken in while she and Ed were playing rabbits. *Or maybe not?* He'd left around six and she'd been dead to the world for the next four hours. She shuddered.

Stupid sodding expression. Surely Ed would have said if he'd smelled paint? 'Timing was most likely between six and ten. I can't pin it down any further. What about the front door, Nat? Was it locked?'

'Front and back. No sign of a forced entry.' He swallowed a mouthful of coffee. 'And the windows? Did you check before bed?'

'Yeah, I'm pretty sure.' On the other hand, she and Ed had been on the pop as well as on the job. Maybe she'd inadvertently provided a literal window of opportunity. Or could Ed have accidentally left the door on the latch? No way. Besides, much as she wanted to believe the break-in was a random act, she'd obviously been targeted. And the writing on the wall couldn't be much clearer.

Nat tilted his head at the message. 'It's to do with the job, surely?'

The red scrawl had dripped like candle wax.

Badger's Copse. 1960. Get digging.

She nodded. 'It's what reporters do, isn't it?' Narrowing her eyes, she slid off the stool, took a closer look. She'd not noticed them before. Tiny letters. Almost obliterated where the paint had dripped.

'And cops.' Nat shoved her phone across the bar. 'You need to call them now.'

'No, hang fire.' She traced a finger over the initials: CR. It struck her the tip-off this time

169

could have come from the horse's mouth. *CR wants you to dig.* 'I'll do a bit of groundwork first.'

Unearthing treasure wasn't high on Caroline's expectations, but Caitlin seemed to think something had been buried.

Or someone.

TWENTY-SEVEN

'Paulie, Paulie. Where are you?' Susan whimpered. Gingerly, she raised her head a few inches but it hurt; she felt dizzy. She must have hit it when she went flying. Even without her glasses, she could see the root that tripped her from here. But no Pauline. Susan crossed her legs, whimpered again; if she wet her pants her mum would kill her. Wincing, she gently traced the outline of a huge bump at the back of her ear. Her fingers came away streaked with blood. She wiped it on her shorts. Oh my God, they were ripped. She was going to get a smack. She must have knocked herself out. How long had she been lying here? If Pauline had scooted off home, and right now was having her tea, tucking into spam sandwiches ... Some friend, huh? Susan clenched her fists, tears pricked her eyes.

She struggled to her knees, then remembered

why they'd fled into the copse. Even though her head spun, she cast wary glances round. No sign of him. And still no sign of Pauline. Susan covered her face with her hands and started to cry tears mingled with blood, snot, dirt. She remembered how the man had shouted at her to get lost, to leave Pauline alone. She felt a warm trickle down her thighs. This was the worst day of her entire life. Then she gasped. Through her fingers she saw just the edge of Pauline's sandal. The little monkey was hiding behind that tree.

She'd get a hiding alright. Susan ran the back of her hand across her mouth. A damn good slapping's what she'd get an' all when Susan got hold of her. Fear forgotten, she was hopping mad. Breathing heavily, she stomped over, hands on hips.

'You're gonna get it, you are, Pauline Bol—' Her brain couldn't – maybe wouldn't – collate what her eyes saw. 'Are you messing round?' *Playing dead?* Pauline lay on her back a few feet from the sandal, arms stretched like broken wings. But the sandal wasn't white any more. It was splashed with red. Susan took a tentative step towards her friend. Where had the jam come from? Pauline's face was smeared with the stuff, great blobs all over her dress, her knickers. Wasps and flies buzzing round. Pauline didn't even flinch when a great fat bluebottle landed on her eye.

'No,' she whispered, then ran to her little friend, grabbed her in both arms, shook her

171

again and again. 'Wake up, Paulie, wake up. I didn't mean it.' For a while Susan held her tiny body close, cuddled her, then held her out again, willing her to breathe. Everything sagged. Pauline's head lolled like a rag doll's; limp, lifeless. Susan gagged, slapped a hand to her mouth. Pauline dropped like a dead weight.

The noise started with a wail, then a loud howl, eerie, ear-splitting. Then another and another, endless. Susan had never heard an animal like it before. On and on it went – why wouldn't it stop? Please make it— Startled, she pressed a hand to her cheek. The slap smarted but it was OK because the noise had stopped. Then she saw Mrs Bolton's ashen face as she clutched Pauline to her chest. And knew nothing would ever again be OK.

Susan's whole body shook; she couldn't control the convulsions, couldn't breathe, couldn't breathe...

Other villagers appeared; she heard more approaching through the trees. Someone swung her round.

'What happened here?' Her mum looked frightened but sounded cross, crosser than Susan had heard anyone sound. 'What happened here, Susan?' Her shoulders hurt where her mum's fingers still dug in. Writhing, she started to sob again.

'Mum. A man...' She could hardly get the words out. 'A man came...'

TWENTY-EIGHT

'If you ask me the guy was bigging himself up.' Harries was huffing and puffing like an asthmatic pigeon. 'Jake Portman takes on an old dipso trying to get his leg over the school wall? It's hardly up there with Captain Marvel, is it?'

Sarah observed the strop over the rim of her cup. Portman could tackle the red army single-handed and Harries wouldn't give him a used tissue. 'Back off, Dave. Portman thought the weapon was real. He had no idea it was a water pistol.' Not until he'd over-powered the bloke anyway.

'Big wow.' Dave stabbed a fried egg with his fork; he was lucky the exploding yolk didn't hit him. 'So why bring the incident up at all? He must know it can't be related to Caitlin's abduction. It happened weeks ago. And dipso-man's drying out now.'

'Yeah. I heard he was admitted with self-inflicted wounds.' Her lip twitched. She reckoned the crack was hilarious. Almost as comical as Dave's pompous-prick act. She wouldn't mind but they'd already discussed it *ad infinitum*.

Harries tightened his mouth big time, then

caught her eye and laughed with her. 'For you, that wasn't bad. Seriously though, there's never been any suggestion Caitlin was snatched by an intruder. Security at the school's tighter than a nun's ... Well, it's tight. And someone would have seen something.'

She sighed. It always came back to that. And still no sightings anywhere. The hotlines hadn't even taken par-for-the-course nut calls claiming Caitlin had been abducted by little green men or devoured by giant lizards.

'Come on.' She nodded at his plate – sausage, egg and chips. 'We've not got all day. And that's getting cold.'

Like the trail. She curled a lip. Her cheese salad was hot by comparison. She'd discarded it after finding a not-so hungry caterpillar helping her out with the lettuce. Not the canteen's finest culinary hour. She took Dave's point though. For a minute or so back at Queen's Ridge, she'd thought they were looking at a break in the case. She was pretty sure Portman hadn't deliberately misled them. What motive would he have? As for the search team at the school, so far it had come up with zilch.

'I reckon Posh Boy was out to impress you, boss.' She caught him sneak a glance at her from under his fringe. If Dave thought she'd rise to the bait, he had another think coming. Turning her head, she looked through the window. Her gaze followed a jet trail just discernible between fluffy clouds. Cumulus? Cumuli? Who gave a

fuck? She sighed. Was it conceivable Caitlin had
left the country? Details had been circulated to
ports and airports but perhaps with a false pass-
port, some sort of disguise ... But that would
have meant weeks of planning. And, again,
why? Was Caitlin hapless victim or happy col-
luder? Sarah wasn't convinced either way.

'Oh, inspector, do give me your card.' Harries
disrupted her train – make that plane – of
thought. The Portman voice was near perfect.
'I'll be sure to call. Has it got your home number?'

She masked a smile. So that's what had rattled
Dave's cage. Portman's harmless bit of flirting.
Given Jude Fox's winning way with words, two
could play at that game. 'Silly me, Dave,' she
simpered, held his gaze, 'that took a second or
two to sink in.' She didn't add 'like seeing your
dentist at the butcher's' and hadn't adopted the
teacher's husky tones, but Dave had clearly
cottoned on.

'Touché.'

'As opposed to touch-ee?' Eyebrow raised,
she scraped back her chair. 'I'm off. Catch you
later.'

Harries watched Sarah leave, her head high,
shoulders back. 'Whip the cuffs on any time you
like, boss,' he muttered under his breath. Sighing, he pushed the plate plus congealed contents
across the table. He'd give his right arm if she
said the word. Actually, no, he'd need both arms

175

to sweep her off her feet. He gave a wry smile. Like that was going to happen. He knew the arguments, of course: Sarah was The Boss, he a lowly DC, nearly a decade younger and work relationships rarely – for want of a better word – worked. Either the brass frowned on them or station comics dined out in style on the material.

And yet ... He grabbed his jacket, headed towards the door. He fancied the pants off her. More than that, her cool analytical brain fascinated him. So where was she coming from? He knew she'd not had a partner since the solicitor guy. And equally convinced she wasn't as frigid as some of the blokes made out. He couldn't believe she went in for one-night stands. Or trod the celibate path. Maybe she just didn't fancy him. Get real. He'd read the signals. OK, subtle signs. He knew she valued his opinion as a cop, and on the social side, he made her laugh, helped her chill. He'd just have to persist without being pushy.

'Penny for them, Dave?'

Glancing up, he saw Paul Wood approaching along the corridor. *It'll cost you more than that, mate.* 'You'd need a mortgage, sarge.'

Shona Bruce was having a quick nose through Luke Holden's letterbox. 'Bloody hell.' The detective glanced up at her partner. 'Call an ambulance, Beth.'

The rented Selly Oak bed-sit was like thousands of others across the city. Except for the

176

smell. It certainly wasn't gas, Shona was dead sure of that. Scrambling to her feet, she slipped a phone out of her pocket. 'I'll ring the DI.'

'What do you mean not well? He was at a funeral.' The logic sounded flawed and the volume loud even to Sarah.

Standing in the DI's doorway, Hunt raised a palm. 'Hey, I'm just the messenger, ma'am.'

'Sorry, John. Carry on.' The ear-bashing was not intentional, the edge in her voice down to concern.

'Don't know much more. He took ill in church and a mate drove him home. The mate just rang. Reckons the chief might not make it in for a few days.'

She frowned. Baker couldn't even pick up the phone to tell them? She muttered a distracted, 'Right, thanks, John,' but addressed the door. Hunt had left her to it, probably to extract the flea from his ear.

Sarah sat back, crossed her legs, flung her pen on the desk. It wouldn't just be a head cold. Baker had never taken time off sick as long as she'd known him. Certainly explained why she'd not heard back from him though. Given Mrs B had buggered off months ago, presumably he'd be on his own in the house? Sarah pursed her lips. Wondered if the old boy liked grapes? As she reached for the phone, it rang. 'Shona? Hi.'

After a minute or so, she hung up, pensive.

She hoped Luke Holden liked hospital food.

The only food Luke Holden would be sampling for a while would be via a tube in his nostril. He looked whiter than the sheet he lay on. Even through the glass of the IC unit, Sarah could see he wasn't up to visitors, let alone a formal interview. She could also see why Caitlin had got mixed up with the guy. Despite his critical medical condition, he was well fit, strong features, fine bones. Quite the sleeping beauty. So why try to kill himself?

Shona and Beth had found Holden lying face down in a pool of vodka-stinking vomit. He'd supplemented the booze with enough sedatives to fell a bull elephant. If he was seeking a bit of shut-eye, the syringe sticking out of his right arm seemed superfluous. The oblivion could easily have become permanent according to the medics. When Shona had entered the bed-sit his breathing had been so shallow, she thought they'd already lost him. The CPR she'd administered at the scene almost certainly saved his life. The coma he was in now had been chemically induced.

'I couldn't find a pulse at first, ma'am.' Standing alongside Sarah, Shona kept a steady gaze on the patient, steadier than her voice. 'If we'd not got there when we did...' Her hand trembled when she held a bottle of water to cool her forehead. What little colour the redhead's complexion normally held had faded, and the freckles

178

looked darker, more pronounced.

'Good work, detective. You did well.' Sarah briefly considered patting her arm, but Shona was no-nonsense Glaswegian; she'd shrug off any sign of moral support or physical contact. Besides, Sarah didn't do the touchy-feely stuff.

'I was glad to see the paramedics, ma'am. They got a drip in, gave him oxygen. Called in the details to A&E. Those people are brilliant.' Typical Brucie, modest, self-effacing. 'A neighbour let us in. That saved a wee bit of time too.'

While the drama unfolded, Beth had scouted round the place; apparently neither room had cat-swinging potential. Nor any other kind from what Sarah had heard. As well as being small, it was sparse, surprisingly neat. No pictures, books, CDs – nothing personal, nothing linking him with Caitlin Reynolds. Beth had found a donor card and next-of-kin details in Holden's wallet. His mother lived in Devon and had sounded less than grief-stricken, according to the officer who spoke to her. Mrs Holden would, quote, 'try and get up there early next week'. If Sarah was in the same boat, she'd get a move on. Looking at Holden, she reckoned the donor card could come in useful any time.

She voiced her next thought. 'But no note, Shona.' No indication why? It wasn't a given; only about a third of suicides left some sort of explanation.

'Not that we saw, ma'am. I guess it might have been a cry for help?'

Booze, pills and a shot of heroin?

Thank God somebody heard it then, because to Sarah it sounded like overkill.

TWENTY-NINE

Nicola let herself into the house, leaned her head against the door, squeezed her eyes tightly shut. Deep breaths helped slow her heart beat, but nothing would soothe her mind, rid it of the poignant image: the little girl in the sundress, smiling, clutching the teddy bear. The little girl her parents called their princess. The little girl Nicola's mother had murdered.

She sank to her haunches, buried her face in her hands. Other pictures surfaced in her mind's eye: Pauline proudly holding her mum's hand, Pauline splashing in a paddling pool, Pauline in the school nativity play with wonky wings and half-mast halo, Pauline's father carrying a tiny white coffin into a village church.

'Dear God, no,' Nicola murmured again and again.

The air in the library had been lifeless. She'd spent an hour there surfing the net, scouring news archives. If she'd not seen the stories herself, she wouldn't have believed them. With

180

growing horror, she'd skimmed report after report, printed out the most shocking, furtively slipped them into her bag.

All those column inches, and in all these years not one word from her bloody mother.

Nicola shucked off her coat, slung it over the banister, headed for the kitchen intending to make a drink. Sod that. Tea wouldn't do it this time. She diverted to the sitting room, poured a large Scotch, swirled most of it round her mouth. She drained the glass, picked up the bottle then placed it back. No more; she needed a clear head.

She'd felt uneasy in the library, as if people knew what she was, as if 'murderer's daughter' was tattooed on her forehead, as if they could read secrets with their prying eyes. She needed to look at the articles properly, try to get her head round the impossible. By God she'd seen her mother in a new light, all right. She kicked off her shoes, settled on the leather sofa, reached into her bag.

Headlines leapt at her:

Babe in the wood killing – man arrested
Builder released, accuses girl, 10
Ten-year-old held on suspicion of murder
Girl, 10, charged with child killing
Susan Bailey guilty of manslaughter
Susan Bailey detained at Her Majesty's
Pleasure

181

The same photograph appeared alongside every report. Nicola tried but failed to see her mother's features in the ten-year-old Susan: the dark pudding-bowl haircut, fat moon face, mean little eyes behind National Health specs. Glowering and surly, she looked every inch the spiteful bully prosecution witnesses had described. Nicola guessed it was a police mug shot. Surely if her mother's family owned a better picture they'd have given – if not sold – it to the press? Maybe papers didn't pay back then, though? From Nicola's reading, the reporting certainly wasn't as sensational, the tone and language restrained by today's standards. The story didn't need sexing-up anyway. A ten-year-old girl bludgeons her best friend to death then tries to blame it on an innocent man?

Nicola snorted. Un-fucking-believable.

She lit a cigarette, sucked smoke deep into her lungs. She scanned another print-out, desperate to locate any mitigating circumstances. Anything that could help her understand why? A defence lawyer hinted at an abusive background. Several bruises had been found on Susan's body during a medical examination. Her father was known to be handy with his fists, especially after a drink. She'd also come in for a lot of stick from the village kids, bullying, name calling. Big deal, Nicola thought. At least her mother had lived to tell the tale. *Tell the tale?* Yeah right. What a joke.

She glanced round for an ashtray, headed for

the kitchen. The way she saw it Susan bloody Bailey had got off lightly. Her Majesty's Pleasure had turned out to be a meagre ten years. Two tabloids had carried the story: *Babe in the wood killer released on probation*. That was 1971 and the last references Nicola had been able to find. There'd been none of the subsequent press hounding that had dogged Mary Bell, the only other female child killer Nicola had heard of. Shame really. The media had run Bell to ground and she'd been forced to tell her daughter the truth about who she was, what she'd done. Nicola had spent her entire life in ignorance. Blissful? Not now it sodding wasn't. She saw it as utter betrayal.

She leaned against the sink, ashtray in hand. All these years of living a lie, hiding behind a false façade. Had the police given her mother the new identity? Maybe she'd ask – when she could bring herself to speak to the old bag again. Even today, she'd clammed up about it, literally turned her head against the wall. Claimed she couldn't remember. Christ, did she think Nicola was thick or something? Patently, her mother hadn't imagined the tongue, the mystery man, a whisper in the ear. 'Speak no evil' hadn't been a warning to keep her trap shut in the future. It referred to the web of lies she'd spun in the past. She *must* have known the significance when she'd begged Nicola to visit. Selective amnesia? Memories dead and buried? In deep denial, more like. Her mother had protected her own miserable existence for years. And the way Nicola felt now, she'd never forgive her.

And neither, she realized, would the man holding Caitlin.

The pieces were falling into shape; Nicola was beginning to see the picture. Pauline's murder was the motive for Caitlin's abduction. Sins of the fathers? Sins of the grandmother.

Crime and punishment.

Nicola and Caitlin were paying the price. That was why they'd been targeted. But who was exacting revenge? And what would be the cost?

Stubbing out the baccy, she pricked her ears. Didn't recognize the ring-tone at first, then almost dropped the ashtray. She ran next door, fumbled for the phone in her bag. 'Hello? Who is this? Hello? Hello?' *Damn, damn, damn.*

'Took your time, didn't you, Nicola?' She heard the smirk in his voice. Funny guy. Dead funny.

'What do you want?' she snapped.

'What do you think?' Curt contempt.

She took a calming breath, softened her voice. 'Look, please, I just want my daughter home.'

'Pauline's mum and dad wanted her home too.' Silence, deliberate pause. 'Just not in a coffin.'

Nicola tasted blood in her mouth. 'I'm truly sorry about the little girl. But please, you have to believe me, until a few hours ago I knew nothing about the murder.' Her eyes smarted with tears. 'You can't blame Caitlin or me for any-

184

thing, surely you can see that?'

'I'll tell you what I see, shall I, Nicola?' His tone implied it would be the last thing she'd want to hear. 'I see an eye for an eye.'

'Oh my God, the tongue...?' She pressed a hand to her mouth to prevent more words and thoughts escaping.

'Neighbour's nosy dog. It needed silencing.' Dismissive tone. Minor detail. Back to the point. 'An eye for an eye, a tongue for a tongue.'

A child for a child? The ultimate retaliation. Nicola swallowed. 'You want—'

'Justice.'

'But Cait—'

'Not Caitlin. Your mother. I want to spit on her grave.'

'She's an old woman for God's sake.'

'Too old. She's a waste of skin. Just do it, eh?'

Nicola showered until the scalding water ran cold, scrubbed until her skin was raw. The symbolism wasn't lost on her: a psychiatrist would wax lyrical about 'washing away sins' – out, out, damn spot and all that. Maybe there was an element of that but in reality, she'd felt unclean, contaminated, even now she felt her skin creep. Hugging both arms tightly round her waist, she paced the bedroom. When she'd helped the old bitch on her way, he'd let Caitlin go. That's what he'd promised. Could she trust him? A man who revelled in taunting her, who'd snatched her daughter, hacked out a dog's tongue? She swallowed bile. Thank God, she'd not reported that touching little tableau. All bets were off if she contacted the cops, he'd warned. *Bets?* Crass bastard.

Pensive, she perched on the dressing-table stool. Surely the police would know her mother's real identity anyway? Weren't released murderers on licence or something? Details were supposed to be kept on record, surely? Circulated to the relevant authorities? Still thinking, she ran a brush absently through her hair. It could certainly explain why her mother had insisted they move round so much when Nicola was growing up. All those new towns, tatty council houses, different schools. Clearly her child-killing momma had a hidden agenda. She'd given them all the slip. She could've given Mary Bell a few lessons, Nicola sneered. Even now Bell attracted media interest, made the occasional headline. While for more than forty odd years the erstwhile Susan Bailey hadn't made a paragraph in a free sheet. She'd lived a boring life, kept her nose clean, not picked up so much as a parking ticket. The biggest crime – to an outsider – would be the occasional library fine.

An outsider? That's what I am, thought Nicola. She'd never really known her mother. And now it was too late.

Placing the brush down, she studied her reflection in the three-way mirror; resented seeing traces of the old woman's features, the button nose, the slightly full bottom lip. She raised a speculative eyebrow. Like mother, like daughter? Who knew? When it came down to it, could Nicola actually take a life? Was everybody capable; did everyone have the killer instinct? Let's face it, she thought, if there's a murder gene, I've got a hell of a head start. She gave a brittle laugh, her heart breaking.

She was looking at Catch 22 in a cleft stick. If she killed her mother, Nicola would in effect lose Caitlin anyway. A life sentence was mandatory and she'd be a fat lot of use to her daughter behind bars. It's what the bastard wanted, of course. He wasn't interested in a pound of flesh; he wanted bodies. Nicola would be doing his dirty work and at the same time digging her own metaphorical grave. But if she didn't...

She reached for the silver-framed photograph to her right. Caitlin celebrating GCSE results; her first prom, they'd hired the ball gown. Nicola's warm smile faded. There was no question really. She'd sacrifice anything – anyone – if it saved her daughter's life.

'Nic! You up there?'

'I'll be down in a tick,' she shouted. What was Neil doing here? A quick call first wouldn't have hurt.

'I bought you these.' He stood at the bottom of the stairs, sheepish smile on his face. Garage tulips. 'Oh, and this.' He whipped a bottle of Bells from behind his back. That was more like it.

She forced a token smile as she descended, took delivery. 'What's this in aid of?'

'I thought they'd cheer you up a bit. I've been neglecting you, Nic. I'm sorry.' He opened his arms for a hug. 'I want you to know I'm here for you.' Kind words and sympathy were more than she could take. She broke down, buried her face in his shoulder. He stroked her hair, let her cry. 'Come on, let's dry those tears. What is it, Nic?' She wanted to share the burden but could barely speak. He led her gently into the sitting room, they sat close and he took both her hands in his. 'Is it Caitlin? Is there news?'

Gazing down at their hands, she told him haltingly most of what she'd learned about her mother that day. He had little time for the old woman, he'd made no secret of it – and that was before hearing about her murderous past. As for Nicola's putative murderous future, she'd yet to break that little nugget. 'If you'd rather leave now, Neil.' She made fleeting eye contact. 'I'll understand. No worries.'

'Poor Nicola.' He used a thumb to dash away a tear. 'I assumed you knew about your mother. It's why I never mentioned it. I thought you were protecting her.'

THIRTY

'All I ever wanted was to protect you, love.'
Linda Walker sat in her chair by the fire, talking
to a photograph that trembled in her fingers. The
pose showed Nicola looking a darn sight hap-
pier than when she'd stormed out hours ago. 'I
thought I was doing the right thing by keeping it
from you.' The old woman stroked her daughter's cheek then pressed the picture – damp with
tears – to her lips.

With hindsight, she realized she'd protected
no one. The past refused to be buried; secrets
and lies had been unearthed. She'd exposed her
daughter to pain and shame and would never
forget the look of horror on Nicola's face. She
wouldn't want to see her old mum again,
certainly not when she found out more. It would
be easy enough to check back; the case had been
in all the papers. Mrs Walker shuddered. She
knew reporters had got things wrong. What
would happen if they got hold of the story
again?

She hauled herself out of the chair, shuffled
over to draw the curtains, shut out the darkness.
Blanking it all out was how she'd coped over the

years: Badger's Copse, Pauline's body, the lies, the bullying, the confession, the baying crowds. Closing her mind to it had been the only way she could live with herself, especially after being released from prison. Even inside she'd switched off, tried hard not to give it head room. That way madness lay. She thought she'd gone loopy anyway after Pauline's murder.

How could she not? Frightened, confused, everyone shouting. It had been like a bad dream from which she'd longed to wake. She couldn't remember the last time she'd consciously looked back on the events of that summer. Hazy memories surfaced still, in nightmares, blended with unreal imaginings. Even on the day, she'd found it difficult to distinguish fact from fantasy.

The old woman closed her eyes, tried hard to visualize the scene. Slowly she nodded her head. The man *had* been there that day. Susan knew she hadn't imagined him.

'Man? What man, Susan?'

Susan pulled back, cowered behind a grimy hand. She didn't *think* her mum would hit her in front of people but her voice was scaring the girl something awful. Susan glanced round nervously, quailed at a sea of questioning faces. It looked as if the whole village had turned out: women still wearing pinnies, men straight off the fields with dust in their hair, on their clothes. And everyone waited eagerly, expectant.

'I won't ask again, young lady.'

Susan knew her mum meant the exact opposite and if she didn't get a move on...

'The man what gives Pauline lollies. His shirt was open, I seen his vest. He had a belt with a big shiny buckle. He—'

'What man?' Susan's mum shouted. 'Who's been giving her sweets?'

'Dunno his name. But I seen him on the building site lots of times, Mum. The one with all the tattoos. Anyway he come chasin' us and Paulie and me, we ran like mad ... He was coming up behind. I heard footsteps and I could hear his breathin' and—'

'She's bleeding, look.' One of the old biddies from the almshouses pointed a twig-like finger at Susan's face.

The girl raised her hand instinctively, winced as her fingers touched the bump again, the blood must've trickled down.

'How d'you get that, girl?' one of the men asked.

'I ... I dunno ... one minute we were running ... screaming ... I went flying ... the next I seen...' Everyone's glance followed Susan's to the right where Pauline now lay cradled in Mrs Bolton's arms. Face and hands smeared with her daughter's blood, the woman rocked steadily to and fro, her lips moving in a silent prayer. Susan wondered if she'd left the twins with Grace; she never let the babies out of her sight normally.

'Look at me, girl.' Susan writhed under her

mother's gaze. 'This man. Did he hurt you too?' She'd not even noticed Susan's wet shorts or that she wasn't wearing her glasses.

'I ... he...' Her lips stuck together her mouth was so dry. Out of the corner of her eye, she saw two women cross themselves, mutter under their breath. Sounded to Susan like 'poor lambs'. She heard someone say that Mrs White up at the farm had called the police, that they were on the way.

Susan's legs buckled; she grabbed on to her mother's arm. 'Help me, Mum—'

She woke in hospital. Two police officers sat beside her bed. And then the questions really began.

THIRTY-ONE

Caroline King tapped a pen against her teeth. Cooped upstairs in the home office, she'd barely noticed the light failing outside. Her face was cast in shadow, her focus still fixed on the monitor; the PC had taken quite a bashing. She'd lost count of the stories she'd read, features skimmed, notes made. As a journo, the research had been child's play. The murder of a child in the summer of 1960 was then the most exciting event that had ever happened in the Leicestershire village of Moss Pit. It probably still was.

She swigged the dregs of her Coke then lobbed the can in the bin. Digging out the story had been easy; the harder part was knowing what was the truth and what bearing it might have on Caitlin Reynolds' abduction. And that assumed her lousy interior decorator – she used the term loosely – wasn't a fruitcake trying to drag Caroline into some bizarre fantasy.

Pen tucked behind her ear now, she angled the desk lamp at the pin board on the nearest wall. Pictures of the main players were posted there, plus a few reports she'd also printed out. Leaning back in the chair, the reporter rested both hands on her head and gazed at the girls' likenesses.

Pauline Bolton and Susan Bailey: beauty and the beast. Had Susan had more than a touch of the green-eyed monster? Fatty four-eyes jealous of five-year-old cutey pants? *Something* had driven the Bailey kid to kill. Envy? Retaliation for all the verbal abuse. Forget that names may never hurt. Maybe the village kids had bad-mouthed Susan once too often, pushed her over the edge? And as we all know, Caroline thought, sticks and stones don't just break bones.

Pauline's death was down to a battering with a chunk of wood from a rotting tree trunk, weals on her legs and arms also pointed to repeated use of a thin stick. Police had discovered the weapons partially hidden in undergrowth in the copse. According to the prosecution, concealing

193

evidence meant the girl knew she'd done wrong; it showed a cunning streak. Certainly there was no suggestion in court of diminished responsibility. That she'd tried to blame it on someone else really went against her. The judge said it indicated a 'cold-blooded calculation almost beyond her years'. The really damning evidence came from the builder she'd tried to nail.

Caroline leaned forward, unpinned the reports that had caught her eye earlier and reread a few passages.

Police are questioning a thirty-year-old builder in connection with the murder of babe-in-the-wood Pauline Bolton. The man who can't be named for legal reasons was arrested following information received from the public. It's believed a ten-year-old girl, also in the wood at the time of the attack, was able to provide a description of a man she saw. Detectives have not called off the murder hunt and are still appealing for information.

Yeah right. Caroline recognized police-speak: what the last line meant was that from fairly early on in the inquiry the cops harboured doubts about the girl's testimony. From where she sat, Caroline didn't reckon the builder had covered himself in glory.

Thirty-year-old labourer Mr Ted Crawford

told the court he'd seen the two children playing in the village several times before the day in question. He expressed regret he'd not thought to mention his concerns to the parents before. 'She was always yelling at her, bossing her about,' he said. 'She was much older than Pauline but I felt sorry for the big girl too. The other kids were forever on at her.'

Get on with it. Caroline ran a finger down the page.

'But she went too far that day. I could see they were playing teachers. Susan had this stick, using it like a cane she was, whipping dandelion heads off. When I saw her wallop Pauline I went racing over, shouted at her to leave the little one alone. That I didn't chase after them – I'll regret to my dying day.' When asked why he hadn't ventured into the wood, Mr Crawford told the court he'd been afraid of scaring the children. The first he knew about the murder, he said, was when two police officers turned up at his door the next day. Outside the court, Mr Crawford told reporters, 'I wish her no harm but the fact is if Susan Bailey hadn't eventually come clean, she could've got me hung.'

Hanged, Caroline murmured. She studied Crawford's pic. Not that there was much to see in the single column, head and shoulders: clean-shaven, sleek short back and sides, eyes creased against the light. Crawford hadn't actually witnessed the attack. Was it possible there'd been someone else in the copse? The real killer even? Someone scared that after all these years the truth would come out? Her reporter's antennae twitched but the thrill didn't last long. Susan Bailey had confessed, hadn't she? Caroline ran her mind back over a catalogue of miscarriages of justices. Supposing the girl had coughed under duress? It was twenty-plus years before the police and criminal evidence act – and it had been brought in partly to stop heavy-handed police interviews.

Sighing, Caroline pushed back the chair. Whichever way you looked at it, Susan Bailey was the key to the babe-in-the-wood case. What she couldn't see was how it fitted with Caitlin Reynolds' story. The girl certainly wasn't around to ask. Caroline would just have to make do with the mother.

'I need to run a few questions past you, Mrs Reynolds.' Sarah gave a tight smile. 'May we come in?'

'It's late. I'm tired. Can it wait until morning?'

'We're here now.' Unsmiling, Sarah tilted her head at the door. Like the DI wasn't keen to knock off anyway? After a twelve-hour-plus shift and little to show for it? At least Dave was on overtime. She wondered vaguely why

196

Reynolds was in a dressing gown. Half-seven was hardly the witching hour. 'If we'd not been following leads, I'd have dropped by earlier.'

Nicola nodded, indicated a door on the left. 'Go in. Sit down. I'll be with you in a tick.'

Mentally open-mouthed, Sarah watched the woman drift off towards the kitchen and close the door behind her. The DI perched on the leather three-seater and, keeping her voice down, glanced up at Harries. 'If your daughter was missing...' Shouldn't Nicola have been over them like a rash for latest developments?

'I get the drift.' Harries flopped next to her, helped himself to a tissue from a box on the floor. 'What you reckon she's doing in there, boss?'

Gesundheit. 'Bless you.' She shifted back even further. 'Who knows? Dutch courage perhaps.'

'Double Dutch.' Harries sniffed. 'Ask me, she's already had a few.'

Tired *and* emotional then? Sarah thought the woman certainly looked knackered, distraught even. Must be a nightmare having a child missing, maybe she needed the hard stuff to soften the edges. Sarah cocked her head. Either Reynolds had the radio on or she had company.

Dave was restless already. Peeling himself off the sofa, he flicked the balled tissue at the bin. 'Whoops.' Nicola's aim was as pants as Dave's. He tidied the litter up for her then, hands in pockets, prowled round the room. Sarah pricked

197

her ears. Two voices? Both female?

'Do you want kids, boss?' Dave had his back to her.

'Not right this minute.' She frowned. The ear-wigging was going nowhere; she gave it up as a bad job. What was Mr Snoop holding?

'Fun-nee. You know what I mean – some time down the line.'

If she was honest, no. More than once she'd had to break news of a child's death, witnessed the raw grief of parents, the broken hearts, shattered lives, families ripped apart. In Sarah's book the old saying about children being a hostage to fortune was bang on. 'I can live without them, Dave.'

'No group hug for you then.' Turning, he showed her the photograph in his hand, three generations of Reynolds women: Linda, Nicola, Caitlin, arm round waists, big smiles – all genes together.

Given Sarah's mother – and father – were dead, even if she did have a kid there'd be no Team Quinn pose. 'As I say, I can live with—'

'Sorry about that, sergeant...?' Nicola didn't sound too apologetic.

Sarah sighed almost theatrically. The deliberate demotion for whatsername? Such an original put down. 'Quinn. Detective Inspector.'

'I was in the middle of a call. How can I help?'

Stop raking your hair and taking a seat will do for a start. Sarah bit her tongue. The relationship had started off on the wrong foot and slalomed fast. She found the woman impossible, unfathomable, knew she ought to build bridges. Tough. She was a cop not Kingdom Brunel. 'The argument you had with Caitlin. Why hide it?'

'Argument?' The acting had gone up a notch.

'Blazing row then.' Reynolds still needed a cue. 'Luke Holden?'

'Oh that.' She flapped a hand, squatted on the edge of an armchair. 'As far as he's concerned, Caitlin has a blind spot.'

'Soft spot more like.' What she'd read of Caitlin's diary made that clear.

'He's no good for her. I told her to keep away. I didn't ... don't ... want her hurt again.'

Nicola's hands were folded tightly in her lap but she still had the shakes. 'Why are you asking all this anyway? Holden has nothing to do with what's happening to Caitlin.' The shouting seemed over the top.

Sarah held the woman's gaze. 'You sound very sure about that, Mrs Reynolds.'

She took a deep breath, briefly closed her eyes. 'I don't want you wasting time on him, that's all.'

'I won't be.' Sarah let a few seconds elapse. 'Not for a while anyway.' Holden, she revealed, was in intensive care in hospital after an apparent overdose. Reynolds' surprise seemed genuine though she asked no questions, voiced no concern. Sarah let the silence ride again, then: 'Is there any reason you can think of why he'd try to take his own life, Mrs Reynolds?'

'As it happens, inspector, I'd rather concentrate on ways of saving Caitlin's.'

Harries leaned forward. 'Are you OK, Mrs Reynolds? Can I get you some water or something?'

'No. I'm fine. Just ask your questions and go.'

'That went well, boss.'

'You are so predictable, Dave.' It was the line he always came out with after an interview from hell.

'You and Nicola Reynolds?' He pressed finger and thumb together. 'Not a cigarette paper between you.'

Lots of smoke – and mirrors – on Reynolds' part though. 'Dave, please.' Her grip tightened on the wheel. 'I'm not in the mood.' She'd got naff all out of Nicola; Caitlin was still God knew where; the inquiry wasn't so much stalled as in reverse. On top of that it was Saturday night, it was pissing down and the most exciting thing on Sarah's horizon was hitting Tesco.

'You as good as accused her of lying about being on the phone in the kitchen.'

'I know what I heard, Dave.' Two voices. She'd swear on it.

'Ways and means, boss.' He was digging in a pocket. 'I think you rub her up the wrong way.'

'Thanks for the valuable insight. Now shut up.' She didn't need the lecture. Asking if Caitlin and Neil Lomas were close, perhaps too

200

close, had very nearly got them thrown out, but the question had to be posed. Nicola's apoplectic denial was as predictable as Dave's verdict on the session. Neither was helpful. 'Where d'you want dropping?'

'Back at the ranch? If that's OK?'

'Yeah, why not?' She peered at the screen through wipers that were barely coping. 'That reminds me. The chief. Reckon we should organize a card, bottle of Scotch or something?'

'Thought you said it'd only be a few days.' Could he sound less interested?

'Even so. He sounded well down on the phone, Dave. The guy never takes time off.'

'What's up with him?'

'He wouldn't say.' She cut him another glance. 'What *are* you doing?' He'd been fidgeting like a kid with fleas since getting in the car.

'Checking Nicola's litter.'

'Litter?' Of course, the balled-up paper around the bin. He smoothed out the sheet, blew off flecks of ash. 'Well?'

'Amazing what you can pick up,' he said. 'Nicola Reynolds' kid's missing, right? Why do you suppose she's taking an interest in a child murder from 1960?' As a throwaway line, it took some beating. 'Fancy thrashing it out over a drink, boss?'

Sod Tesco. 'Your shout?' She smiled. He could put some of that overtime to good use.

THIRTY-TWO

Nicola Reynolds opened the door and word-lessly gestured Caroline into the sitting room.

'Bad timing or what?' The reporter gave her now tight-lipped hostess a tentative smile as she slipped past. Like Nicola, she'd certainly not expected Sarah Quinn and the boy David to come calling. Not when she and Nicola had been getting on so well. No worries; they'd just have to pick up where they left off.

Nicola headed straight for the drinks trolley. 'I won't have that woman in this house again. Who the hell does she think she is?' She flashed a bottle at Caroline. Gordon's. 'I've a damn good mind to slap in a complaint.'

'A small one, thanks.' The reporter sank back on the settee, the leather still warm from one of the cops' backsides. Caroline had skulked in the kitchen knowing just how ecstatic Sarah Quinn would have been to see her cosying up to Caitlin's mum. Fortunately the reporter had already played her ace before the Ice Queen showed. The top card – make that cards – was letting Nicola see the photos on her phone, the macabre mural in wide shot and close-up. The fact she and Nicola obviously shared the same mystery correspondent had helped forge a bond of sorts. 'Cheers. The inspector's not everyone's cup of tea.' She tipped her tumbler at Nicola. 'I wouldn't underestimate her though.'

Nicola's snort suggested otherwise. But Caroline knew Quinn wouldn't take long to put two and two together – once the inquiry established the Reynolds-Bailey link. The reporter had elicited it within minutes. She'd taken along a couple of cuttings and could've played snap with Nicola's collection. Snap, not Happy Families, given Nicola Reynolds was the daughter of a child killer. On top of that, the poor bloody woman had only just found out.

Talk about right place, right time – Caroline could hardly believe her luck. What's more, as soon as Nicola saw Caitlin's initials on the pic, she seemed almost eager to tell her tale. And what a tale. The more background that emerged, the more Caroline had to play down her growing excitement. She'd covered just about every sort of story in her journalistic career. This was unprecedented. To die for. A child killer's granddaughter abducted fifty years after the crime. And someone seeking retribution? The news potential was huge, margin for error massive: Caitlin Reynolds' life hung in the balance. Even Caroline felt an unaccustomed caution, a tad out of her depth.

'I really think you should tell DI Quinn what you know.' She studied Nicola over the rim of her glass. With so much at stake the reporter had already decided to bring the cops in. Eventually. That didn't stop her wanting to get as much material as she could first.

'No way.' Nicola shook her head. 'I've told you why. He says he'll kill Caitlin.'

The guy could top Caitlin anyway but Caroline kept that thought back. 'And you've absolutely no idea who's holding her?'

'Believe me, I'd tell you if I did.'

Would she? Caroline wasn't sure. 'What about a member of the murdered girl's family?' she asked. 'The parents would be getting on a bit now, but I wonder if she had siblings, cousins?' The way Caroline saw it, anyone bearing a grudge was fair game.

'How would I know, Miss King?' She put down her empty glass. 'It happened years before I was born.'

Thinking of grudges. 'The builder's a possibility. Ted Crawford? Your mother falsely accused him of the killing.'

'Your guess is as good as mine.' She picked a loose thread from the dressing gown, rolled it between her fingers.

'Guesswork's not going to do it, Nicola.' Logic dictated it had to be someone who was around at the time. Caroline knew how to dig, but the police had instant access to records and the resources and officers to follow trails. 'Time is passing, Mrs Reynolds. The police—'

'No. No. No.' She clamped her hands over her

ears.

OK, OK, I get the picture. Caroline leaned forward, softened her voice. 'So what are you going to do, Nicola?' Conciliatory. Solicitous. She didn't want to lose the woman, or risk the exclusive.

Nicola needed a refill. She strode across the room, topped up the glass then turned to face Caroline. 'You've asked all the questions so far. Let me ask you one. Whoever this ... this ... sadist is who's holding Caitlin ... why's he involved you?'

As much as she once thought she'd been singled out, Caroline had changed her mind. 'I don't think it's me, *per se*. I imagine he's just after press coverage, any high-profile journalist will do. He wants me to deliver.' She just wasn't sure what yet. 'When was he last in contact?'

Slight hesitation. 'Yesterday?' Quick sip of drink. 'Yes. Yesterday.' She walked back to her chair. Cagey and evasive.

Caroline wondered why the woman had lied, what else she might be keeping back. 'Do you know why he's holding Caitlin?' Reynolds' shrug seemed too casual. 'Surely he's told you what he wants out of this?'

'Nothing. No.' She ran a hand through her hair. 'Look, Miss King, I've had a rough day. I need—'

'Of course. Thanks for your time. We'll talk again.' Caroline grabbed her bag, rose to her feet. 'Just one thing, Nicola.' She waited until the woman was standing. 'When did your mother die?'

'Die? What makes you think she's dead?'

'I'm sorry.' She felt her colour rise. 'I assumed from what you said—'

'You misunderstood, Miss King. She has Alzheimer's, her mind's failing. I suppose you could call it as good as dead.'

The Alzheimer's was stretching it a bit but so what? Nicola didn't particularly want a nosy hack knocking on her mother's door. God knows what the old crone might come out with. Nicola wouldn't have been so forthcoming herself but for the pictures on King's phone. It was shock more than anything that had led her to invite the reporter in. Like the look on King's face when she realized the main player was still alive. Lying in bed now, Nicola sighed as she stared at the ceiling. Not giving King the old woman's name and address had only delayed the inevitable. King was a reporter. She'd find out sooner or later. Hopefully, by then it would be too late anyway.

'Try and sleep, Nic.' She stiffened as Neil laid a proprietary arm across her naked stomach. He'd slipped back to the house after midnight. She was aware of where he'd been, what he'd been doing. She'd begged him to help: a few drinks in a few pubs, words in the right – or wrong – people's ears. Everybody hates child killers – even more than paedos. Neil's father, an ex-Fleet Street reporter, had covered the original case. He'd kept tabs on Susan Bailey for years thinking he might write a book about child killers, recognized a photograph Neil had shown him months back of Nicola and her mother. She and Neil had discussed tipping off the press: child killer in our midst, that kind of thing. But Neil said the media wouldn't dare touch a story like that these days. Besides, it would have taken too long and Nicola wanted her daughter back as soon as humanly possible.

'Don't worry, Nic.' She tried not to recoil when Neil traced the curve of her belly with his finger. 'We'll have Caitlin home before you know it.'

'It's the last one on the right, boss.' Slurring just a touch, Harries leaned across her, pointing out the house. His finger was none too steady and pretty superfluous given the street had only one end-terrace. ''S good of you to drop me off.'

Sarah masked a smile, gently nudged him back into place. She blamed his squiffy state on the grappa. Not to mention the beers and wine. DI Virtuous had downed one glass of Sauvignon then switched to tonic water, and they'd split the bill. Mind, they had moved on from a quick jar in the Queen's Head to the full works at Giovanni's. For Sarah, it hadn't been a tough call, they both had to eat and the supermarket wasn't going anywhere. Besides, Dave had been on good form: she couldn't remember when she'd laughed so much. Mind, he'd thought her suggestion about the sergeant's exam had been a joke. At first, anyway.

'A lift's the least I could do, considering.' She braked as a fox shot across the road.

'Considering what?' Dave made to straighten the tie he'd removed hours ago. She saw the end sticking out of his pocket.

'The paper trail?'

'Paper what?' How much had he had to drink? Either he'd taken a drop more than she realized or he'd adopted a new speech pattern.

'Are all your pronouncements going to end in "what", Dave?' She cut a glance in the mirror, nudged the Audi into a parking space.

'Wh—?' The penny dropped and his smile spread slowly. 'With you. Paper trail, huh?'

In his current state, he'd have cottoned on quicker if she'd said 'litter lead'. Sarah had a feeling that Nicola's cast-offs could contain metaphorical gold dust. The printout had been badly creased and covered in ash but enough of the story remained to intrigue. After a bit of net-surfing on Dave's phone in the pub, Sarah had called the squad room, tasked a couple of officers with carrying out more stringent background checks. Someone else would get on to Leicester, ask colleagues there to delve into records. If Nicola's interest in the babe-in-the-wood killing turned out to be more than morbid curiosity, the inquiry needed to know. Like, yesterday.

'Is it a habit of yours then, Dave? Ferreting round in people's bins?'

'It is now.' He cocked his head, suddenly serious. 'Calling me nosy, DI Quinn?'

'Daft sod.' She rolled her eyes.

'Anyway, strictly speaking the paper wasn't *in* her bin.'

'Splitting hairs? Time to call it a night I think.'

'Day.' He nodded at the clock on the dash: 00.05. 'Strictly speaking.'

'Out!' Smiling, she leaned across, opened his door.

'Hey, boss.' His head re-appeared. She'd bet he was holding on to the roof for support. 'Fancy a coffee?'

You are joking. 'I'd best be off. Early start and all that.'

'Instant's quick.'

The gag was glib, but she'd rarely seen him look so serious. 'Dave, I really have to—'

'Sarah. Please.'

'Black. One sugar. Make it snappy.'

THIRTY-THREE

'Come in, sit down.' Unsmiling, Sarah looked up from her desk, played a pen between her fingers. She could only remember entertaining Caroline King in her office once before. It hadn't been a social call. Back then the DI had accused the reporter of screwing privileged police information out of Harries. Screw being the operative word. Harries, who'd shown King up from reception, still hovered just behind her in the doorway. Sarah dismissed him with a smile. 'Thanks, Dave.'

'Ditto. Davy.' Caroline flashed him a wink before sauntering in and taking a seat. 'Thanks for seeing me.' Her smile was perfunctory. She took her time crossing slender legs, smoothing an imaginary crease in a tight skirt. It seemed to Sarah that the reporter, who rarely looked less than immaculate, had gone out of her way to make a statement. The tailored black suit was definitely Armani and she'd teamed it with a crisp white shirt and black stilettos. The get-up shouted: business.

'So, to what do I owe this pleasure?' Sarah leaned back, loosely laced her fingers. *It had*

210

better be good. The desk sergeant who'd alerted her to the reporter's arrival had made it sound as if she'd turned up hand-in-hand with Lord Lucan clutching the Holy Grail. Mind, it was first thing Sunday: maybe Caroline had dropped by on her way to church. Not. Either way, Sarah's more pressing priority was a face-to-face meeting with Nicola Reynolds to establish what exactly interested her in the babe-in-the-wood case.

'You seem very ... laid-back this morning, DI Quinn?' King pursed her lips as she studied Sarah's face. 'Is there something we should know?'

Even Sarah struggled to keep a straight face. Surely to God, Dave hadn't given the game away about last night. Sarah couldn't even blame it on the drink. Unless instant coffee counted. Anyway, sod it. She was a grown woman; her conscience was clear. Ish. 'Like what?'

'Oh, I don't know...' Caroline flapped a casual hand. 'I thought you might have an opening. In the case.'

Bullshit. Yes, the early brief had been a breeze compared with recent ones and Sarah now had a newly energised squad working Dave's paper trail, but King wasn't privy to that. The reporter was on the wind-up. Sarah couldn't be doing with stupid games.

'My mistake, Caroline. I was told you had important information.' Half rising, she rolled

211

the chair back. 'I'll see you out.'

'*That* would be your mistake, DI Quinn. I'd not be here wasting my time if I didn't have something big to share. It's quality intelligence, pukka.' *Another meaningful silence.* 'And it could be the breakthrough in Caitlin Reynolds' abduction.'

Sarah had an idea where she was coming from and sensed a 'but'. 'Go on.'

'Quid pro quo.'

The DI stifled a sigh; the reporter had more pauses than a Pinter play. 'Meaning?'

'I want something from you in exchange.'

Nothing new there then.

Caroline delivered the facts concisely, convincingly. Top line: Caitlin Reynolds' grandmother had killed a child in the 1960s, the abductor wanted revenge. Before the recital, Caroline had carefully laid out two cuttings on the desk in front of the DI. Tilting her head now at the display she said, 'The dish isn't cold. It's absolute zero.'

Continuing silence from the other side of the desk.

'Well?' Caroline gazed at Sarah, still waiting for reaction. She'd already tried mind-reading because Sarah's face sure as hell hadn't given anything away as she heard Caroline out. Frowning, she watched as the DI rolled back the chair again. This time she headed for the window, perched on the sill. For a few seconds she stared at the reporter, then: 'So what is it you want from me?'

Was that it? A miffed Caroline masked her disappointment. On the proverbial plate, she'd handed over the key Reynolds-Bailey connection. OK, Caroline regarded it as a bargaining chip but by rights the detective should be waving her arms yelling Hallelujah not looking like it was yesterday's news.

'Actually, first.' Sarah folded her arms. 'Tell me what you intend doing with the story.'

'Nothing. Absolutely nothing.' Mock horror. 'Not until Caitlin's released and you've got whoever's holding her banged up.'

'Quite sure about that?' She cocked an eyebrow. 'Because if this got out—'

'It's a no-brainer. I'm hardly likely to risk someone's life.' Caroline resented the DI's shrugged shoulder but knew when to hold back. Securing a deal outweighed scoring a point.

'No.' Sarah's smile held no warmth. 'I suppose you're saving it to go towards the king-sized scoop when it's all over?'

You bet. And there'd be a book in it. Quinn was nobody's fool, though. 'Actually that's where you come in, DI Quinn.' Caroline leaned forward, eyes shining as she told Sarah she wanted access all areas, exclusive access. She'd provided the lead, she argued; it was only fair she worked it – within reason – with the police. 'Observing mostly, natch,' she added, 'though with me being a skilled interviewer...'

213

'You're offering your services? How kind.'

'I'm a pro, Sarah. I know what I'm doing. I won't get in the way. Besides, I think you owe me, don't you?'

'You're right, I do.' Nodding, she bit her lip. *Strike while the copper's hot.* 'Oh and I need the grandmother's details. Better still, maybe I could tag along when you go see her?'

'Sure. Anything else?' She strolled back to her seat, took some papers out of a drawer. 'Expense account? Police driver? Shrink?'

Shrink? 'Oh very funny. Big laugh.' Caroline jabbed a finger in the DI's direction. 'Take the piss all you like but until I walked in here your inquiry was going precisely no—'

'Enough.' Sarah raised a palm. Her other hand held a cutting which she positioned carefully over Caroline's. 'Snap.'

The reporter snorted. The line was hardly original. And if the snooty bitch wanted to play, Caroline preferred poker any day. Keeping her gaze on the detective, Caroline reached into her bag for her phone. 'I'll raise you.' She brought the abductor's artwork up on screen, slid the phone across the desk. 'I prefer playing big girls' games.'

Caroline regarded the mural as her winning card, and after Quinn's predictable hissy fit over the incident not having been reported, it partly did the trick. She knew Sarah wouldn't fold completely but she did agree to keep Caroline in the loop. Given the reporter could potentially bring communication with the perp to the table, Sarah digging her heels in would have been counter-productive. That was Caroline's take, anyway. 'Shake on it?' she asked, smiling.

'Don't push your luck, Caroline.'

Halfway to the door, the reporter turned back. 'You could've stopped me sooner.' *Before I made a tit of myself.*

'I was curious to see how far you'd go.'

She'd seen nothing yet. Caroline hoisted her bag on her shoulder. 'Nat sends his regards, by the way.'

'Oh?' Sarah hadn't run into Caroline's lodger for months.

'Yeah. He was in Giovanni's last night. He'd have come over to say hello, but he reckoned it looked like a private party. Dead cosy, he told me.' She fluttered her fingers. 'Ciao.'

The sharp exit would have had more impact if King had a swipe card. She was back within seconds. 'Can you let me out, please?'

After summoning King a police escort, Sarah grabbed her coat and keys, dashed to the squad room and brought the few officers there up to speed on the killer's bloodline.

'Caitlin Reynolds' granny?' Paul Wood gave a low whistle. 'Now that's what I call a turn up.' Going by the stunned silence, he'd voiced everyone's reaction. Until now, the detectives' phone bashing had been little more than speculative. Given the family connection, it had

215

actually been bang on. They'd already amassed a list of names of people they needed to talk to. Near the top were Bolton family members. Pauline's parents were long dead but there'd been an elder sister and a younger set of twins. A retired cop was still around somewhere, too. Harries sat at a desk by the window, making a call. Doubtless the list would grow as the day wore on.

'So we're thinking the motive's revenge?' Wood tucked a pen behind his ear. 'Makes sense, I guess. To a sad git.'

'Yeah, but what's the sad git after?' John Hunt tugged the ring-pull on a can of Red Bull. 'He's had Caitlin for three days now and not a word. If it's Old Testament revenge he's after, I don't fancy her chances much.'

A rookie DC's blank look suggested religion wasn't his thing. Huntie could enlighten the guy later. Sarah wanted out of there, soon as. 'Actually,' she said, '"not a word" isn't strictly true.' She mentioned Caroline King's un-commissioned wall art and the message ostensibly from Caitlin. A communal groan of incredulity followed. 'I know, I know.' She waved it down. 'Tell me about it.' She'd been so furious at the delay in reporting the incident, let alone loss of potential evidence, she'd threatened to slap King with an obstruction charge. She'd have thrown in a perverting the course too if the reporter hadn't agreed to go home and wait for the arrival of a forensic team.

216

'At least King tipped us the wink on the family connection.' Holmes opened the bread roll in his hand, inspected the bacon content. 'Hack doing favours is rarer than a straight coil.'

'Greeks bearing gifts, Jed. Anyway,' Sarah said, 'it's a link not the chain. To hear her bang on you'd think she'd cracked the case.' King had bought them a bit of time, hardly saved the day.

Hunt swivelled in a chair, brawny arms folded across his chest. 'How come Nicola Reynolds blabbed to a reporter anyway?' The tacit corollary? *And not a word to us.*

'Good question, Twig.' And one of the first she intended asking the bloody woman. 'I'll get back to you.' Sarah jangled her keys as Harries ended the call.

'Just coming, boss.' He grabbed his leather jacket, drained whatever he'd been drinking from a paper cup.

'You pair off to Nicola Reynolds' now then, ma'am?' Hunt asked.

'Later.'

She'd cut out the middle woman, deal with the matriarch first.

THIRTY-FOUR

'Boss, about last night?'

Here we go. Sarah tapped the wheel, had been wondering how long it would take. For twenty minutes now, Harries had prattled on about the weather (heavy cloud), the traffic (light flow), the up-coming interview (sooner you than me, boss). She'd not been fooled by the forced jocularity in his voice; it didn't marry with the studiously avoided eye contact, same as at the early brief. Dave wasn't lost for words, she reckoned, just a bit lost. That was no surprise, given Sarah wasn't entirely sure about last night's ramifications either. The promise she made to herself ten years back not to get into bed with another cop had bombed spectacularly.

'Not at work, eh, Dave?' Thank God she hadn't said 'not on the job'.

'I'm just ... you know ... really sorry.' Out of the corner of her eye she caught actual hand-wringing, Uriah Harries.

'No sweat.' She sensed his gaze on her profile. 'Nothing to be sorry about.' Wasn't his fault he'd fallen asleep before they'd got down to business. Blame it on the booze. She certainly

218

didn't see it as personal. A professional failing, perhaps, if they'd gone ahead? 'Next time, maybe?'

He turned to face her. 'Are you serious?'

If the foreplay was anything to go by. Dead serious. Her spirit was willing, his flesh had been weak. He'd get over that. His coffee was crap too and she'd get over that. 'Yes, I am.' She cut him a glance: perky didn't cover it. 'One absolute no-no?' She pressed a finger against her lips. 'Or it's curtains.'

He did the 'Scout's honour' bit, holding three fingers against a temple; the smile was beatific. 'Trust me ... mum's the—'

'Don't even go there, Dave.' The age gap wasn't *that* big. Besides, on current experience, the last person she'd trust was a mother.

Or grandmother.

'You'd best come in.' Linda Walker, in another life Susan Bailey, held the door open and shuffled back against the faded rose wallpaper. She'd smartened her act since last time. Sarah spotted a dab of lipstick, a dusting of face powder, the smell of fabric conditioner wafted from the get up of black skirt, baggy jumper; her down-at-heel slippers had been replaced by court shoes. Had the old girl been expecting a police visit? A knock on the door?

Until less than an hour ago, the house call was more than Sarah had anticipated. In fifteen years as a cop she'd never come across a similar scenario. A child killer's granddaughter abducted half a century after the crime? Shame there was no handy police guide. She'd have appreciated hearing the chief's take, but her calls to him had gone straight to voicemail. Knowing Baker, he'd barge in and grab the woman by the metaphorical balls. Might not be a bad idea.

Masking her distaste, Sarah brushed a load of cat hairs off the settee before taking a seat. At least the feline itself wasn't in sight, though the stink of pee lingered. The room was like an oven; Sarah unbuttoned her coat. Mrs Walker stood in front of a blazing coal fire, smoothing her bun. 'Would you like a cup of something?'

The DI shook her head. 'Sit down please.' The brew last time had been undrinkable, and besides they weren't at a tea party. 'When were you going to tell us? About Pauline Bolton?'

Her amber eyes narrowed a touch behind the thick lenses, sinking on to the wing chair, she clutched her chest. Sarah sensed Dave's concern but she was unmoved. Clearly feeling differently, he leaned forward, asked if she needed water, pills, tea, anything.

'No thank you, dear. I'll be alright in a minute.' She used a *Radio Times* to fan her face. 'I suppose Nicola's been talking?'

Weird response. Nicola had been as forthcoming on the bloody subject as her mother. Sarah stared at the woman, found it nigh on impossible to marry the ordinary appearance, bland features with a child-killing past. She re-

220

called her first impression, mentally likening Caitlin's granny to a Russian Babushka. Bang on there then. 'Pauline Bolton, Mrs Walker. Soon as you like.'

She sighed, shook her head. 'It was all so long ago. You have to understand I've not thought about it in years. I block it out, it's too painful.'

For who, Sarah wondered? Either way Walker needed to get her head round it now. 'Did it not occur to you that your conviction for the child's murder could be a significant factor in Caitlin's abduction?'

'No, never,' she said, clinging to the arms of her chair. 'I've told you, for me it's in the past, dead and buried, over and done with.'

'*Was* in the past, Mrs Walker.' Coal shifted in the grate, sparks flew to the hearth. Impassive, Sarah waited for Walker to break her silence. Surely it was inconceivable that the woman hadn't put two and two together?

'If anyone hurts Caitlin, I'll ... I'll...'

Didn't say. Walker dropped her head to her chest and started sobbing. Harries delved into a pocket for a tissue. Sarah shook her head, stayed the offer with a raised hand. 'Never forgive yourself?' she prompted. 'Is that what you were going to say? Because I'd say whoever's holding Caitlin likely feels the same way.'

Harries cut her a don't-hold-back look. She wouldn't. Walker had held back and look where that had got them. If she'd revealed the pointer first time round, the inquiry could be a lot

221

further forward. Walker's emotional angst didn't cut it with the DI, not when Caitlin's life was at risk. She drummed her thigh with three fingers, mentally counting to twenty, reached fifteen.

Mrs Walker sat up straight, wiped tears with the heels of her hands before folding them loosely in her lap. 'I'm sorry, inspector, but I don't think there's anything to forgive. I paid for the crime. I'll regret to my dying day what happened to Pauline. But I was locked up for ten years. I was bullied inside, beaten, spat on, verbally abused every day.' Her fingers kneaded the skirt. 'Believe me, prison's no picnic. But I took the punishment, I served the time and I've tried to live a decent life since. I keep my head down, nose clean, never hurt anyone. Early on in life I learned a very hard lesson.'

Sarah nodded. The attempt at dignity touched her slightly more than what she regarded as Walker's previous histrionics. She took the point too, but clearly someone out there didn't share the view. 'Problem is, Mrs Walker, I think somebody's trying to teach you another lesson. An even harder one.'

'I'm an old woman. He can do what he likes to me. But not Caitlin. Why punish her?'

'He?' Sarah and Harries exchanged glances.

'He, she, they. You know what I mean.' Walker broke eye contact. 'Slip of the tongue.'

Was it? Sarah pressed her on whether anyone from the past had been in contact recently; whether she'd spotted anyone/anything odd over the last few days/weeks. Fast denials, firm head shakes. Too fast? Too firm? But why would she lie? She ran names past her, people who'd lived in the village, given evidence at the trial. Walker had no memories of them, she claimed, apart from the Boltons and the builder.

'The man you tried to frame.' Sarah said. It wasn't a question.

'He died while I was in prison.' Walker nodded. 'Hanged himself in the copse apparently.'

'Who told you?' Sarah asked.

'One of the warders. I never got visitors.'

'Never?'

'Just the one. Pauline's sister. Wanted to know why I'd done it. Grace, I think her name was.'

'Was?' Sarah glanced at Harries who was already making a note.

'I read in the paper that she died.'

'When?'

'Years back.' Sighing, Walker took off her glasses, started polishing them with a sleeve. 'I never got no cards neither. Birthday. Christmas. Not a single one. Everyone took against me, uncles, aunts, even my brothers and sister. My mum and dad never spoke to me again after Pauline ... died.'

Matter-of-fact tone, no self-pity. Sarah bowed her head briefly. Reports she'd read suggested the Baileys were no great shakes as parents but it must've been tough for a ten-year-old kid despite what she'd done to be disowned by her own flesh and blood. After her release, Walker

223

told them, she had no home to go back to and never put roots down again. She kept on the move, changed her name a couple of times. To keep a roof over her head, she cleaned houses, took in ironing, worked in shops. Never married though, partly afraid it would all come out.

'So Nicola's father?' Harries asked.

'He didn't want to know, did he?' Nicola was the result of a one-night knee trembler round the back of a chippie in Walsall. 'I never told her that neither.'

Neither? Sarah frowned. So why had Walker assumed Nicola had opened her mouth? 'She didn't know about your past?'

Walker shook her head. 'Nothing. I cut myself off from the past completely. By the time I had Nicola it was like the whole thing happened to somebody else.'

No wonder Nicola hadn't breathed a word. 'So when did she find out?' Sarah asked.

She stared down at her hands. 'Yesterday. She was here. Someone sent her a message on her phone.'

Secret pasts, hidden truths, buried lies. The Walker-Reynolds set-up was less tangled web, more weaving convention. Spiderwoman Nicola had some more explaining to do. Sarah made 'go' motions at Harries who nodded, stowed away the notebook. Walker was still in a world of her own. Sarah touched her lightly on the shoulder. 'We're off now, Mrs Walker. I'm not sure you should be staying here alone.'

'Don't worry, inspector.' Lifting her gaze, she forced a wan smile. 'It would've been easy any time for them to bump me off. It's not me they're after, is it? And you know what? I'd rather die any day than see Caitlin hurt.'

Sarah nodded. She'd ask uniform to keep an eye on the place anyway. 'Don't get up. We'll see ourselves out.' Her business card was still on the table where she'd left it. 'My numbers are there. Please call me, any time.'

'Thank you, dear. And thank you for not asking.'

Sarah paused at the door, turned her head. 'Sorry?'

'For not asking why I killed Pauline.'

Everyone had. Police, lawyers, reporters outside court, people in the reform school, prison warders, fellow inmates, probation officers, psychologists, therapists. When she was first locked away, Pauline's parents had posed the question several times in letters. The correspondence dried up when she failed to reply.

Why did you kill Pauline? Why did you kill our little princess?

They'd have visited, they wrote in one letter, if they could stand to be in the same room as her. Presumably why they'd sent Grace that time. God, if looks could kill. Thank God there had been a table between them and a couple of guards on duty.

Shuddering, Mrs Walker wiped her eyes,

threw a damp tissue on the fire. Her glance fell on the business card. She fancied she could still feel the detective's gentle touch on her shoulder. It stirred a memory that made her flinch. Another detective. Another hand. Not gentle. She'd recoiled at any form of physical contact ever since, but DI Quinn seemed if not to sympathize then at least not to judge too harshly. She felt guilty not telling her about the intruder but she'd promised Nicola. Something to do with keeping Caitlin unharmed. And Mrs Walker had meant every word when she said she'd rather die than see Caitlin hurt. At least that had been the truth.

As to why she'd killed Pauline?

Sighing, she leaned forward in her chair, stared unblinking into the fire. Reflections of flames danced across the thick lenses of her glasses. Her focus was on the images flickering in her head, jerky black and white pictures, jagged flashes of scarlet, dashes of dandelion yellow, tantalizing snatches of Pauline hopping in and out of frame – now you see me, now you don't.

Keep still, keep still, Paulie.

Mrs Walker shook her head, desperate to dispel the disjointed visions, to dredge the full picture from her mind. It had to be swirling round in the depths. If she could only concentrate, coax it out. Sitting back in the chair, she slowed her breathing, squeezed her eyes tight, willing herself to see, transporting herself back to August 1960, Badger's Copse, the heat wave, the relentless stream of questions. The ghost of a smile parted her lips as a child's image slowly developed in her mind's eye. The plain face, barrel chest, defiant hands on chubby hips.

She barely recognised herself...

'Answer me, Susan.' The detective wasn't a kind man. Not any more. He sounded like her headmaster, only not so posh. He'd been nice to her in the hospital, but that hadn't lasted long. She'd quite liked the fuss at first. That hadn't lasted long though. Susan liking it – not the attention. She couldn't escape it now if she tried. They were in the police station again, a small windowless room with sickly green walls and a wobbly steel table, a nearly full ashtray slap bang in the middle. The detective smelled of Woodbines and Brylcreem. He didn't ask about the shouty man any more, but for what seemed like weeks now, he kept on and on and on. About why she'd hurt Pauline.

'You're not a baby, Susan. Take your hands away from your ears. Look at me properly, please.'

Not so easy when she didn't have her specs. They'd still be lying in the grass somewhere but her mum hadn't bothered looking. Susan was supposed to be getting a new pair, but no one seemed in a rush to sort it for her. She could still see, of course, but everything was a bit fuzzy round the edges, and she felt lost without them. A little dizzy too, cos the place was hot and stank of sick and wee and she was tired and she was hungry and she was...

'Sit up straight. And please stop yawning. Why did you hit Pauline?'

She winced again. It hurt when she shuffled her bum, the back of her clammy thighs stuck to the wooden seat. 'I already told you, mister. We were playing schools.' She wondered when he'd lost the front tooth and the button on his blue shirt; one of the cuffs had frayed too. He reminded her of her granddad, only he died ages ago.

'And I've told you, young lady. I'm Detective Chief Inspector Southern.' She budged back when he pointed a fat finger at her. 'You call me sir. And "playing schools" isn't good enough. Why did you hit her?'

The younger bloke sitting next to Susan nudged her gently in the ribs. She couldn't remember his name either, or ever seeing anyone so skinny. Like a stick of liquorice with a tie on, he was. They said he was her solicitor, looking after her interests or something. Funny that, cos he barely spoke to her and never looked her in the eye. The pretty police lady opposite didn't smile at her any more either. Jenny, her name was. Only she'd told Susan yesterday not to call her it again.

'I already told you that an' all, sir. She got in the way when I was swinging the stick.'

'How many times did you hit her, Susan? Once? Twice? Twenty?'

'Once. Cross my heart.' She eyed the last custard cream on the paper plate; the fly buzzing round fancied it too. Funny how it reminded her of the picnic, the Midget Gems, the jam sandwich she snaffled when Paulie wasn't looking. She started to smile then caught the expression on the detective's face, the tightening of his fist on the table. Her insides had gone all wobbly. 'Please, mister, I need the—'

'Why were you covered in her blood, Susan? Why was it on your clothes, in your hair, under your nails?'

'Cos I picked her up, cuddled her.'

'Why?'

She crossed her legs. 'Cos she was hurt, bleeding. And cos she was my friend.'

'And you were sorry for what you'd done?'

'I didn't mean no harm. I told you. The man chased us. Me and Paulie ran. I fell. Please, mist—'

'Mr Crawford says he didn't run after you, Susan. He says he saw you bully Pauline, shout at her, beat her with the stick.'

She squeezed her thighs even tighter. She'd not be able to hold it in much longer.

'The murder weapon has your hairs on it, Susan. Cotton from the clothes you wore.'

She whimpered as hot pee seeped into her knickers.

'Did Pauline bother you, Susan? Pretty little girl, popular, bright as a button? Did you resent her?'

Resent? She didn't even know what it meant. 'Susan. It would go so much easier for you if you told the truth. Why did you kill Pauline?'

Like the last time and the time before and the time before that, she rested her head on the table and started to weep. And when he placed a firm hand on her shoulder and told her he'd understand if it had been an accident, somehow it just seemed simpler to agree.

She'd had a while to think about it but Caitlin still had trouble taking it in. Lying on her back, her vacant gaze swept the filthy ceiling; the occasional flake drifted down, sprinkled the sheet dandruff fashion. A five-legged spider scuttled round and round near the light fitting, like her thoughts, not quite spinning. Caitlin had always found it difficult to picture her granny as a child, let alone a child-killer. Some of her mates' grandmothers she could easily imagine shimmying down a cat-walk, strutting their stuff, but Caitlin's was *Last of the Summer Wine* vintage: Nora Batty tights, grey bun, Cornish pasty slippers. If she'd thought about it at all, she'd have put the premature ageing down to a hard life, not a life sentence. But Granny Walker hadn't been sent down for life. That was monkey man's beef. And why – as he so predictably put it – he wanted a pound of flesh or two.

Caitlin hauled herself up from the mattress, paced the pitted concrete floor yet again. If increased blood flow was good for the brain, she needed to get a couple of marathons under her belt. It helped that she wasn't drugged up to the eyeballs any more. The fog was beginning to lift, letting tantalizing shafts of light fall on how she got here. First she had to work out how to get out. Not easy when after sixteen years of thinking one way, some weirdo comes along and snatches not just the rug from under your feet but the whole sodding planet. Get used to the idea, he'd said, then legged it. Get used to the idea? Some bizarre episode of *Who Do You Think You Are?* How long had she got?

Still pacing, she wrapped her arms round her waist. She'd always loved her gran to bits. Often felt closer to the old dear than her mum. Family folklore had it that gran had been orphaned as a kid, brought up in care, widowed in her twenties. In monkey man's version, she'd been disowned by her parents, banged up in jail, never tied the knot. Making the family folklore a fucking fairy tale.

Caitlin balled her fists remembering how he'd thrust a news cutting in her face. Try as she might, she'd not been able to see her gran's features in the grainy pic. It didn't help that she'd never seen photos of her as a child, the earliest likeness she recalled was gran doing the proud mum bit, beaming down at a newborn Nicola cradled in her arms. Come to think of it, none of the old albums had childhood snaps, family shots. It figured, given she'd been inside for a decade. Caitlin shook her head. Mind blowing.

Like being told your mum was going to take your granny out, but not on a day trip. Or a picnic. That was when he started humming again. De-dum-de-dum-dum-de-dum-de-dum. If you go down to the woods today ... Oh how the dumb fuck had laughed. He thought he was so funny. Dead funny.

'Yeah, well, over my dead body,' she murmured. And it would be if she didn't do something about it. She was convinced the mad freak would never let her go, he'd told her too much. Far too much. Not just about her gran and how the crime had destroyed other lives too, but also about Luke Holden. Monkey man had obviously tailed Caitlin for weeks if not months, observed her with what he called that 'junkie piece of shit'. He reckoned drugs were pure evil, relished describing how he followed Luke home and gave the bastard a taste of his own medicine.

Monkey man had nothing to lose. Caitlin knew she had to act to save her life. And the mad git was going to help – he just didn't know that yet. Simple really. She gave a tight smile. She'd be playing him at his own games.

THIRTY-FIVE

It wasn't rocket surgery or brain science. Slunk in the back of a parked black cab, Caroline checked the mirror for the millionth time. She'd put herself in Quinn's mental jackboots. If – God forbid – she was SIO in the Caitlin Reynolds' inquiry, who would she be keenest to interview? Who'd be top of the tree? The family tree? Exactly. Caroline's journalistic priority was the same as the cop's. If it wasn't getting tired she'd say 'snap'.

She'd only had to wait ten minutes for the DI to emerge from the station after what Caroline thought of as their negotiating session. With Dave in tow, and a purposeful stride, Sarah certainly wasn't en route to the hairdresser – though God knows she could do with a new look: that school ma'am bun was so passé. Ordering the cabbie to 'follow that car' had given Caroline quite a frisson: felt like she was in a movie. OK not quite...

The driver's running commentary plus rank BO was the only downside. Who gave a flying fart about the state of the roads, the crap weather, or last night's telly? Small price to pay though, since for the last half hour Caroline's sights had been set on a poky bungalow in a seedy side street on the Monkshead estate in Small Heath. The Ice Queen and her bag man were in there and if Caroline wasn't much mistaken, the target under the grill would be Caitlin's granny, child killer of this parish. Of course, it would help if she knew the woman's new name.

The driver turned in his seat a fraction, threw Caroline a lop-sided smile. 'You're that reporter off the telly aren't you?' She nodded, mentally rolled her eyes. *Here we go.* 'I knew it.' The knowledge clearly gave him intense pleasure. Yawn. 'I bin tryin' to place the face.' Motor Mouth's face was pretty good though the bodywork left everything to be desired. His paunch had already popped a button and two more looked as if they were on the way out. The green tidemark round his neck meant his Ali G chain wasn't twenty-four carat, or he'd been sold a pup. 'What you doing sniffing round here then?'

Wouldn't you like to know, sunshine. She'd tell the world – once she had the full story. 'Sightseeing.'

It took a few seconds for him to get it, and even then the laugh was uncertain. 'I could tell you a thing or two. I hear stuff in the back of that cab that'd make your hair curl.'

'You should stay in more.'

Hint taken, he gave her a back view of his head. Sighing, Caroline checked her watch. Get a move on, ace detective. How much time could an interview take, for pity's sake?'

'How long you plan on needing me, darlin'?'

'Just till—' Movement in the mirror caught her eye. Hoo-bloody-rah. The cops had come out and were walking to the DI's Audi deep in conversation. What Caroline wouldn't give to be a fly on the car roof. 'I'll settle up now.' Smiling, she handed him a twenty and almost threw in a tip: use a deodorant. As it happened, she'd been glad to have the guy's bulk around. The area was rundown, dirt poor; youths strutted round as if they owned it and pit bulls appeared to be the weapon of choice. Caroline had a cautious streak these days. She'd been attacked by a girl gang the year before last and, though loath to admit it, knew the physical violence had left mental scars.

The driver stuck a thumb's-up out the window. 'Watch how you go, darlin'.'

You bet. She had a lot to play for. After she'd picked her way along a stretch of pavement strewn with dog turds and chewed gum. The bungalow was the last in a fairly forlorn row, a patch of scrubby grassland lay beyond, handy given gardens were the size of a stamp, and most of those had been concreted over. Up close, twenty-two looked even tattier than the others. Pebble dash always put Caroline in mind of puke and the front door hadn't seen a lick of paint since God was a girl. Ringing the bell, she inhaled like there was no tomorrow, just knew the place was going to stink inside. Tough. Securing the interview would make the difference between writing a few news stories and producing another book. A doco even? Assuming the woman was up to it.

Caroline strained her ears, rang the bell again. It didn't sound as if she was up at all. She took a couple of steps to the side – she'd hesitate to call it a lawn – peered through a grimy window. The old dear sat in a chair by the fire. She couldn't be dozing; the cops had only just left. Caroline smiled. Must be the Quinn effect. The reporter pressed her nose against the glass, watched tears trickle down the woman's cheeks. Not sleeping, weeping.

Pensive, she stepped back on the path. Now she had the address, she could come back any time. It would definitely be kinder to let the old girl have a good cry, get it out of her system. Yep. Definitely. She knelt, shouted through the letterbox.

'Let me in. I'm a friend of Caitlin's.'

Mississippi Diner was a rip-off MacDonald's sandwiched between a balti house and a bookie's in deepest Small Heath. It wasn't often the detectives broke for lunch. Sarah felt like nipping next door and placing a bet this would be the last time Dave got to choose where they ate. She slid her phone to one side of the table so he could dump the tray of goodies.

'I still don't think you believed her, boss.' He

sank into the orange moulded plastic chair opposite. Classy.

Sarah had sat on comfier walls. 'Come on, blanking out bad memories is one thing. But killing a child, spending years behind bars? I can't see how your mind censors that kind of trauma.' She watched askance as he took a massive bite from a burger seeping yellow goo. Not so much fast as ooze food. Sarah had opted to fast. The foul taste in her mouth after encountering Linda Walker wasn't appetite-conducing either. Dave had yet to make a comeback and she was pretty sure his silence wasn't down to mastication. She stirred more sugar into what masqueraded as coffee. 'Spit it out, Dave.' *And the burger while you're at it.* 'I can see you're not with me.'

He shrugged, dabbed his mouth with a paper napkin. 'Maybe the bigger the horror, the deeper you have to bury it.'

'They don't make shovels that size.' She widened her eyes. Dave was certainly shovelling it down. Not a pretty sight. Half-turning, Sarah glanced round at the clientele. The place was packed, youths mostly, a few families; the loudest racket came from a kids' party kicking off in the corner, all balloons, painted faces and party hats. The birthday girl had a big grin and kept pointing to a bright yellow badge shaped in a six. Sarah smiled back then turned away, in her mind's eye the image of another little blonde girl, only Pauline Bolton never got beyond five.

'Help yourself.' Dave jabbed what was left of the bun at his chips. She took one without thinking, about food at any rate. Sarah's head housed a whole gallery of pictures, crime scenes, victims of violence she knew she'd never be able to let go. Dave-dog-with-a-bone hadn't dropped the topic. 'If she really did manage to bury it,' he said, 'it explains why she never put two and two together. About Caitlin, I mean.'

Sarah knew what he meant, and didn't buy that either. Linda Walker must have realized there was a connection with her past and Caitlin's current predicament. 'Ask me? She's in total denial.'

The burger paused midway to mouth. 'There's a difference?'

She held his gaze. 'Can't see. Won't see.' Deliberate blank refusal. Ostrich fashion.

He chewed that over for a few seconds, then: 'You heard what she said about Caitlin, boss.' *I'd rather die than see Caitlin come to any harm.* 'If she'd harboured even an inkling – I can't believe she wouldn't have said something to us that first time.'

'Don't bank on it, Dave.' She leaned forward, lowered her voice even more. 'I grant you it was a long time ago but that woman killed a child. Tried to frame an innocent man. Her whole life's been built on lies and deception. And I'd not be surprised if she's still lying through her teeth.' There had been too many shifty looks, evasive answers, furious denials.

'Watch it, boss.' Unsmiling, he tilted his head. 'It's slipping.'

She frowned. 'What is?'

'The black cap.'

Frigging cheek. 'Don't be ridic—' She pushed back from the table, just caught the cup before it toppled, grabbed napkins to mop the overspill.

'She committed a crime. She went to prison.' He shoved away the remains. The happy meal wasn't living up to its name. 'Seems to me you're sitting in judgement all over again.'

'Bollocks.' Or was it?

Dave gave a laboured sigh. 'Sorry if I happen to believe people can turn their lives round.'

'And I don't?' Christ, if she didn't believe crims could redeem themselves, she was in the wrong job.

'If the cap...' His lip twitched. 'Slip of the tongue. Sorry.'

'Not funny.' She opened her mouth to remonstrate, thought better of it. Maybe he had a point. Irrational maybe, but every time she recalled the second or two when her hand had touched Walker's shoulder, Sarah's skin crept. 'Fair enough, Dave.' She shucked into her coat. 'Forgive and forget. End of. Will you tell the mad bastard holding Caitlin? Or shall I?'

Dave caught up with her before she reached the door. 'Point is – what's he going to do to her, boss?'

'Point is, we need to nail him before he does anything else.' They waited for a gap in the traffic before crossing. Even on a Sunday, the main drag was busy. Sarah was half surprised to find the Audi still intact. Mind, she had parked in plain view.

'Any ideas then, boss?' Dave fastened his seat belt.

She waited for a Tesco wagon to trundle past before pulling out. Home deliveries wasn't a bad notion. Not the point Dave was driving at though. She curved a lip. 'I reckon we need a little help from our friends. In the fourth estate.' She'd decided to hold a news conference late afternoon. Go for broke. Make a direct appeal to the perp, try and get Nicola on board as well. The man had made contact twice with Caroline King, so he couldn't be that publicity shy. Control freaks had to dictate the pace, call the shots, she'd no doubt the abductor fitted that category. Given he had his own agenda, it would be a fine line between drawing him out and pissing him off. Instinct told her that even alluding to the babe-in-the-wood case was a no-no. Might be an idea to run it past the profiler they called in from time to time.

'You and King mates now then, boss?' She heard the amused smirk in Mr Irony's voice.

'Besties, Dave. 'Specially after this morning.' She told him the reporter's proposed deal – demand more like – about working the case alongside the police in return for interview master classes. 'As if.'

'Cheeky mare.' He sniffed. 'Sounds more like

"you scratch my back, I'll have a lifetime supply of free loofahs".'

She cast him an old-fashioned look though got the drift. 'I had to tell her I'd keep her in the loop.'

'No way?' He was digging in a pocket.

'Thing is, the perp's in touch with her, Dave. Could be useful. Plus she's sitting on a big exclusive. I can't risk anything getting out until we've collared the bastard. I know it goes against the grain but I'm going to have to keep her sweet.'

'Talking of which.' He pulled out a bag. 'Fancy one?'

The tell-tale grease marks said it all. 'Dough-nuts, Dave? Purlease.' The cop in her saw them as edible clichés.

'Dunno what you mean, boss. They're power rings, these.'

'I'll pass, thanks.' On the keeping King sweet front, she might as well throw it in. 'By the way, Lois Lane knows where we were last night.' The chewing halted and she sensed his gaze on her.

'And is that going to make a difference?'

'I shouldn't think so, Dave.' *Only if she starts sniffing round, trying to make trouble.*

THIRTY-SIX

'I only want to help, Mrs Walker.' Caroline King had more than a foot in the door. Both heels were planted on the sludge-coloured carpet in the cramped gloomy hall. The handily placed envelope on the table had been a great help providing the woman's moniker. Getting in had been comparatively easy; staying in was proving less so.

'But you said you were Caitlin's friend. And now you tell me you're a reporter.' The woman looked fit to drop, clung on to the wall with one hand for support.

'And I'm really, really sorry. I *so* hate ly— not telling the truth. Cross my heart.' She did with both arms, threw in a bright smile. 'I'll be completely honest with you from now on.' The full beam usually worked but needed eye contact; Walker wouldn't meet her gaze.

'No. I don't think so, dear. I think you'd better go now.'

'That is *such* a shame.' Caroline's mock concern masked impatience. She knew she'd get there in the end, she always did. Boy had she been right about the place stinking. It wasn't just

242

cat pee making her journo nose wrinkle. She sniffed news like there was no tomorrow. The murder of a child told by the killer fifty-something years on? Even without the abduction it was sensational stuff. If – no, *when* – she got this woman to open up, she'd have a story to die for. 'You see, I really think I can help the police find Caitlin.'

Walker rubbed a hand over her face. Plain, unprepossessing, anyone looking less like a child killer Caroline couldn't imagine. But that was part of the beauty. This woman could pass unnoticed in every street, every gathering, yet she had a unique story. Caroline didn't just want to get inside her sodding sitting room; she wanted temporary residence inside her head. Then tell the world what secrets, thoughts and emotions lurked there.

'Look, if you don't mind, I've had a rather trying time of late.'

Had quite a few trying times if you asked Caroline. 'Of course, Mrs Walker.' Mentally bracing herself, she gave the woman's arm a gentle squeeze. 'I was only thinking of Caitlin ... being at the mercy of a man like that.'

'Like what?' The voice snapped; her gaze locked on to Caroline. Alzheimer's? No way. Caroline reckoned Nicola had been telling porkies. Fleetingly she registered something in the woman's eyes that sent a shiver down her spine. The pause it gave was momentary, she told herself not to be stupid. Glancing round conspiratorially, she lowered her voice. 'I shouldn't really tell you this, Mrs Walker, but ... the abductor's been sending me messages. He wants me ... Are you—?' She shot out both arms to steady the woman. 'There you go. Look, forget I said a word. I'll just wait until you've got your breath back and I'll be on my way.' Another pat, another concerned smile. If that didn't open more doors, Caroline would begin to suspect she was losing her touch.

'You'd better come through, dear. I need to sit down.'

Bingo. Full house – well, bungalow.

'Let me help.' Caroline linked arms with the woman. 'Lean on me, Mrs Walker.'

Losing her touch? Yeah right.

'Come sit next to me when you're done?' Caitlin pulled a face behind his back as she patted the mattress. 'I hate being on my own.'

'You've changed your tune all of a sudden.' Monkey man, still divvying up fish and chips, turned his head, flicked her a casual glance. 'Hungry?'

'Starving.' Switching on a smile, she circled a hand over her stomach. Its wild churning meant even keeping water down would be a big ask. Nerves not nausea. Given the size of the challenge she'd set herself. Changing the tune was part of it. From screw-you to screw-me. Only the segue had to be a lot subtler, her performance faultless.

'Why don't you give me a name I can call you?' She twisted a strand of hair between her fingers. 'Monkey man's so lame. And it's not very nice, is it?'

He stood gazing down for a few seconds before handing over her share. 'You want to play nice now, eh?'

'Yeah, why not?' She held his gaze as she nibbled a chip. 'No sense biting the hand that feeds you, is there?' It wasn't the greatest line, but she giggled anyway. 'Not to mention clothes.' She stroked her fingers down a slender thigh. 'The jeans fit great by the way. I should've said thanks. You taking a pew, or what?'

He shrugged. 'Shove over a bit then.'

She did, but not too far. 'Go on then. What shall I call you?'

'Stick with monkey man. I kinda like it.'

Weirdo. 'I wouldn't tell the police or anything, y'know.' His shrug said 'who-gives-a-fuck?' Caitlin interpreted it as another sign he had no intention of letting her go. 'Hey, it's not fair. You've got more than me.' Playful, teasing, she leaned across to snatch a chip, made sure a boob brushed against his arm.

He batted her hand. 'Life's not fair, is it? I thought the cuttings made that clear.' She knew what he meant but a discussion of crime and punishment would hardly lead to bedtime stories.

'Sorry.' Licking grease off her fingers. 'It was only a little joke.' She caught the smell of fish on his breath. The guy was gross. How could anyone make so much noise eating? She hoped to God she'd be able to go through with it when the time came.

'Lighten up a bit, hey?' Very gently she tapped him on the forearm. 'It's OK for you. You get to go out. I'm stuck here with only the walls for company.' And the odd spider. Hop-along was still doing the not-so-rounds up there. 'What's happening in the world?

'Don't worry, it's still spinning.'

'Time goes so slow though. Any chance you could bring some DVDs in? I love movies. How about you?' He turned his mouth down, non committal. She ploughed on regardless as they ate, reeling off favourite films, actors, précised the *Twilight* plot: man bites girl. She played to her audience with verve, threw in impersonations and extravagant hand gestures, all the while casting covert glances at his face. He cracked the occasional smile, made the odd comment. He seemed edgier than of late though. 'Hey.' She laid her hand on his shoulder. 'How about you grab popcorn, hot dogs, ice cream?'

'I shouldn't get your hopes up if I were you.' He screwed the wrappings, tossed them in a corner.

'Why not?' Casual but his words had sent a chill down her spine.

'You might not be here much longer.'

Shit. 'Great. That means I'll get to see Mum again.'

'Course you will.' Smiling, he got to his feet, patted her shoulder. She saw a flake of fish lodged in the lying bastard's teeth. 'Laters, babe. I've got a few things need sorting.'

'You're not going, are you? I hate being on my own in this place. Gives me the creeps.'

'And I care because?'

Knob end. She dropped her head. 'I thought you did, just a little.' Could she force a tear or two? Oh, yes. And a shudder.

'Come on, Caitlin, don't cry.' He reached out a hand but didn't touch her this time. 'I won't be long.'

'Go then. Leave me. You don't care.'

'Look, I'll try and pick up a film for you, OK?'

'Promise?' She counted five before lifting her head, meeting his gaze. 'Is there any chance I could clean up a bit? I know I'd feel better. The wipes are almost gone and—'

'I'll bring you a bowl, heat some water. Next time I'm back.' He smiled. 'That do you?'

'Ace.' She pursed her lips. 'A mirror, too?'

He shook his head. 'I'll see.'

You bet you will, arse wipe. She heard the key in the lock, his footsteps fade. Finally relaxed. Thank God, he'd gone, hopefully he'd shower, smarten up a bit before getting back. She'd seen the gleam in his eye, the way he ran his gaze over her body. She had no doubt he was warming to her, but he hadn't yet got the hots. No point going off half-cock.

Caitlin smiled. The performance had only been a curtain raiser for the second act.

Slowly, slowly catchy fucking monkey man.

Nicola Reynolds opened the front door wearing a winter coat and a face like thunder. 'I was just on the way out.'

'No worries.' Sarah gave a tight smile. 'I'll give you—'

'I've got transport, thanks all the same.' She made to close the door. Difficult with Harries' size ten in the frame.

'A lift to the station. Do it there.' Sarah folded her arms. 'You've got ten seconds to change your mind.'

Without a word she stepped back, flung the coat on the stairs, stormed down the hall. Sarah and Dave shrugged in sync before tailing through to the kitchen. He muttered some sarky line about Rizlas. Sarah glanced at the luridly stained dishes in the sink, didn't need detective powers to suss Reynolds' partiality to Indian food. She was already slumped at the table, legs crossed, arms clamped. Sarah and Dave took the same seats they'd used the first night. The DI picked a hair off her skirt. Dave opened his notebook. Sarah was curious to see how or if Reynolds would break the silence as well as how long it would take. Twelve seconds.

'Get on with it then.' Snarling, Reynolds reached for the inevitable nicotine hit. Sarah stifled a sigh then breathed one of relief. The smoker was fresh out of fags. She screwed the pack, chucked it across the room. If deprivation made her any jumpier, God help them. She was like a human pressure cooker with no safety valve. Her current heightened state made those first-night nerves look laid back and she'd been on a knife edge then.

Again, Sarah was surprised Reynolds hadn't asked about developments, her seeming indifference to the inquiry. 'Why didn't you tell us about the message?' If she'd not been looking out for it, she'd have missed the momentary darkening in Reynolds' eyes, the tightening of the lips. The question had hit home and then some.

'What message?' She twisted a silver ring round her wedding finger. The tremor in her hands made her apparent nonchalance risible.

'Coat. Now.' Sarah pushed back the chair. 'I'm not playing games; we'll do this at the nick.'

'Please. No.' Her voice was very near a scream of fear. She'd raised both palms to back up the plea. 'You don't understand.'

'Damn right, I don't.' The cooler the tone, the closer Sarah was to snapping. Right now, arctic was an under-statement. 'I don't understand why you're obstructing *my* inquiry into *your* daughter's disappearance. I don't understand why you rarely answer my questions and I don't understand why – when you do – you seem incapable of telling the truth.'

Glaring, Reynolds balled her fists on her thighs. A few tense seconds passed then her defiance – and defences – crumpled. She hunched over, shoulders heaving. Inevitable really. Days of stress, not helped by the recent discovery of her mother's past, something had to give. Sarah made a T with her fingers, Harries took the hint. By the time the brew was on the table, Reynolds had calmed enough.

'Right.' Sarah slipped her BlackBerry in a pocket, a quick check had revealed the earth was still intact. 'Who sent the message?'

'I don't know. Honest to God I'd tell you if I did.'

Sarah held out a hand. 'Give me the phone. Now.'

'No way.' Her eyes widened. 'What if—'

'Now.' She'd no intention of taking it away. Cutting the perp's line of communication would be risky, could be fatal. Besides, he was no fool, the mobile was probably a pay-as-you-go registered to a Mr M Mouse. Whatever, she'd lay bets they'd not be able to trace the owner. Sarah scrolled through texts checking whether Reynolds had kept anything else close to her chest. Assuming she hadn't deleted anything, there was just the one: *Ask your old lady about Badger's Copse.*

'Have you actually spoken to the guy?'

'Just the once.'

'And?' Reynolds couldn't be that dense surely? 'Come on, give. Does he sound young, old?

High pitch? Low? Lisp? Accent?'

Reynolds turned her mouth down. 'Young-ish? Quite softly spoken but creepy if you know what I mean?'

Not a clue. 'Would you recognize it again?'

'Definitely.'

Thank God for small mercies. 'If and when he contacts you, I'll be the second person to know. Right?' She slid the phone across the table but kept hold, waited for Reynolds to make eye contact. 'Right?'

'I want to cooperate, really I do, but how can I?' The palms she held out were empty. 'He says he'll kill her if I have anything to do with you.' Her voice was softer, body language slightly less stressed but she was still singing from the same can't-help hymn sheet.

Sarah sighed, shook her head. 'What *you* have to understand, Mrs Reynolds, is he could kill Caitlin anyway.' Reynolds slapped a hand to her mouth. Harries turned his sharp intake of breath into an unconvincing cough. Tough. Pussy-footing hadn't worked. 'I've no idea what's going on in his head or what his agenda is, but he clearly enjoys toying with you. We have to draw him into the open, get to him before he does any more harm.'

'I see that, inspector.' She pushed away the mug. 'But it's not your daughter he's holding.'

'If it was...' Sarah paused, held the woman's gaze. 'I know damn sure what I'd do. And it wouldn't be playing mouse to a psycho cat.'

She nodded, pensive, then wandered to the sink, poured and drank a glass of water before turning to face Sarah. 'If it helps Caitlin – I'll do whatever you say.'

Sarah secured various promises from Reynolds, prime being she'd call the minute she heard from the abductor. She'd also consider having an experienced detective in the house, someone skilled in communication, negotiation. Theory being, he could help Reynolds lead the conversation, tease out information. In practice, he'd act as minder too.

'Tell me, has he been in direct contact with your mother?'

She shook her head. 'Not as far as I know.'

'Would she tell you?'

'Tell me?' Reynolds snorted. 'Course she would; her life's an open book, isn't it? Oh, no, wait. It isn't. She forgot to mention one or two *minor* points.'

Like killing a child and spending ten years in prison. What could Sarah say that wouldn't sound trite? She took a sip of tea, grimaced. No wonder the woman was on water: Dave's PG was on a par with his coffee.

'It has to be connected, Mrs Reynolds. You do see that?'

'Not one word in all these years.' Staring at the floor, Reynolds could have been talking to herself. 'How could she do that?'

'With the inquiry on-going I'm not sure she should be left on her own,' Sarah said. The woman still stared at the lino, circling her toe. 'Mrs Reynolds?'

She lifted her glance. 'Yes, you're right. I'll have her stay here a few days. To be on the safe side.'

'Has he told you why he's holding Caitlin, Mrs Reynolds? What he wants out of this?'

'I wish I knew.'

'Maybe next time he gets in touch.' Sarah nodded at Dave. As they walked to the door, she told Reynolds there'd be a news conference late afternoon, the cameras would be there, she'd make a direct appeal to the abductor. 'I'm hoping it'll have the desired effect. I want to smoke him out.'

'Smoke him out? For what he's doing, I'd like to see him burn in hell.'

THIRTY-SEVEN

'Can I get you anything, Mrs Walker?' Iced water, cold shower, industrial fan? How the old girl could sit so close to the fire was beyond Caroline. Just helping Walker settle in the wing chair had brought the reporter out in a sweat. The small space was like a furnace on full blast, airless and odorous to a stultifying degree. Still, looking on the bright side. 'Would you mind awfully if I slip off my jacket?' One arm was already on its way out. The unwitting hostess stared into the flames. Caroline doubted she'd even taken the request on board.

Smiling solicitously, she perched on the settee as close as she could get bar taking up berth in Walker's lap. *Perish the thought.* Caroline found the woman's stale odour abhorrent but the art of persuasion called for close proximity. Soon she'd start mirroring Walker's posture, pick up the speech patterns. It was in the journalist's DNA: insinuate, ingratiate, imitate then extricate the truth. *God,* she thought, mentally tossing back a theatrical head, *how I suffer for my art.*

Leaning forward, she rested her elbows on her knees. 'How about I rustle you up a cup of tea? I'm sure I can find my way around the kitchen.'

'No,' she snapped. Behind the smeared lenses her eyes looked huge, unfocused. 'All I want to know before you go is what this man's game is? He's sending you messages, you say?'

'That's right.' Caroline hugged her knees. The Manolos weren't under the coffee table yet. 'He came to my house once, too. I wasn't in but he left a note.' Of sorts.

Walker gasped as her liver-spotted maw grasped Caroline's small delicate hand. 'Surely you have been in touch with the police?'

'You bet I have.' How she didn't flinch, Caroline would never know. 'In fact I met with the senior investigating officer first thing. DI Sarah

254

Quinn?'

Walker frowned, gave an uncertain smile. 'So it'll all be over soon?'

Caroline sighed her regret, gently removed her hand from the woman's clammy grip. 'I'm afraid it's not that simple.' The messages, she said, hadn't been explicit. The cops still had no clue where Caitlin was being held or by whom. 'But they think they know why.' Girding mental loins, she took a deep breath. 'And I do too, Mrs Walker.'

She gazed at her lap. 'You know about my past, don't you? Did he tell you?'

'Not in so many words.' Caroline described the crude painting on her kitchen wall, the instruction about Badger's Copse. When Walker heard about Caitlin's initials, she closed her eyes, murmured what sounded like 'dear God'.

'He's getting back at you through your grand-daughter, isn't he?' The woman held her face in her hands as if it was about to fall apart. Caroline shook her head. 'Well, I'm sorry, Mrs Walker, but I think you've suffered enough. I think he's a cruel, callous coward.' Ingratiate, ingratiate. Christ she sounded like a dyslexic Dalek.

'But what will he do to her? And why contact you and not the police?'

'Assuming he's punishing you because he believes you got off lightly, I shouldn't imagine he holds the law in high regard. Which is a shame because DI Quinn's a good detective. She's given me her blessing to help with the inquiry.' The endorsement could go either way: Walker's past dealings with the cops couldn't have been great. On the other hand, anything that added gravitas and credence to what Caroline now saw as her increasingly less precarious position was worth the risk.

Walker nodded. 'Yes. She's been here.' Of course she had. Quinn hadn't long left the place; her card still lay on the table. Caroline clocked the woman's mouth soften slightly so presumably the Ice Queen couldn't have put her foot in it too much.

'As for why contact me?' She opened her arms. 'I'm a TV reporter, Mrs Walker. The abductor wants publicity, press coverage. But if he thinks he can manipulate me, he's got another think coming. And I'll tell you this for nothing, I won't be writing a single word until Caitlin's safely home where she belongs.' Like it was a big favour.

'Thank you, dear.' She wiped a tear from her eye.

'Tell me about Caitlin, Mrs Walker. Off the record, naturally. I'm very interested. From what I hear she's a lovely girl. And I can see you're terribly close.' She tilted her head at the mantelpiece, gazed admiringly at a pic of the two of them. Softener like that always worked. Walker relaxed slightly, started spouting off about her 'wonderful granddaughter'. Talk about *This Is Your Life*. Caroline stifled a yawn, smiled politely and made the right noises, all the while gauging how best to put her proposal. Asking a child-killer whether you can write her life story didn't happen every day. Last thing she wanted was to blow it.

'I'd like you to tell it, Miss King.'

Had she heard right? 'Come again?'

'I've never really had my say. I'd like my story told. You say the man thinks I got off lightly? I beg to differ. I made a mistake and I've paid for it ever since and now my daughter and granddaughter are paying too.'

As mistakes went, it wasn't exactly down there with spilled milk. Was the woman seeking public sympathy, understanding? Either way, Caroline had well and truly landed on her feet. She struggled not to show her elation. 'I'd be honoured, Mrs Walker. Yours is a unique perspective. I've read contemporary newspaper reports and back then they called you a monster but every story has two sides. Look, I just happen to have a recorder with me.' She reached down for her bag: no time like the present – or past.

'Every story has at least two sides. It's about time people heard the truth.'

Caroline's hand stilled, she raised her gaze, frowning. 'The truth?'

'It wasn't me.' Walker had taken off the glasses, now polished them with a cloth. 'I didn't kill anyone, Miss King.'

Caroline paced up and down outside the bungalow. Where the hell was the fucking cab? Talk about brass monkeys! After the heat in there, she'd catch her death if it didn't show soon. She glanced at her watch, scanned both sides of the street, willed the familiar boxy shape to emerge through the near dark. Shoving both hands in her pockets she continued pacing; it helped alleviate the frustration too.

If she thought she had a cracker of a story before, Walker had handed her an explosive. The child killer who wasn't. A-fucking-mazing.

Potentially.

Neither the goods nor bads had been delivered yet. Until she knew the detail, she'd no way of assessing its worth. Walker could be talking double bollocks with fairy lights but if the tale stood up, it had legs that could run the equator. To what would now be an unsolved child murder add criminal police and judiciary incompetence, wrongful imprisonment, miscarriage of justice – the old girl could even be in line for compensation. And Caroline was hanging round waiting for a bloody taxi. Not through choice.

All polite, Walker had asked her to leave, said she felt sick, needed time to collect her thoughts. Like she hadn't already had fifty-odd years? The reporter curled her lip. She'd tried every trick in her journalist's collected works, but Walker wouldn't/couldn't do it now, told Caroline to come back tomorrow. She'd literally shown her to the door. Short of squatting, Caroline had no option but to walk.

Never mind wild horses, rabid buffalo would not keep her away in the morning. Did buffalo carry rabies? Who cared? She didn't give a monkey's jockstrap as long as the old girl didn't bottle out by then. Besides, the thinking time cut both ways. Caroline still hadn't decided whether – no, when – to share the stop-press news with Quinn. That the cop had to be told was a no-brainer, but if Caroline could put some flesh on what was currently a bare bone, the story would carry more weight.

'Wotcha, babe.' Tap on the shoulder. 'Not from round these parts, are you?'

'Well spotted...' Eyes blazing, she spun round. She was about to add 'pet' when she clocked the youth's heavy-duty acne and his four-legged friend.

'Wanna drop?' He staggered, waved a can of Red Stripe too near her face. Spotso was only an inch or so taller, stick thin and a good bit older than she'd first thought. A year ago she'd prob-ably have told him to go fuck. The aftermath of the attack undoubtedly played a part in her tongue-biting but more than that she counted over his shoulder four, five, no six of his mates enjoying the floor show. They'd clearly been congregating on the waste ground beyond the bungalow. Doubtless gathered to say their prayers. Not.

She stepped back casually, smiled amiably. 'I'm on duty. Otherwise...' Making light of it, but her heart was on double time, its beat audible in her ear. Showing fear was almost the worst thing anyone could do in the circs. Besides, glistening strings of slaver swung from the pit bull's jowls; if it shook its head she'd need a shower, and if it got any closer maybe a tetanus jab. He had it on a tight rein but she could still smell its rancid breath. Hint of something else in the air too. Smoke? Maybe they'd lit a fire to keep warm.

'Oh, yeah?' He hooked a thumb in a belt loop. 'What's your line a work then? Undercover cop?'

'Got it in one.' She gave a brittle laugh, inched back further, calculating if she could get to the pepper spray in her bag before he'd worked out what she was doing.

'Mounted variety?' Sniggering, he nudged a steel-capped toe into Fido's rounded rump. 'Or dog division?' The animal bared its lips, emitted a low growl, so did the guy. His coterie started barking, howling, guffawing. 'Bet it's bitch branch.'

The guy's sharpish comebacks suggested she'd under-estimated him. She needed to get away, but at the same time was nearly paralysed with fear. 'Look mate, what do you want?'

'What do you think, babe?' He made a kissing motion, swung his hips. She'd rather eat shit.

'If it's money you're after...' Head down, she delved into her bag.

Snarling, he kicked the can out of her hand. 'Yeah, definitely bitch branch.'

'Please.' She hated the whimper in her voice. 'Just tell me—'

'Hey, Bounce, how's about a sniff round? Get to know the nice lady a little better?'

The dog strained at the leash, gasping for breath, the guy loosened his hold a touch. *Mother of God.* Bounce wasn't the dog's name. A youth in a hoodie had peeled off from the gang and loped towards them. 'Nice one, bro. Oh yeah. This one's a hottie.' He danced around her, sniffing, pawing. 'Fac' I reckon she's on heat.'

Her legs were about to give way. Would it stop if she screamed?

'Hey, you lot.' Mrs Walker rapped on the window. 'Leave her be. I've called the police.'

'We've bags a time then, ain't we, Granny?' Bounce's quip unleashed another round of guffaws and growls from the gang. From the corner of her eye, Caroline glimpsed four hunched, hooded figures, swaggering ever closer. In the street light, she caught the glint of a blade. Her legs buckled again and she fought not to faint; instinct told her if she hit the ground she wouldn't stand a—

'Fuckin' ell.'

She hit the ground. The bastard had released his grip. The thugs tore off whooping and bark-ing back towards the waste land. Caroline heard the twos before catching sight of the blues. She'd never been so happy to see a cop car even though it barely slowed down. By the time the cab pulled up she was on her feet, brushing God knows what shit from her designer gear. She knew one thing for sure: the driver could whistle for a bloody tip. Remembering Walker's intervention, Caroline turned to wave but the window was closed, curtains drawn.

The cops had got there so quick, Walker must have been calling the yobs' bluff, not triple-nine. Either way, Caroline was grateful. The woman jailed as a child killer had almost certainly saved her life.

THIRTY-EIGHT

'He's not dead, boss.' Head down in a notebook, Harries strolled into Sarah's office, straightening his tie.

Attilla the Hun? Jimmy Savile? 'Come in, do. Who?'

'The builder?' The dig was lost. Dave sank into the chair uninvited as well. 'Ted Crawford. Linda Walker said he hanged himself?'

'In the copse. That's right.' Frowning, she pushed a sheet of A4 to one side. She'd asked Huntie to hold the late brief so she could put down a few thoughts for the up-coming news conference. 'Didn't some prison warder tell her?'

262

'Well they got it wrong.' *Wrong or wilfully misleading?* Dave flashed his notes at her. 'I checked it out. Had a word with his missus. They're living in Worcester. Retired there ten years back. Three kids, all grown-ups now of course.'

She nodded. He'd be getting on a bit these days, early eighties. Even so they'd need to dig a bit deeper. Crawford had been a major player that day. 'We'd best—'

'He'll see us first thing, boss.'

She smiled, should've known Dave would have it sorted. 'And the retired cop?' Another interview she wanted to handle.

'Jenny Purslow. Sat in on the early interviews. She's happy to talk.' For sure they'd not be chatting to the boss man. DCI Ken Southern had gone to the great interview room in the sky twenty-odd years back. Mind he'd been near retirement at the time of the murder. Which reminded her. The chief was still incommunicado. She added a note to an ever-lengthening mental list. Dave handed her Purslow's number on a slip of paper.

The code didn't ring a bell. 'Where is this?'

'Texas. She married an American.' He smiled at the bleeding obvious. 'As opposed to an alien, you understand?'

'I got the drift, Dave.' She tapped a pen against her teeth. 'Bloody cruel, wasn't it?'

'Making her live in the States?' The gag was limp as well as tortuous. He apologized, excused it on the grounds he was in a good mood. He'd got two tickets for a gig, a Birmingham bluegrass band. Sarah reckoned Birmingham bluegrass sounded like an oxymoron but she'd agreed to give it a whirl. 'I know what you mean though, boss. Telling Walker the builder had topped himself was a pretty shit thing to do.'

'Precisely. Whoever told her couldn't have got it that wrong. Presumably they just wanted to pile on the guilt? How is Crawford?'

'He was out playing golf but from what the wife said, he sounds pretty compos mentis to me, boss.'

'Good. Shame the same can't be said for Luke Holden.' Holden's condition remained critical. Shona Bruce was keeping tabs with the hospital. She'd told Sarah she hoped to be on hand for the interview when Holden came round. Could hardly say no. It'd be in no small way down to Brucie *if* he came round.

'Have you seen this, Dave?' Sarah held up the forensics report. One of the guys had left it on her desk. Top line? No evidence pointed to the presence of a third party at Holden's passing-out parade. Given the bed-sit could have doubled as a pharmacy it was beginning to look likelier that the overdose was deliberate and self-administered. So what had driven Holden to try and take his own life? And did Caitlin Reynolds' abduction figure in his reasoning?

'I saw the quantities,' Dave said. 'Reckon he was supplying the stuff?'

'Have a word with Mel in narcotics.' Sarah slipped into her jacket. 'See if Holden's on their radar.' Drug deals bombed, suppliers made enemies, coincidences happened. Maybe there was no Reynolds' link.

'Before you go, boss' He slid a print-out across the desk. 'At least we know the sister's not done a Crawford.'

Frowning, she reached for the sheet of paper. 'Sister?'

'Grace Bolton? Pauline's older sister? She's definitely pushing up the daisies.' The article was from the *Leicester Mercury* dated July 1994. There were only a few paragraphs and no mention of a babe-in-the-wood family connection. Forty-nine-year-old Grace Bolton had died from an overdose of anti-depressants and sleeping pills. Her teenage son had found her dead when he came home from school. An open verdict had been recorded.

'So the coroner couldn't have had enough proof she did it on purpose.' She handed it back to Harries.

'Either way she wasn't a happy bunny, boss.'

'I wonder why neither of the twins mentioned it?' Pauline's younger siblings lived in Cornwall. Both women had been traced and eliminated.

Dave turned his mouth down. 'Maybe didn't think it worth it. Or maybe the memory's still too painful.'

The ripple effect, Sarah always thought of it.

One death, God knew how many people dam-aged in its wake. 'We need to track down the son, Dave. He'd be, what, thirty-five now?'

'Jack Bolton. The lad was taken into care. Seems to have slipped the net, but I'm on it, boss.'

Course he was. He'd walk the sergeant's exam. 'Thanks, Dave.' She drained her glass of water, picked up the notes.

'Good luck.' He held the door for her. 'I won't say break a leg.'

'You just did, dahling.' She smiled, ready for her close-up.

It hadn't been so much a bank of cameras, more a small ridge. Sarah – not a natural performer – hadn't been disheartened. Radio and newspaper reporters had put in an appearance and she knew the press office was following up with regular posts on the police Facebook and Twitter pages. The abductor only had to see or hear her appeal once. It had been tailored in line with the pro-filer's insight. Not dissimilar to hers and the squad's. For 'intelligent, arrogant, manipula-tive', read 'smart-arsed control-freak cock'.

She checked the mirror, pulled out of Tesco's car park. Her lip curved as she cast her mind back. Who says the camera never lies? Bullshit. She'd been tighter with the truth than Pinoc-chio's aunt. She'd implied throughout that the guy could walk free if Caitlin was released un-harmed within twenty-four hours. *For whatever reason you're holding her* had been the key line. Sarah had shared the profiler's conviction. It was vital the abductor believed he was streets ahead of the inquiry and that the cops were still stumbling in the dark over motive.

She glanced at the dash. The clock showed 18:04. Flicking on the radio, she thought she might just catch the appeal on WM. Nah. They were on the weather already: cold, wet, same old. Just as well, she hated hearing her own voice. Besides, she knew every word. She'd wound up the piece to camera by urging the abductor to ring a special number, assured him she'd take the call personally. *Bring it on, sunshine.*

Even if he didn't take the bait of the police hotline, she hoped the plea would prompt him into contacting Nicola again. The more he gave away, the more they'd have to go on. Right now, it seemed that particular cupboard, if not bare, was running low.

Unlike the Audi's boot. She allowed herself another smile. It had enough food and drink in it to keep a small army going. Not to mention a DC with hollow legs. She'd promised Dave – God help him – to rustle up a bite for them after the gig on Thursday. First, though the lucky man didn't know it, she had another date.

'I hate flowers, fruit makes me fart and I'm on the wagon. What the bloody hell do you want?'

'You sure know how to talk to a girl, chief.'

Sarah's wry smile masked deep shock, and she could only see Baker's face.

'Quinn, if I ever called you a girl, I'd be waving bye-bye to my boll—'

'Yeah, yeah, yeah.' She flapped a hand. Chianti, daffs and a bunch of grapes were tucked under the other arm. 'Do I get to come in then or what?'

'Another day, eh?' He scratched his head. 'Place is a right mess.' And its owner. God knew when his jowls had last seen a razor; same went for the hair and a comb. At least food stains down rumpled pyjamas showed he was still eating. Tomato ketchup at least.

'Give you a hand then, can't I?' She held an arm out.

'Naff off, Quinn. I'm not a sodding invalid.'

'I meant with the hoover.' Her smile wasn't returned. He was clearly weighing it up and the decision could go either way.

'Come on, before I change my mind.' Opening the door, he stepped back. 'First right.'

The sitting room was neat, near immaculate: clean lines, classy furniture, duck-egg blue and ivory décor. His wife must've had good taste. Sarah couldn't imagine Baker leafing through colour charts and comparing swatches. She'd half expected to see a buffalo head mounted on a wall and a display of his favourite whips – horse whips. Mind if she'd not seen it with her own eyes, she'd not have been able to picture Baker looking so knackered, so ... pinched.

'Take a pew then.' He grabbed a dressing gown. Paisley. 'Can I offer you a drink?'

'You're all right, chief. I'll not stop long.'

'Thank God for small mercies.' Baker hadn't lost his bark – she wasn't sure about the bite, sensed he might be going through the motions for her benefit.

Two cream sofas faced each other across an expanse of taupe carpet, a glass coffee table divide held a huge bowl of fruit and a half-empty bottle of single malt. The place only needed a vase of roses and he'd have spun three lies on the doorstep. Sarah placed the goodies on the table then plumped for a low stool not far from the sofa where he'd clearly been sitting and, given the dregs in a glass on the floor, falling spectacularly off the wagon. She waited and watched while he lowered himself into a nest of cushions.

'Thought you were off the booze.'

'I only said it to get rid of you.' He folded his arms. 'Never could take a hint, could you, Quinn?'

'Mincing your words? Not like you, chief.'

'Would straight talking have made a difference?'

'No.' Her glance fell on a framed photograph, a young Baker in uniform, holding up some sort of gong. He was probably in his early twenties and though she'd die rather than tell him so, he looked seriously tasty. 'What did you do to get that, chief?'

'Rescued a mouse up a tree.'

'Yeah right.' She strolled over, took a closer look.

'Nosy sod, aren't you?'

'Some mouse.' Press cutting on the back read he'd saved two kids in a house fire. Entered the place twice before fire crews arrived.

'Ancient history, Quinn. Look, can you get on with it?'

She replaced the picture, retook her perch. 'You're ill, you live on your own, you're not taking any calls, not responding to texts.' That he'd not called in to keep up with the Reynolds' case spoke volumes. 'I'm allowed to show a bit of concern, aren't I?'

'I need a few days off, is all.' Gingerly he reached for his drink. 'You don't need me, any road.' He tilted his head at the TV. 'You pitched it good, Quinn, hit the right note. Let's hope the bastard responds.'

Three compliments in a row? He was definitely off colour, or changing tack. 'Nice try, chief. I'm still worried. Frankly you've looked better.'

'Tell it like it is, Quinn.' Swirling the glass meant he didn't have to make eye contact.

'OK, you look shite.'

He shrugged, carried on swirling.

She leaned forward on the stool. 'So have you seen the doc?'

Again, she watched him decide whether to say anything. 'Consultant. Couple weeks back.'

Consultant. Right. 'And?' A clock ticked in another silence that stretched.

'Should've seen him earlier.'

Sarah swallowed though her mouth was dry; she stilled his hand with her own. 'Talk to me, chief.'

Baker held her gaze for several seconds. 'I've only known for sure a few days. I needed a while to get my head round it. It's cancer, Sarah. They're not sure they've caught it in time.'

For a split second she waited for the punchline then felt the colour drain from her face. She watched a tear leak from the corner of his eye. That and the fear still there moved her almost as much as what he'd said. 'But...' She stopped herself: stupid bloody thing to say.

'Never had a day's sickness in my life.' He'd ignored symptoms, dismissed his wife's nagging. By the time the diagnosis came the prostate cancer was in an advanced stage. There would be surgery, radiotherapy. 'They'll do what they can, Sarah. But by God it's hit hard.'

She could hardly begin to imagine. 'Fred, I don't know what to say.'

'Nothing to say, lass.' He dashed away the tear with the back of his hand. 'I was going to keep it to myself for a while. The funeral must've brought it home. Reality hadn't sunk in 'til then. All them bloody lilies and Sinatra warbling on about his way. And the ... the...'

Sarah closed her eyes briefly, saw her parents' coffins, open graves. 'I know.'

'I was gonna retire and ... grow veg. Now I might not even see sixty.' She put down his glass, took his hands in hers.

'If there's anything I can do, Fred. All you need do is ask.'

'You're a good kid, Quinn.' He gave a thin smile. 'Fact is – it's in the lap of the gods. And you know what? I'm scared shitless.'

Sarah, who didn't do touch-feely, didn't even think about it. She knelt, held him in her arms and gently stroked his hair. 'I'm here for you, chief. Whatever you need.' That was when the strongest, most macho man she'd ever known broke down and wept. She doubted he'd shown an iota of vulnerability in front of anyone since he was a kid. In a weird way, Sarah felt almost privileged. The episode didn't last long, no more than a couple of minutes before he straightened. Resting on her haunches, she watched him dry his eyes. 'Trust me, chief.' She held his gaze. 'I won't tell a soul what I've just seen.'

'Too right, Quinn.' He winked. 'Or I'd have to kill you.'

THIRTY-NINE

Linda Walker lay in bed praying for the comfort of sleep. Having finally decided to speak out, she'd imagined rest would come more easily. Laying ghosts was one thing, she supposed, exorcizing thoughts another. Now and then her unfocused gaze trailed car headlights as they chased shadows across the low ceiling. She heard the occasional blast from a horn, distant sirens, the plaintive bark of a dog. She ached for morning to come. She had the story worked out now, wanted to be word perfect for the reporter. She'd felt no guilt about turfing the woman out. Mind, if the police car hadn't turned up, she would have called 999. Those bloody yobbos made people's lives a misery, got away with murder some of 'em.

Sighing, she turned on her side, pulled the duvet over her ears. A neighbour had dropped by earlier to tell her he'd found her cat dead in the next road, looked as if a car had hit it. He offered to bury the body to save her the grief. She'd shed a tear, shed another now, but on reflection thought it for the best. Ginger dying was one thing less to worry about. The more she thought, the more it made sense: she had to be the abductor's real target, which meant Caitlin's abduction was almost certainly a smokescreen. Mrs Walker felt her fate was probably sealed but the story she'd give to the reporter would probably tip the balance in favour of her granddaughter's release. It wasn't the worst thought to drift off to sleep with.

She woke disorientated – two minutes, two hours later? – convinced she was still dreaming. It had been so vivid, even now it prompted a fond smile. Village bonfire night. Pauline and her so happy, so excited, whizzing sparklers round, standing so close the heat almost burned their cheeks. Screaming as the blazing Guy flopped and disappeared into the licking flames. Squealing as a shower of sparks lit the sky.

But she still heard noises.

Frowning, she propped herself up on an elbow. She smelled smoke, petrol; heard breaking glass, gloating chants; saw hooded figures, flashing lights.

Burn witch burn. Burn witch burn.

Smoke caught in her throat, nostrils, stung her eyes. Red glowed in the gap round the door, a brick shattered the window, shards of glass landed on the bed. She screamed in fear, frustration.

Burn witch burn. Burn witch burn.

She had no means of escape, no wish to survive. She lay back on the pillow, crossed her arms, prayed for death.

FORTY

'You can't blame yourself, boss.' Dave took the seat next to Sarah, handed over a coffee from a machine at the end of a seemingly endless white corridor.

'I can do what I bloody well like, Harries,' she snapped, placed the cup on the floor at her feet. Slouched opposite, two surly youths broke off fiddling with their phones and glanced up at the exchange, probably thought they had ring-side seats. One had a Pudsey-style bandage round an eye; the other looked like he'd need a nose job any time soon. They were a pair of A&E's walking wounded as opposed to Linda Walker who, according to one of the medics, could be on her way out. Permanently.

Sarah shuffled off her coat, wished to God they didn't keep these places so bloody hot. She'd picked up the gist in a call from an inspector at the crime scene. Just after two a.m. a guy driving past had smelled smoke, heard breaking glass, called 999. Fire crews and uniform were on site within six minutes. That and the guy's heroics were the only reason Walker hadn't perished in the blaze. According to a nosy – or insomniac – neighbour the good Samaritan had literally driven away half a dozen hooded figures by mounting the pavement and motoring on round the side of the property. Shame he hadn't careered into one of the bastards. Even greater shame he'd not given the emergency operator a name and address.

Dave sat forward, laced his fingers between his knees. 'Beat yourself up if it makes you feel any better, but if you ask me—'

'I'm not.' She blew on the coffee. She'd failed to protect a vulnerable woman known – OK, strongly suspected – to be at risk from a retaliatory attack. That was the way Sarah saw it. Serve and protect? Fuck-up and fail, more like.

'You were going to ask patrol to keep an eye on the place.' *Until Nicola Reynolds said she'd have her mother to stay. And where exactly was the loving daughter?* Sarah shook her head. Nice try, but it smacked of buck passing. Sarah hadn't established when Walker would move out, and even if she had mentioned it to uniform, an eye on the place wouldn't have been enough. The situation had called for round-the-clock surveillance.

'Shut it, will you, Dave? I'm not interested.' Lack of sleep didn't help either. She'd not left Baker 'til gone midnight then spent hours tossing and turning in bed until control's call-out had woken her at half-five. Having asked Dave to meet her at the QE, she was beginning to wish she'd let him have a lie-in. 'You got anything for a headache?'

'Parrots do you?' He pulled paracetamol out of a pocket. She held a palm open. He dropped two tablets in, counted the nods, added another couple. 'I've got a pair of glasses as well if you want, boss.'

'Sorry?' Hand halfway to mouth.

'Give you perfect hindsight.'

She gave a token half smile before dry swallowing the tablets. Dave was a decent guy, but it would take more than a one-liner or five to gee her up. On top of everything else, she couldn't stop thinking about the chief, ached to tell Dave what was going on. In characteristically bullish fashion, Baker had sworn her to secrecy. He'd announce it his way, he said, like Old Blue Eyes. He'd winked at that, told her if anyone chose Sinatra at the funeral he'd come back and haunt the buggers. Brave-faced bravado. Again, she thought he'd put it on for her benefit. For his, she'd agreed to keep him briefed via daily phone calls.

'Anyway, boss, the fire might be unrelated.' Dave had dropped his voice but not the subject. 'Who's to say—?'

'Get real, man.' If she believed that, she might as well believe unicorns went in for deep-sea diving.

'Fucking give her one if I were you, mate.' Nose job getting in on the act.

She shot to her feet. 'You offensive little shit.'

'Let it go, Sar—'

'And tuck your sodding legs in, do us all a favour.' She cut the pair of them a final glare before retaking her seat.

Her heart rate was up, she leaned her head back against the wall, took a few deep breaths. The smell of toast cut through the scent of latex and antiseptic. She sighed. 'Why do you think they had the paint then, Dave? Reckon they were going to do the place up for her?' She caught the minuscule flex of his jaw. It said, 'enough already'.

'Beneath you that is, boss.' He took a swig of coffee. 'Leave the sarky digs to Baker. Past master he is.'

'Don't bring him into this, Harries.' She turned her head and muttered something about not being so bloody naïve. Aerosol paint cans, red, had been found scattered at the scene. The arsonists had only got round to spraying one letter: A or K apparently. Her money was on the K. As in killer. How they knew about Walker's past, she'd still to establish. Yet again, she checked her mobile for messages from the squad room. They'd let her know the minute last night's appeal had any effect. Zilch.

Sighing, she glanced at her watch: 7.15. A word with Walker could go a long way but they were waiting on a senior medic's say-so. If it was out of the question, Sarah was keen to get off, wanted a look at the crime scene before heading out to Worcester. 'Where's the doc got to? He said a few minutes max.'

Swing doors flew open. Four heads swivelled in unison. A white-faced Nicola Reynolds ran down the corridor. She stood in front of the detectives, struggling to catch her breath. 'Is she dead?'

Sarah shook her head, wondered why the woman had taken her time getting here.

'Will she make it?'

'I think you need to speak to the doctor, Mrs Reynolds. I'm told she has a fighting chance.'

'Dear God.' She sank down on the chair next to Sarah. 'In that case, it's you I need speak to.'

Caroline had it all worked out. She'd whisk Walker away in the motor. Take her to a decent hotel for a night, maybe two. No expense – well, not much – spared. With a bit of luck she'd swing it on expenses anyway. Every news desk in the UK and beyond would want a slice of the story. And that was before the book. She needed to make sure she had enough goodies to go round. Ergo: there was no point rushing the interview. It merited several sessions and it would take a while to get Walker chilled, confident, confiding.

Caroline admired her perfectly painted pout in the driving mirror. *Just call me Mother Confessor.* The pout took a sudden dive: the BMW had better be safe outside Walker's poxy bungalow. She tightened her grip on the wheel then eased off. How long could it take to pack an overnight bag? She'd just have to keep an eye out, call the cops at the first sign of trouble.

She'd certainly be relying on her own wheels from now on. Last night's drama had left her seriously spooked; she didn't fancy another episode. It'd be worth it though once she had Walker's life on tape. Then she'd share with Quinn: the look on the Ice Queen's face would be priceless. Worth a picture at least.

Smiling, Caroline tugged down the visor, reached for her shades. Even the sun had come out to play. All she needed was a decent sound-track. She hit shuffle, laughed out loud at the unintentional irony. 'Sympathy for the Devil' featured in *Interview with a Vampire*. She tap-ped along in time on the wheel, couldn't quite picture Walker in the Tom Cruise role. Mind she couldn't see herself as a blood-sucking hack either, though one or two names hurled her way in the past had only been a few letters out.

She dropped the smile, sharpened up. Play this right and it was a story that would make her name. OK, she enjoyed a bit of fame with TV news, but Caroline still harboured ambition. With even more industry clout plus a potential best-seller, her career would be on the up. Why not peak-time presenter, current affairs anchor, chat show host? Eat your heart out Pax—

What the hell? Her face froze; time seemed to slow if not stand still. Police cars, white transits, crime tape, a burly uniform pacing the pave-ment. Outside Walker's. Caroline pulled the Beemer over, grabbed her bag. She had to resist the urge to run, approached slowly, taking in the scene en route. The acrid smell of smoke gave the first clue, the tell-tale blackening of bricks round what was left of the blistered door and window frames the next; the water lying round in filthy oily puddles clinched it. Not a fire engine in sight so presumably the blaze started in the early hours, even the damping down had been done and dusted. *A spark from Walker's fire?* Yeah right. That's why forensics were out in force, there were so many bunny suits in there it looked like *Watership Down.*

'What happened, officer?' She might as well ask, because the guy wasn't going to let her get any nearer.

'What's it to you?' PC Jobsworth. She'd met the kind before: if she told him who she was he wouldn't give her a used teabag let alone the time of day.

'I had an appointment with the woman who lives there.' She flashed a one-size-fits-all card, nodded at the bungalow. 'Social services.'

'Bit late for that.' He wiped a hankie round his bull neck. 'Funeral services maybe.'

Her heart sank. 'Christ, she's not dead is she?' He turned his mouth down, waggled a hand. *Callous sod.* 'I've a good mind to report you for that.'

'Let me know. I'll buy the paper.' Clearly, she'd not flashed the card fast enough and/or he'd recognized her. 'Don't try it on with me, love,' he said.

Fair dos. It had been a stupid move to make. 'I'm sorry.' She raised a placatory hand. 'I just can't take it in. When I left here yesterday...' She narrowed her eyes. Walker had told half a dozen yobs she'd dobbed them in to the cops. *Coincidence?*

'What?' he asked.

She shook her head. Monkey. Organ grinder. 'Does DI Quinn know about this?'

The grimace was gormless. 'Who?'

'Yes, she does.' Caroline turned to see a forensics officer, tall, probably trim under the suit and – now he'd removed the headgear – definitely blond. 'Caroline King, isn't it?' Easy authority, natural confidence, she'd bet he was top bunny. 'Ben Cooper, crime scene manager.'

'I've seen you around.' She smiled, shook the proffered hand. 'Good to meet though.' *Exceptionally so.*

'I've just been on the phone with the inspector.' He smoothed a hand over mussed hair.

Lucky inspector. 'And?'

'As I say, she knows about the fire.'

Big help. Not. 'It's arson, isn't it?'

'You sound pretty sure on that score.' He nodded towards one of the transits. 'I need to grab a case.' As they walked in step he asked, 'Do you know something I don't, Miss King?'

Plenty. 'I had a meeting scheduled this morning with the woman who lives here.'

'Go on.'

'She has a story to tell and I'm thinking...' *But*

how did that figure with the gang of youths?

'That someone doesn't want it coming out?' Cooper voiced the rest of her thought. Not just a pretty face then.

'It's possible, isn't it?'

'I'd like to help but I think you need to speak with Sar— DI Quinn.'

So did Caroline. Pronto. And not on the end of a line. 'Is the inspector still at the hospital?'

'Far as I know.'

She tapped a temple. 'Catch you later.'

It hadn't been a total punt. Not if Walker was still alive.

FORTY-ONE

'You have to convince him it's true.' Nicola Reynolds fixed her gaze on Sarah, hands clasped in what could have been a prayer. 'I'll get down on my hands and knees if it helps.'

'What would have helped is you being straight with us from the word go, Mrs Reynolds.' They sat in a small room, the sort of impersonal space where doctors break bad news, cushioned armchairs round a low wooden table, anodyne prints on magnolia walls, a cheese plant that needed a dust. 'Now you're asking me to lie as well.'

She shook her head. 'If he believes my

mother's dead, he'll let Caitlin go.' Reynolds made to touch Sarah's arm. 'Why can't you see it?'

The DI saw a woman in danger of losing it, a woman who'd consistently misled the inquiry, a woman whose failure to tell the truth – forced or not – had led to the arson attack at Linda Walker's home, a woman who'd been told by the abductor he wanted to spit on her mother's grave. 'But she's not dead, is she?'

Reynolds turned away, murmured something that sounded like 'she is to me'. Sarah and Harries exchanged glances. If she'd read his right it said, 'charge her now'. Reynolds took a few deep breaths, tried composing herself, came back with the same tune as if there had been no break. 'I don't understand why you won't do it. He's not to know she's alive.'

Reynolds wanted Sarah to issue a news release reporting a woman's death in a house fire. It would name the victim as Linda Walker, give age, address and contain an appeal for witnesses. And, hey presto, according to Reynolds, Caitlin would walk free.

'It's not that simple,' Sarah said. She'd no intention of letting the perp get away with it. Her brief was to put the bad guys away, not give them a get-out-of-jail-free card.

Reynolds tightened her mouth. 'If your daughter's life depends on it, anything's simple, inspector.'

Anything? Hasten your own mother's death?

284

The chances of the arson being a random attack were so infinitesimal that Sarah wouldn't even give the thought house room. What she had to establish was if Reynolds was in any way implicated.

'Please, inspector, if you back me up on this, I'll do whatever you want.'

'The fire was started deliberately.' Sarah stared at Reynolds. 'What I *want* is you to tell me what you know.' *Because without that – no chance, don't even think about a deal.*

'Honest to God, I...' Maybe she was sick of lying; maybe she'd heard the tacit corollary; maybe she really would do anything to help Caitlin. Sarah struggled not to wince as she watched Reynolds rake her hair with her fingers. 'OK, inspector. I'll tell you everything.'

'How could she do it, boss?'

Nicola Reynolds had put the word out round the Monkshead estate. No names, no pack drill, just 'the woman at number 22 is a child killer'. Pass it on. Rough justice. Lynch-mob mentality. Faceless vigilantes. The estate had no end of likely suspects but they'd close ranks, plead ignorance, and if the squad couldn't gather the evidence, they'd get away with attempted murder as well as arson. If she wasn't a cop, Sarah could almost admire the woman's duplicity.

'You heard her, Dave. When she said anything...' Sarah pointed the fob at the Audi. 'Is your motor here?' She wanted them travelling together.

'It'll be OK.' Harries nodded at the police business notice in the MG's window. 'Y'know you're wrong, boss,' he said, fastening the seat belt. 'It wasn't absolutely anything. Reynolds drew the line at murder.'

'Only by her own fair hand, Dave.' Reynolds had learned from a puppet master: the abductor had ordered her to do his dirty work, and she'd passed on the assignment. 'I can't see the courts making any distinction.'

Incitement was just one of the charges Reynolds would face, in addition to obstruction, perverting the course of justice, withholding evidence, plus a few more. But 'would' was the operative word. She was at liberty but under police guard for a while. The DI had decided to issue a bogus news release announcing Walker's death. Last night's appeal had signally failed to flush out the bastard. Maybe Walker's obituary notice would do the trick. Meantime, Beth Lally and Jed Holmes were sticking to Reynolds like super-glued honey. There'd be no more secret sweet talking with the abductor.

'Actually, boss, when I say how could she do it...?'

She picked up a telling inflection, cut him a glance. 'You're thinking she had help?'

He shrugged. Said he couldn't see Reynolds bonding with the Monkshead lowlife somehow. 'You need to know how to approach people like that, how to connect.'

She nodded, pensive. 'The descriptions she came up with were crap too.' Totally worthless in terms of identifying anyone. Because she couldn't? 'Let's hang fire an hour or two with the news release. Apply a bit more pressure on her.' Switching on the engine, she told him to give the press office a bell then have a word with Beth. Reynolds needed to be pushed on the accomplice angle. 'Good thinking, Dave.' Her smile faded as a BMW with its lights flashing headed down the parking bays, blocked the Audi's exit. She caught a glimpse of the driver. 'Tell me it isn't, Dave.'

'It isn't Brad Pitt, boss, but...'

It was Caroline King. Sarah lowered the window. 'I could probably do you for speeding.'

'Please, Sarah, no dicking round. Is Linda Walker dead?'

There was something in King's voice, the look in her eye that made Sarah ditch the obvious comeback. 'No. Why?'

'Because I don't think she killed anyone.'

FORTY-TWO

'This is on condition you keep it buttoned. Clear?' Sarah glanced in the mirror at the back-seat passenger.

'Yes, ma'am.' Caroline gave a mock salute.

'I'm serious. One word out of place and that's it.' Letting King hop in had seemed like a plan back at the hospital. The DI and Harries had already been pushing it to get to Worcester for nine-thirty. The reporter appeared to be sitting on a story that for once Sarah thought worth hearing. They'd discussed Walker's shock retraction en route but with only the one line to go on – apart from speculating – they couldn't really take it any further. That wasn't the case with the yobs that had milled round outside Walker's home. Caroline had half-decent descriptions and Harries had phoned in the details. By now they would have been circulated to door-to-door teams and patrol cars on the estate. Rightly or wrongly, Sarah had reluctantly yielded to King's request: the reporter was being allowed to keep a watching brief on the Crawford interview.

'Nice pad.' King gazed up at a pristine terrace

288

in a Worcester side street a stone's throw from the cathedral. The black door looked as if it had just had a paint job; the brass lion knocker glinted as Harries did the needful.

'Remember what I said,' Sarah warned. The reporter pulled an imaginary zip across her lips.

For a man in his eighties, Ted Crawford wasn't in bad shape. Around six-two and with a rangy frame, his slight stoop could be habitual rather than down to age. He ran a spade-like hand through a shock of white hair. 'Police? The wife said. Come in, come in. She's out shopping as per.' He led them down a narrow hall to a sun room at the back of the house, lots of wicker furniture, padded floral cushions, plants on every surface. A pair of wire-framed glasses lay on an opened newspaper. 'Doreen left a pot of coffee.' Crawford pointed to a tray on a table with three cups and saucers. 'I'll go and grab anoth—'

'Not for me, Mr Crawford,' Caroline said. 'I've already drunk my own weight in the stuff. In fact...'

He smiled. 'Upstairs, last door on the right.'

Once she'd got the intros over, Sarah elaborated on why they were there. That a Birmingham teenager's abduction could be linked to the babe-in-the-wood murder. A woman in Small Heath had been outed as Pauline Bolton's killer and arsonists had fire-bombed the house. Watching Crawford carefully, she let the silence ride for a while. He flexed his jaw a couple of times before wiping his eyes with a hankie. Sarah thought the moistness was down to age rather than emotion.

'Well, inspector, if anyone should bear a grudge, then I guess you've come to the right place.' She was intrigued it was the first thought in his head, or at least the first he voiced. Her raised eyebrow asked for more. He blew ripples on the surface of his drink, all the while holding Sarah's gaze. When King re-entered, no one reacted. Muttering an apology, she took the seat next to Harries.

'However,' he said, 'I can assure you the fire's nothing to do with me. If you really want to know, even back then I felt sort of sorry for Susan Bailey. It was clear from the start that she'd killed little Pauline. Like a cornered rat, she was desperate for a way out and thought I'd do.' He gave a hollow laugh. 'I can see you're having difficulty with that, inspector. But trust me, I was there.'

Unsmiling, Sarah nodded. 'Tell me about it.'

He placed the cup on the tray. Apart from adding colour and a sense of place and the blazing summer heat, his account didn't differ with anything she'd read. God knew what she'd hoped for. A mad axe murderer hiding up a tree wearing a name badge?

'Was there never any suggestion that someone else could have carried out the killing?'

'Apart from me?' He stroked finger and thumb down his chin. 'Not as far as I know.'

290

She asked about other people around at the time, whether he thought any of them could be seeking revenge after all these years. Chin cupped in hand, Crawford shook his head. 'What I do know, inspector, is that Pauline's murder damn nearly killed her parents. They had to keep going, of course, because of the other kids, but...' His spread palms invited her to fill in the blanks.

Sarah nodded. 'We've spoken to the surviving siblings.' And eliminated them from the inquiry. 'The eldest daughter, Grace, died twenty years ago.'

'How?'

'The inquest recorded an open verdict.'

'Top herself, did she?' He didn't wait for an answer she wouldn't give anyway. 'Poor kid went off the rails after the murder. I always reckoned she blamed herself, being the big sister and that. Grace doted on Pauline.'

'Define "off the rails".'

'Drinking, smoking, hanging round with lads. Left home at sixteen. Last I heard she'd got herself pregnant.'

'You seem very well-informed, Mr Crawford.'

'Village life, inspector. People knew their neighbours in them days. Not like now when—'

'You lived there?' She was surprised, assumed the workforce travelled to the site each day. The question also stemmed a lecture she could do without.

'Eventually. I moved in to one of the new houses.' He gave a lop-sided smile. 'Least I knew it was well built.'

In Crawford's shoes – given the proximity of the girls' families – it would have been the last place Sarah would choose. 'That couldn't have been easy?'

'Didn't worry me. The Baileys did a moonlight flit before the case even got to trial. I think the Boltons saw me as a victim too.' He eased a finger round his collar. Sarah doubted the gesture was unwitting.

'OK, I think that's it for now, Mr Crawford. If you could just give us your sons' details we'll leave you in peace.' He baulked at first, eventually gave Dave the names then slipped the glasses on to read their numbers off his phone. Two lived in the States, a third in Manchester. As Sarah gathered her bits, Crawford half rose in his chair.

'Why did you feel sorry for Susan?' Caroline had other ideas. The question prompted a puzzled frown from Crawford. Sarah's was more pissed off than nonplussed. 'You were saying when I came in?' Caroline helped out.

He opened his mouth twice before words emerged. 'Do you know the expression spare the rod, spoil the child?' She nodded. 'Well, the Baileys never spared it. Or the belt, or the fist. Great role models, eh? With parents like that, it's no surprise she lashed out at someone smaller.'

'That's not how she remembers it,' Caroline said. 'And besides—'

'Thanks for your time.' Sarah handed him a card.

'I'll see you out, inspector.' As they walked down the hall he asked about the fire, whether Walker had died.

'The place was a death trap, Mr Crawford.' She might as well get used to bending the truth: once the news release was issued there'd be no turning back.

'What part of "button it" don't you understand, Caroline?'

Caroline shrugged as she slipped into the back seat. 'Condescending git.'

Sarah's hand stilled on the way to the ignition. 'What did you say?'

'Crawford, not you.'

'For what it's worth,' Harries said. 'I thought he was full of shit too.'

'That's another thing.' Sarah glanced in the mirror. 'What took you so long?'

King held up her phone. 'I took a call.'

'All that "right from the word go" stuff.' Harries hadn't finished. 'I thought he was a builder not a bloody trick cyclist.'

'Aren't you going to ask who from?' King again, another flash of the phone. Her straight face and pointed delivery were answer enough. 'He wants an end to it. He's set a deadline – twelve hours.'

FORTY-THREE

Short and not sweet. The abductor's call had been so brief King hadn't had time even to think about recording his voice. Half an hour later, Nicola Reynolds received the same warning in a text. Both were enough for Sarah to green light the release. Success wasn't guaranteed but what else had they got? The lie surfaced first on the police Twitter account. *Small Heath fire death, woman named as Linda Walker, 64.* Facebook's slightly longer version was posted a minute later. Local radio was broadcasting the fairy story on the hour and half-hour. First paper to carry it was the *Birmingham News*. Sarah held the lunch edition in her hands.

FIRE DEATH

A woman's died in an arson attack at her home on the Monkshead estate in Small Heath, Birmingham. The victim's been named as 64-year-old Linda Walker. Mrs Walker suffered extensive burns and was dead on arrival at hospital. The fire broke out in the early hours of this morning. West Midlands police are appealing for witnesses.

Short and not sweet times two. In fact it sucked. Shaking her head, the DI tossed the paper in the bin next to Harries' desk. It had been a tough call. Sarah Quinn had never deliberately crossed the line ferrying a bent rule book. Releasing false information went against everything she believed in. Having made the decision, she'd kept very few people in the loop: hospital authorities, a handful of squad members, news chiefs. She'd discussed ethics with only one detective.

'Come on, boss. Baker would've done it without a second thought.' Though the squad room was fairly quiet, Harries kept his voice down. He'd intuited her thinking or read her face because Dave wasn't the officer she'd discussed it with. And he was dead right about the chief. Sarah heard his voice again: *What you waiting for, Quinn? It's a no-brainer.* She'd put in a quick call to see how he was doing as much as anything. She'd already known what his take would be. Had she also expected his typically brash offer? *If it goes tits-up, I'll carry the can. It's not like I'm going to miss out on my pension is it, lass?*

And if she let him, wouldn't that push her so far over the line there'd be no way back?

'Boss. I said—'

'I heard what you said, Dave. Just get on with it, eh?' He was still trying to track down Jack Bolton. Grace's son hadn't just slipped the net.

After absconding from the care home, he appeared to have gone off the radar. Not even the twins – his aunts – had been able to shed any light. Sarah wandered over to the water cooler, nodded at Hunt who was talking on the phone. He and Twig were on standby taking calls. Beth Lally and Holmes were still at the Reynolds' place. Nicola had named Neil Lomas as her muck-spreading go-between on the estate. She'd been warned the release wouldn't be issued if she didn't give up a name. The abductor's deadline had proved a more powerful spur than Sarah's threats. Lomas would soon be helping with inquiries. The hero driver who'd raised the alarm was proving elusive too. She hoped he'd respond to the witness appeal – that was genuine if nothing else.

Sighing, she crushed the paper cup in her hand, jettisoned it in another bin. She wondered too about King's current whereabouts. Last seen, the reporter had been getting into her car at the hospital. Didn't mean she'd driven away though. Sarah knew King wanted the interview with Linda Walker more than she'd ever wanted anything in her career. Knew too there wasn't much to which King wouldn't stoop. Sarah gave a crooked smile. The reporter used to keep a white coat and stethoscope in the BMW, just in case. It wouldn't work this time; the medics had been tipped off.

Restless, she strolled over to the window. With most of the squad out working the estate, she reckoned all the inquiry irons were in the fire. Whoops. What an analogy. Either way, right now it was a waiting game. The wall clock read 13:00. Given the deadline expired in around nine hours, they didn't have long to play. Pressing her forehead against the glass, she murmured, 'Make a move, you bastard.'

'Come on, boss.' Dave must have heard. 'You said it yourself; he's only got to see it once.'

'Victim?' Monkey man thrust a newspaper in Caitlin's face. She felt his spittle land on her cheek. 'Victim? That is so fucking rich.'

She grabbed the local rag out of his hands, scanned the front page with narrowed eyes. She hadn't a clue what his problem was but boy was he in a strop. 'I can't—'

His jabbing finger pointed out the item, an affected newsreader voice provided backup. 'The victim's been named as Linda Walker. Bitch is no more vic—'

Gran's dead? Caitlin frowned as she read the few short lines. Arson attack? Extensive burns? Poor bloody woman. What a god-awful way to die. Tears welled but she couldn't risk him seeing her distress. Letting the paper drop to the floor, she walked away. 'Where's the champagne then?'

'Victim.' He snorted. 'Fucking killer is what she is.'

'Was.' She made heavy weather of a yawn. 'So when are we celebrating?'

'*We?*'

'You've got your revenge.' She lay on the mattress, legs slightly splayed. 'I get to go.'

'Yeah, course you do, babe.'

'When?'

'Tomorrow. Let the heat die down a bit, eh?'

He'd never let her go, she knew that. Like him, she had nothing left to lose. 'Why don't we make a night of it then? Champagne, DVD, Indian.' She licked her lips. 'The Raj is just over the road, isn't it?'

He lifted a corner of his mouth. 'Worked it out, have you?'

Guesswork mainly but she nodded. 'Sure have.'

'When you were going on about loving films and all that crap, did you know then?'

'Had a damn good idea.' He'd just inadvertently confirmed it. 'This is the old Picture Palace, isn't it?' The disused cinema on the main drag through Kings Heath, place was falling to rack and ruin, dusty greenery sprouting from crumbling brickwork. The bulldozers should've been sent in years ago. Apart from tell-tale smells and voices, she'd remembered the taxi rank right next door, recognized call signs, engine noises. 'Are we in a store room then? Admin office or something?'

He cocked an eyebrow. 'Who's a clever girl?' Then clocked what her fingers were doing inside her thigh.

'Do I get a prize?'

He blew her a kiss. 'That's on account for when I get back.'

She watched him leave, ditched the forced smile. He could come back when the hell he liked as long as the night was one she'd live to remember. Then it hit home. Her gran, the fire. Caitlin buried her face in the pillow and sobbed.

FORTY-FOUR

She'd only seen the outside, but Sarah doubted Linda Walker would ever live in the place again. Fixing blackened brickwork and blistering paint was one thing, but the images inside a head were difficult to shift. That Walker would pull through now looked more likely. The smoke inhalation turned out not as severe as first thought; she'd been taken off the ventilator; burns had never been an issue. Only Sarah's pants had been on fire. Like Mark Twain, reports of Walker's death had been greatly exaggerated. Especially the ones in the press.

'You here for the guided tour?' Ben Cooper headed her way jabbing a thumb over his shoulder. 'I've just been admiring the artwork round back.'

'Picasso?' She arched an eyebrow. 'Good to see you, Ben.'

'More like Pollock.' He returned her smile. 'Or would've been if the handiwork hadn't been interrupted. Follow me.'

Chatting, they fell in step towards the poor man's Tate. Sarah got on well with Cooper. The FSI boss was good at the job and easy on the eye. They'd tried giving a relationship a whirl, but it hadn't worked out. Professionally though she had lots of time for him, knew the feeling was mutual.

'Wish I'd placed a bet now.' Sarah nodded at a foot-high jagged red mark to the side of the boarded-up window. 'In my book, that was definitely going to be a K.'

'I won't argue with you.' Ben tapped the plywood. 'Bedroom's through there by the way.'

She shuddered. An unwanted image in her mind. 'Anything?'

'Half a house brick. Shards of glass. Nothing to write home about. The aerosol cans were clean, by the way.'

No prints. No DNA. No surprise there. He told her they'd tagged and bagged a load of stuff lying round outside, drinks cans, butt ends, bottles, matches, bits of wood. 'But you can see for yourself. There's no fence and it's all a bit of a dumping ground.'

'I won't hold my breath then.' She pulled her coat tighter as they headed back.

'Do you want to take a look inside, Sarah? We're just about done now.'

She shook her head. 'Thanks, no.' No need. She'd dropped by the estate to show her face to the troops, boost morale, pick up any whispers, decided to have a nose at the bungalow's external damage while she was here. Pointing to the land at the side of the property she asked about the tyre marks on the grass.

'The guy who raised the alarm? I think he must fancy himself as the next Jensen Button.'

She frowned. 'Have you spoken to him?' It was more than she had.

'No.' He grabbed a bottle of water from the Transit's passenger seat. 'The house over the road there? I got a blow-by-blow account from the owner.'

Mr Insomnia? 'Thanks, Ben.' She tapped her temple. 'Later.'

Ray Castle could rabbit for Europe. By the time he'd talked her through it, Sarah felt she'd been there. For once, a person's verbal diarrhoea didn't bother her. Nor the fact the earlier door-to-door sweep had missed Walker's elderly neighbour. He'd been out back, he said, wouldn't have heard the knock. A touch deaf he might be, but there was nothing wrong with his eyesight. In more ways than one he'd had the vision to scribble down the number plate. While Castle banged on, Sarah had called it in to Dave who'd run it through the PNC.

For Jensen Button read Jake Portman. The name had rung an immediate bell. And a faint alarm. There could be an innocent explanation but what the hell was the caretaker at Caitlin Reynolds' school doing driving past Linda Walker's house at two o'clock in the morning?

The late brief – 18:00. A team of DCs and half a dozen uniforms were still on the estate, knocking on doors, stopping drivers, canvassing people in the street. Two youths had been brought in for questioning on the strength of Caroline King's descriptions. Dozens more statements had been taken. Sarah had read every word and still had no answers. The Portman question had been going round in her head for hours; she'd just put it to the squad; it was their turn now.

'He didn't just drive past, boss,' Harries said. 'If the neighbour got the right end of the stick, Portman went out of his way to foil the attack.'

'Drove straight at the buggers, didn't he?' Hunt propped up his patch of wall, pen tucked behind an ear. Twig for once sat at a computer.

Sarah nodded. She stood at the front, hand in jacket pocket. 'So why didn't Action Man stop? Or at least supply a name and address?'

Twig turned his mouth down. 'Could've been pissed. You'd need bottle to do what he did.'

'Skin full, presumably,' Hunt said deadpan.

Twig rolled his eyes. 'You know what I mean. It could explain why he didn't hang around. If he'd had a drop, he'd not want the law on his neck.'

'Christ, Twig, have you been to the pun shop?' Hunt again.

'Enough,' Sarah said. 'Besides, he'd be sober as the proverbial by now.' So where was he? Portman hadn't turned up for work. He wasn't answering calls. There had been no sign of life at his Balsall Heath flat. Sarah had pushed a note and numbers through his door.

'The background seemed to stack up, boss.' Dave ran a pen down his notes. 'Father dead. Small inheritance. Started at the school in January.'

'Could be coincidence, ma'am,' Hunt said.

'Could be complete fabrication,' she countered. The abductor would have had years to work on a story; a meticulous almost foolproof plan.

Dave sniffed. 'Reckoned he was Jack-of-all-trades, didn't he?'

Sarah narrowed her eyes. *Jake*-of-all-trades was what he'd actually said. For Jake Portman read Jack Bolton? Portman was about the right age and they'd still had no joy tracing him. Could he be hiding in full view, as it were? 'What if Portman's been keeping an eye on the place?'

Dave voiced what half a dozen looks said. 'How does that work?'

'Not sure.' She was still working on it herself. 'Let's get a pic of Portman. Flash it round the estate. Start with Ray Castle.' If Portman had been hanging round recently...

'If Mr Neighbourhood Bigwig had the number plate, ma'am, how come he didn't call it in?' Twig asked.

'He reckoned he only took it on the off-chance,' Sarah said. 'He caught the witness appeal on the news just as I turned up.'

'Much bloody good that's done us so far,' Twig chuntered. He was one of the few who knew the release was a tissue of lies.

She thought about picking him up on it but ceded that – as far as the bigger picture went – he had a point. The abductor had yet to make a call, let alone a move. Logic dictated he'd make contact with Nicola Reynolds sooner or later. Beth and Holmes hadn't let the woman out of their sight. Reynolds was at home sitting on the phone, tearing her hair out according to Beth. Sarah intended heading out there straight after the brief. It had to be the place to be and she certainly wouldn't be knocking off any time soon.

'I've been thinking, boss,' Harries said.

'Bad for the health that, lad.' Twig winked at Hunt.

'About the deadline.'

'Even more fatal.'

'Zip it, Twig,' She heard him mutter something about Baker. Sooner the chief's back, something like that. The older guys, Twig particularly, didn't like having strips torn off them by a woman. The fact that Baker would have their bollocks off was neither here nor there. The chief would be a hard act to follow and right now only Sarah knew he'd likely be making an early exit. It was another pressure she could live without. 'Go on, Dave.'

'The abductor set twelve hours. Said he wanted an end to it. I kind of assumed that meant for Walker to die. Then he'd let Caitlin go. Surely, he has to know the woman's dead by now? What if he's changed the goal posts? Has a different end in mind?'

'For Caitlin?' She raised an eyebrow. 'I don't think he's changed a blind thing, Dave.'

Sarah had never regarded the girl's release as an option.

FORTY-FIVE

The call came at 19:00. Jed Holmes had alerted Sarah, who had been en route to Reynolds' home anyway. Beth had a transcript ready and the recording cued for when the DI arrived. Harries had gone along for more than just the ride. He'd been here with Sarah at the start, told her he wanted to be around for what could be the end-game. If the recent exchange on the phone was anything to go by, it sounded that way too.

'One more time please, Jed.' Sarah slipped off her coat, the heat getting to her.

'No,' Nicola wailed. 'I can't bear to hear it again.' The DI nodded at Beth who put an arm round the woman's waist and steered her out of the sitting room.

Sarah needed a second listen: the voice wasn't immediately Portman's. On the other hand, if he suspected for a second the police were in on the act, it wouldn't be. Like he'd be thick enough not to disguise it. She lifted her pen. Jed took his cue, hit play.

Did you really think you'd get away with it, Nicola?

Where's my daughter, you bastard? You swore you'd let her go.

Language, language. Caitlin's going nowhere. You said you'd kill the old cow.

She's dead, for Christ's sake. What more do you want?

I told you what I wanted.

God damn you to hell, my mother died in agony.

You didn't kill her.

A five-second silence was broken only by Sarah's pen scratching the paper.

I know everything, Nicola. Like I know you'll never see your darling daughter again.

Harm her and you're dead. I swear to God I'll

kill you with my bare hands.

*Like mother, like daughter. I'll call later ...
you'll probably want to say goodbye.*

The final words sent a chill down Sarah's
spine. In marked contrast to Nicola's screamed
abuse, the abductor's delivery was utterly de-
void of emotion.

'Cool bastard, isn't he?' Harries folded his
arms.

'Dry ice.' She lifted her gaze. 'And deadly.'

'Bloody crackpot if you ask me.' Jed sniffed.

'That's the last thing he is.' The perp wasn't a
step or two ahead of the cops; he was so far in
front he was out of sight. *Like Caitlin.* There'd
still not been a single sighting of the teenager
since her last day at school. *School. Jake Portman. A caretaker with keys. Access to the entire
building.* The DI shook her head. Queen's Ridge
had been searched twice. If Portman was their
man, he couldn't have Caitlin holed up there.

'What is it, boss?' Harries heard her out, then:
'There's no way she's on site now but...' He
narrowed his eyes, imagining scenarios. 'I guess
it would've been easy enough for him to grab
her, spirit her away in a store room, an outbuilding, somewhere like that.'

She nodded. 'Or just come up with an excuse
for her to show him where he could find ... God,
I don't know ... a book or a classroom or something.' Portman was good-looking, plausible.
Caitlin would have no reason to fear him.

'All he'd need do is bide his time until every-one left.'

'Before bundling her into the back of a motor.' And taking her God knew where. She glanced over at Holmes. 'Get on to the incident room, will you, Jed? See if Jake Portman's pic is ring-ing any bells. And ask if Leicestershire Social Services has come up with anything yet.' Jack Bolton had been in a couple of its children's homes, hopefully there would be a photograph on file.

'I still don't get it, boss.' Harries frowned. 'If Portman was there last night, doing what he did probably saved the old girl's life.'

'I think the answer's here.' She showed him the transcript, pointed out what she'd under-lined.

'"You didn't kill her."' He glanced a query at Sarah.

She shook her head. *'"You* didn't kill her."'

His eyes widened as the implication sank in. 'Nicola had to do it herself?'

'I think he drove the yobs away so they *couldn't* kill her. He wants Walker's blood on Nicola's hands.' Make that *wanted*. Sarah reck-oned the option no longer existed; time had passed for that – and for Caitlin was still running out.

Harries cracked a knuckle. 'Sadistic bastard.'

She nodded, wondered if the original deadline held. In which case, they had two and a half hours to play with. Or Caitlin did.

FORTY-SIX

The congealed remains of lamb rogan josh lay in foil dishes on the concrete floor; the air stank of cardamom and coriander. Caitlin reclined on the mattress, playing a strand of hair through her fingers. 'What time is it?'

'Why?' Smiling, he propped himself up on an elbow.

She parted her lips a fraction. 'It feels like bedtime.'

'Again?' He laughed. 'I'm knackered.'

'Good.' She giggled artlessly. *Fucking good.* That had been the general idea, even though she felt she'd never get rid of his smell. She made a playful grab for his wrist, checked his watch. 'Hey, it's only eight. We've not seen the film yet.' Kneeling now, hands on thighs, she asked what he'd brought.

He pointed to an Asda bag on the far side of the room. 'Take a look.' She knew he just wanted to ogle her naked body as she padded over. She bent over, threw in a wiggle or two. Feast your eyes, monkey man. *I Know What You Did Last Summer.* Sodding joker. Straightening, she clutched the DVD to her boobs. 'Hey, I love this movie. Ace choice.' She sashayed back, reached down for her glass, tilted it towards him. 'Cheers.' The cheapskate hadn't run to champagne but the Chianti wasn't bad. He'd downed a couple of lagers as well, didn't look particularly out of it though.

'Wanna stick it in?' She cocked an eyebrow, angled a toe at the laptop.

'Sure, and the disc.'

The film had barely started when he slid into her from behind. The booze hadn't touched his sex drive.

'A neighbour's fingered Portman, ma'am.' Holmes covered the mouthpiece with his hand. 'Want a word? It's Huntie.'

Sarah took over the phone. 'John. What've we got?'

Ray Castle. The one-man Neighbourhood Watch had clocked a guy mooching round on the pavement outside his house several times in the last month or so. The man paced up and down, smoked a fag often as not. Castle went out once to ask what he was playing at. The guy told him he was an undercover cop and Castle was jeopardizing an operation.

'Almost got to admire the bloody cheek,' Hunt said.

'Castle's a hundred per cent?'

'Recognized the photo straight off, ma'am. Portman was definitely the driver last night.'

'I want it out there now, John.' Social media,

TV news, web sites, press. Bloody sandwich boards if need be. "Have You Seen This Man?"'

Huntie knew the drill. Pensive, she handed the phone back to Jed. She wished to God they had more to go on. But if Portman had nothing to hide, surely he'd come into the open?

'Reckon Portman's our man then, boss?' Harries asked.

'Who the hell's Portman?' Nicola stood in the doorway, Beth just visible over her shoulder.

'He's a person of interest. Someone we need to talk to.' She brought the picture up on her phone. 'A caretaker at Caitlin's school.'

She stared at the screen then shook her head. 'Never laid eyes on him.' Sarah recoiled at the sour smell of vomit; Reynolds didn't just look sick.

'Why not go and lie down, Mrs Reynolds? Try and get some rest?'

'I'm waiting for a call, remember?' Her voice dripped with contempt. 'To say goodbye to my daughter.'

Caitlin hardly dared breathe, let alone move. She felt the rise and fall of his clammy chest against her spine, fancied she could feel the beat of his heart. Out of the corner of her eye, she saw his eyelids droop. His phone lay just out of reach. *Sleep, you bastard, sleep.*

Linda Walker slowly opened her eyes. Each time she regained consciousness she'd seen

things more clearly. Not just the sterile surroundings of the side ward; her own ghostly
reflection in the window. She knew she had to
act quickly before her resolve weakened. She
had to talk to DI Quinn, the detective who'd
touched her in more than one way. She rang the
buzzer. A nurse popped his head round the door.
She asked him to bring a phone and pen and
paper.

'Where are you? We have to talk.'
Sarah sighed. 'Not now, Caroline.' She was en
route to the hospital, Harries behind the wheel.
The summons from Linda Walker had sounded
serious. Reynolds had refused point blank to go
with them. Beth or Jed would make sure the DI
knew when anything moved. It was now 20:05
– sooner the better.
'I've seen him before. Jake Portman.'
'Where?'
'In person or not at all.'
She rolled her eyes, no time to argue, knew
King wouldn't budge a gnat's anyway. 'Can you
be at the QE? Ten minutes.'
'Main entrance. Don't be late.'

Caroline had a head start. She was there already.
Nothing ventured, nothing blah-blah. She'd
turned up halfway through visiting time and
tried – again – to blag her way in. The reporter
had moved on by now from just seeing Walker
as her ticket to the top; she was genuinely

312

fascinated by the story, convinced she could do it and the woman justice.

She'd actually given up the blag as a bad job – just for the night – and was sitting in her car when she checked the cops' Twitter feed. Portman was a dead ringer for a pic she had on her phone. What you might call a snatch shot. One of several taken during her comfort break at Crawford's pad. The landing walls held more family snaps than the National Portrait Gallery. It's not just old habits that die hard; Caroline never missed a digital trick these days. One of her mantras being: you never know...

She didn't know what Jake Portman was doing posing with Ted Crawford at a barbecue but the picture would be worth a lot to Sarah. Far more than a thousand words with Linda Walker.

'Why the hell didn't you let me see this earlier?' Sarah snapped, handing back the reporter's phone. The question was stupid – she knew that. Until this evening, the cops themselves had no idea of Portman's POI status. King had only realized twenty minutes ago, couldn't have contacted Sarah any quicker if she'd tried. Harries was back in the car calling in the new intelligence to the squad room; soon every available detective would be working the angle. Even as she stood here arguing the toss with King an unmarked car should be en route to Worcester to pick up Crawford. Initially at least, he'd be helping police inquiries.

Caroline's tapping foot echoed in the hospital corridor. 'You just can't stand the fact I've bailed you out yet again, can you?'

'Bailed me...?' The DI wasn't often speechless. With Caitlin Reynolds' life still at stake and the deadline ever closer, bailed out was the last thing Sarah felt. Floundering up a creek with a paper paddle maybe. She watched Caroline raise a finger, knew what was coming.

'I hand you the Reynolds-Bailey link on a plate.' A second finger. 'I tell you Walker's retracted her confession.' A third. 'I pass on info from the abductor.' A fourth. 'I place Portman with Crawford. Four-nil, DI Quinn. Strikes me a bit of gratitude wouldn't go amiss.'

Sarah tightened her mouth. Loathed feeling beholden to the bloody woman. King's smug superiority didn't help either. Fact was her words held a grain of truth. The DI had already made up her mind on the score. King just had to shut up and listen. 'This gratitude? It wouldn't be in the form of letting you come in with me to see Linda Walker, would it?'

The reporter shrugged. 'Could be.'

Sarah turned on her heel, called over her shoulder. 'What are you waiting for?'

'You're serious?' The killer heels clacked as she power-walked to keep pace.

Of course. A mental clock was ticking. 'If Walker agrees, it's OK with me. One condition, Caroline.' She cut her a glance. 'I talk, she talks, you—'

'Listen.' Caroline nodded.

Sarah stifled a sigh. Bloody woman still hadn't got the hang of it.

Caitlin's piss-take comments on the movie had long since dried up. They'd not been funny in the first place, more a means of making him think she was happy. She was dead serious now. For what seemed hours, she'd made not the slightest sound. She'd even matched her breathing to his, the frequency, the depth, every rise and fall in complete harmony. As fucking if. She curled a lip. Mind, there was nothing she wouldn't do to get out of the place. The foul stickiness between her thighs proved that.

Had the bastard dropped off yet? Gently, so very gently she moved her hand an inch towards the floor. What was it she'd said? *Slowly, slowly catchy monkey man.* She daren't rush anything anyway; she knew she'd only get one crack at it.

FORTY-SEVEN

Linda Walker lay propped on a mound of pillows, her hair hung loose like twists of steel cable; the finger and thumb on her right hand picked compulsively at the top sheet. Sarah and Caroline perched on armchairs either side of the bed. Walker had almost seemed to welcome the reporter's presence. The sooner people knew the truth, she'd said, the sooner Caitlin would be released. Sarah hadn't disillusioned the woman or filled her in on the current state of play. Dave would call from the car the second anything changed.

'You told Miss King you didn't kill Pauline?' Sarah coaxed gently, itched to still Walker's fidgeting, force her to look up. Perhaps she found it difficult without the glasses to hide behind?

'I did kill her ... in a way.'

'In a way?' Sarah exchanged glances with Caroline.

'I ran off. Left her. I was a coward. If I hadn't fallen ... got knocked out ... maybe Pauline would be here now.'

Sarah tapped a finger against her lips. 'But

316

you confessed to her murder, Mrs Walker.'

'Not at first. I was confused. When I came round there was blood all over my dress, my hands. I suppose I was concussed. I told them about the shouty man. Then the ambulance came and took me away.'

'The shouty man?'

Walker shuddered. 'The builder. He used to give Pauline sweets and lollies. He chased us into the copse. Thing is, I didn't see him hurt her and they said it couldn't have been him who killed her.'

'They?'

'The police, his boss, his work mates.' She nodded towards a glass of water on the cabinet. Sarah passed her the drink, registered the tremor in her hand. Registered, too, that King wasn't taking any notes. Either the reporter had total recall or she had a recorder on her. Sarah sighed, opted for the latter. 'I still don't understand why you confessed, Mrs Walker,' she said.

'I did hit her. With the cane. We were playing schools. But it was an accident. Then there was this detective. He didn't believe me. He twisted my words. Kept saying I did it. It got so I couldn't think straight. He said I had her blood on me and the murder weapon had my hairs on it. I was confused, scared. I just wanted him to shut up, leave me alone.'

'But you were jailed,' Sarah said. 'Sent away from your family.'

For the first time, she made eye contact. 'My

father was a monster, DI Quinn. I didn't even know what he did to me was wrong. I'd never heard the word "incest".' Water spilled down her chin as she held the glass to her mouth.

Sarah handed her a tissue. 'You could've tried to get the conviction quashed when you were released.'

'What would've been the point? Why stir it up? You know what people say: no smoke without fire. They didn't believe me when I was a kid, why believe me ten, twenty years later? Besides, if I'd raked it up, everything would have come out. I didn't want Nicola to know. I wanted to protect her from all that.'

Sarah bit her lip. So Walker had lied and the killer got away. Maybe she'd read the silence.

'I swear if there'd been another murder I'd have come forward.'

Sarah glanced at the wall clock. 21:05. 'So who do you think killed Pauline?'

'I always thought it was the builder. That he hanged himself out of guilt.'

Sarah waited for Walker to make eye contact. 'Ted Crawford didn't hang himself, Mrs Walker.'

The colour drained from her face. Sarah had to relieve her of the glass. 'But they told me he was dead. Why would anyone do that?'

She shrugged. To stop her seeking redress? If she thought Crawford had killed himself...

'Oh my God. Speak no evil.' She placed a hand across her mouth.

'I think you need to explain.' Sarah listened impassive as Walker told her about the intruder in her kitchen, the tongue. Why the hell hadn't the woman spoken sooner?

'I thought he meant the lies I told in the past. But it was a warning to keep my mouth shut now.' Her voice – and panic – was rising. 'I shouldn't be speaking to you. He's scared I'll say I didn't do it. It's why he's holding Caitlin, isn't it? No, no, ridiculous.' She shook her head. 'He's an old man now.'

Sarah nodded at Caroline. 'I'd like you to look at a photograph, Mrs Walker.'

Squinting, she held the screen inches from her face. 'Holy Mother of God.' The voice was barely a whisper; the phone fell on the bed as she shrank into the pillows. 'He's the spit of Grace.'

Sarah reckoned it was a bloody good job the woman was already lying down. Walker looked as if she'd seen a ghost.

They were at the door when she called: 'Miss King. A word before you go?'

FORTY-EIGHT

One banana, two banana, three banana ... Caitlin
counted the seconds in her head: monkey man
hadn't moved for twenty-three minutes. Not so
much as an eyelash. Not since he'd asked what
the fuck was going on.

Slowly, cautiously, as the film played, she'd
inched away from his sweaty musky embrace.
The last tiny shift had clearly disturbed the
bastard but not enough to rouse him. She'd murmured sweet nothings and hadn't budged since:
nor had he. Twenty-four minutes now. But she
had to act soon: the DVD hadn't long to run, and
in what would be a sudden silence, Caitlin
reckoned she'd have even less chance.

Gently, she turned her head on the pillow, eyed
the phone. By now it was well within reach. It
wouldn't be her first port of call. God knows
what planet she'd been on, imagining she could
summon help with monkey man in earshot.
Planet of the Apes? She allowed herself the thin-
nest smile: an action movie was more what she
had in mind.

Mentally, she'd run through the scene a couple
of times, worked out the moves, calculated the

distances, clocked the props. Timing was all.

No, she thought, the phone was a bad idea. Besides the glass was nearer.

She reached out a hand. 'Just grabbing some wine, babe.' Sleepy murmur. She even took a sip. Did he know what hit him when she smashed it in his face? Oh, yes. She saw the look of pain and terror that spread when she rammed the ragged stem in his eye. Screaming in agony, he made a fumbling grab for her, glass still embedded in both eyeballs, blood poured from deep cuts.

'Fucking bitch.' He caught her a glancing blow with his fist – more by luck than judgement. 'What the fuck have you done?'

'Nowhere near enough.' Standing now, Caitlin watched as he staggered to his knees. Swaying and sobbing, he could barely see through a veil of blood and tears. Shame. Holding the bottle over her head in both hands, she wondered if he wanted more wine. The noise when the glass shattered his skull was one she thought she'd never forget. She knew she'd remember the sound of the laptop: the DVD was still playing when she brought it down on his face. Again and again and again...

Then she reached for the phone.

The call came in at 21:50.

'Triple nine, ma'am. Body in that disused cinema in Kings Heath?'

'And you're telling me why, Huntie?' Like

Sarah didn't have enough on her plate. She and Harries were in the motor heading back to Nicola Reynolds' house. If the abductor could be believed, he was cutting it fine.

'Caitlin Reynolds called it in, ma'am. She's still there.'

The scene that greeted Sarah put new meaning into deadline. Jake Portman had been battered almost beyond recognition. Drenched in his blood, Caitlin Reynolds was near catatonic. Irony was: soon as the girl was fit, she'd be charged with murder.

FORTY-NINE

CUTS days, Sarah thought of them. Cleaning up the shit. Some inquiries left more than others. After seventy-odd hours of shovelling, the Caitlin Reynolds case was still mired in the stuff. The leaning stack of files on the desk was testament to that. Sarah circled her shoulders, eased a crick in her neck. Definitely time to call it a day. Resting her head against the chair she gazed at the far wall. Pictured a row of vertical penises. Cock-up didn't do it justice. *Justice?* She snorted. What was that when it was at home?

And why hadn't she seen the crucial link before? The case keys should have been staring her in the face. Without sightings of Caitlin, the thrust of the inquiry should always have been at the school. A school where a caretaker had access to every room, every outbuilding. A caretaker with a warped mind who'd fabricated an utterly fictitious background, biding his time before moving in for the...

Sarah had gleaned some of Portman's thinking during lengthy interviews with Caitlin. As he saw it Susan Bailey hadn't just killed Pauline, the bitch had destroyed his mother and devastated his life. Grace had only turned to drugs to cope with the pain of her sister's murder. Her increasing addiction meant Jack/Jake had spent much of his youth in care. As he grew older, so did his scalding hatred and thirst for payback. Eighteen months ago, he'd sought out Ted Crawford desperate to learn more about the tragedy that happened long before he was born. Maybe Crawford had fuelled Portman's resentment? Maybe Crawford felt partly responsible? Either way, he'd made Portman welcome, invited him back for the odd family event. Sarah strongly suspected there was more to it than that but Crawford vigorously denied involvement.

Caitlin maintained throughout that Portman's motive was revenge; it was certainly Nicola's belief. How ironic, given the only person Linda

Walker had killed was herself. On what would turn out to be her deathbed, Walker had confessed to lying all those years ago. Two days after opening up to Sarah, she'd taken her own life. Had the news about Caitlin driven her over the edge? Sarah sighed: should she have seen that coming too? Whatever. Walker had been found with a plastic bag over her head. With her breathing laboured anyway after the fire, the medics had been unable to save her. They were having better luck with Luke Holden, who still clung to life in intensive care. Caitlin had revealed Portman's role in the apparent suicide attempt. The rough justice he'd meted out had been for Holden too. Sarah shook her head.

Ripple upon ripple upon...

Move on, damn it. She strolled to the window, checked if Dave's car was back. She didn't really fancy going out tonight but a promise is a promise. Her aim was to get quietly hammered. She'd not had a drink all week. Operation Vixen was the only investigation she'd ever worked when there'd been no piss-up at the end. Not that the end had been pretty. The savagery of the attack on Portman had been appalling. Even with extenuating circumstances, Caitlin was looking at years behind bars. Nicola Reynolds and Neil Lomas had already been charged with incitement, perverting the course of justice. Whatever punishment the courts dished out, it wouldn't touch what Nicola would go through seeing her daughter jailed.

The squad had been sober in more ways than one since finding out about Baker's health. The chief had yet to show his face at the station but she'd spoken to him on the phone a few times. She hoped he'd make it tonight.

Smiling wryly she wandered back to the desk, surveyed the day's detritus: empty crisp packets, KitKat wrappers, six coffee-stained polystyrene cups. She swept everything into the bin, wished she could do the same with the fallout from the case.

The wall clock showed half-seven. Time enough to touch up the mascara, finger comb the hair. She told herself that ditching the bun had nothing to do with Walker's version, but the pixie crop still came as a shock every time she looked in the mirror. Ten minutes later she was drumming the desk with her fingers. Sod it, she'd meet Dave out back; a bit of fresh air wouldn't go amiss. Her phone rang as she reached the door. After glancing at the caller display, she almost didn't answer. King had kept a low profile since Monday night.

'Caroline?' She arched an eyebrow. 'Finished the book yet?'

'You missed your vocation, Sarah,' King drawled. 'Is it true?'

'What?' She stepped to one side as a mop-wielding cleaner passed in the corridor.

'Walker. Is she dead?'

What? 'How do you—?'

'She is then. There's something you need to

325

see, Sarah.' The voice brooked no argument; the DI didn't even try.

'This had better be good,' was Sarah's opening gambit when King turned up in reception twenty minutes later. 'Follow me.'

The reporter pulled a face as she clocked the surroundings. 'An interview room?'

'Just want you to feel at home, Caroline,' she quipped deadpan. Hopefully the ambience and eau de Jeyes meant the reporter wouldn't hang around. Sarah had already called Dave, said she'd see him at the gig.

'That night in the hospital.' Caroline reached into her tote bag. 'When I was leaving? And Walker called me back? She gave me this.'

Sarah studied the envelope, read the writing. 'Have you re-sealed this by any chance?'

'How dare you? She narrowed her eyes. 'It says quite clearly—'

She flapped a hand. 'I see what it says, Caroline.'

Only to be opened after my death.

Walker's last words covered barely one side of the unlined sheet of paper. Sarah read them in silence.

I had to kill Pauline. She saw me and Ted Crawford in the copse. The nosy little beggar didn't even know what we were doing but she threatened to tell my dad. He'd have killed me if he thought I'd done them things with someone

326

else. Crawford helped me, held her down. He was always nice to me, gave me sweets and stuff, told me I was a good girl. Said he'd look after me. I thought when I came out of prison he'd be waiting. Fat lot I knew. I can't live with the lies any more.

Sarah folded the paper, slipped it back in the envelope. 'Knocks your story on the head, doesn't it? Miscarriage of justice, false imprisonment and all that.'

'Ain't that the truth?' Caroline grimaced. 'Still I—'

'Fell into that?' Sarah shook her head. 'Despicable woman.'

'Hey!'

'Not you. Walker.' She stood, held the door. 'Let's go.' Back in reception she faced the reporter. 'You know, Caroline, I'm not sure it's worth the paper it's written on.' Crawford would be dragged in for further questioning but given it was his word against Walker's, Sarah wouldn't be counting chickens. 'She only ever said one thing I actually believe.'

'Oh?'

'She'd rather die than see Caitlin harmed.'

Caroline sniffed. 'That worked then.'

'See you around.' Tapping her temple, she gave a half smile.

'Ciao.' Caroline paused in the doorway. 'Don't fancy a drink, do you? Drown your sorrows?'

327

'Sorrows?'

'The hair. Was there a power cut?' She winked. 'Only joshing.'

The Toy Hearts were in full western swing mode
in an upstairs room when Sarah arrived at the
pub. She stood with Caroline at the back waiting
for a break between numbers. Through the
crowd, Sarah spotted Dave who'd bagged one of
the few tables going. Judging by the empties
he'd been there some time or had a drinking
partner. Yup. A beer buddy. She smiled. It had
taken a few seconds to recognize Baker. He sure
had dressed the part: blue denims, loud checked
shirt. Knowing the chief he'd probably brought
along his Stetson.

Pouting, Caroline pointed her glass. 'Isn't that
your boss?'

'Sure is.'

She nudged Sarah's arm. 'You didn't tell me it
was a foursome.'

Cue applause, whooping, cheering. 'That was
for the band, Caroline,' Sarah drawled before
weaving a path through the packed house. Tapping the chief's shoulder she said, 'Still on the
wagon, I see.'

Baker beamed, raised his pint. 'Where've you
been, Quinn? You're missing a treat. Hello,
hello, hello.' He waggled a lascivious eyebrow.
'If it isn't the lovely Lois.'

'Ms Lane to you.' Caroline pecked him on the
cheek. 'How's my favourite super ... cop?' She

328

nodded at the stage as she parked her butt. 'Great band, aren't they?'

'Cracking.' Baker was a big fan, seen them loads of times. 'If you ask me, it's in the genes.'

Sarah frowned. 'Jeans?' The vocalist and guitarist – lovely young women – wore minuscule dresses and vertiginous heels.

'Keep up, Quinn. They're sisters.' He pointed his glass at the guy with a steel guitar. 'That's their dad. Can't you feel the chemistry?'

'Blood thicker than water, eh, Fred?' Caroline dabbed wine from her lips with a finger.

Sarah kept schtum, wondered if it went for bad blood too. Ironically, the derelict cinema where Caitlin had been found covered in gore was just up the road. As for family chemistry – it could be a toxic blend.

She smiled wryly when the blonde singer introduced the next number: 'Femme Fatale'. Listening to the lyrics, the DI reckoned they held a weird sort of resonance too: *the lies fall softly from her lips ... I have heard it said the devil is a woman.*

What had King come out with earlier? *Ain't that the truth.*

Sarah told herself to let it go. Glancing round she saw Baker in his element: tapping a cowboy boot, drumming his thigh, singing along – softly thank God. She watched King lean across, whisper something that made him laugh. He reached under the table, pulled out a hat as if he was busking. Aren't we all? Sarah bit her lip, had to look away. Catching Dave's gaze on her face she returned his warm smile. He was a lucky boy; she'd decided he could wait to sample her culinary delights. They'd eat out tonight. She might even pick up the bill.